take
the
lead

JAQUELINE
SNOWE

MW01125256

HAPPY READING!
Jaqueline Snowe

Published: 2022
Published by: Jaqueline Snowe
Copyright 2022, Jaqueline Snowe

Cover Image by Floral Deco
Cover Design by Katie Golding
Editing by Katherine McIntyre
Formatting by Jennifer Laslie

All rights reserved. No part of this publication may be reproduced, stored in a retrieval system, or transmitted in any form, or by any means, electronic, mechanical, recording or otherwise, without prior written permission from the author. For more information, please contact Jaqueline at www. jaquelinesnowe.com.

This is a work of fiction. The characters, incidents, dialogue, and description are of the author's imagination and are not to be constructed as real. Any resemblance to actual events or persons, living or dead, is completely coincidental.

ACKNOWLEDGMENTS

This book wouldn't have happened without Kat. You've been such an amazing editor to work with. You've kicked my ass and I'm so thankful for everything. This series wouldn't be where it is without you.

I know I'm a needy client, but a huge thanks to my husband who created these covers for me. They are beautiful and perfect.

Lastly, a huge thanks to Sil (@thebookvoyagers) and Nick (@romancefiend) It sounds dramatic but when you both read *From the Top* last year and posted about it, it changed my author path. Your reviews reached so many new readers and I honestly cannot thank you enough. Bloggers and readers are why authors write stories and having you read my words is a real gift.

TAKE THE LEAD

Daniella Loughlin might seem put together in her dance gear and captainship, but on the inside, she's figuring out who she is without her mom's beauty pageant influence. Constantly being critiqued and set up by her mom, she dreads going home for the holidays.

Enter her best friend's older brother, hockey captain Gabriel Van Helsing. Dani and Gabe have been friends for two decades, and sure, she's harbored a secret crush on him forever, but she never acted on it because his sister would've killed her. Gabe's a player, on and off the ice, and the longest relationship he's had is with his hockey stick. He offers to drive her home for Thanksgiving break and proposes the most bonkers idea—they should fake date until New Year's to get her mom to leave her alone.

Gabe might wear the C on the ice, but he's always been passive. Here for a good time, never rocking the boat. But after his latest hookup wouldn't take a hint, he uses Daniella's predicament for the perfect solution: if he was unavailable, then people would leave him alone.

Things begin easily with their friendship, but with every touch and *fake* kiss, Daniella can't hide her feelings anymore. And for Gabe, who sets deadlines for every fling he's ever had, he struggles to fight for what he wants. When their timeline is up, Daniella's insecurities clash with Gabe's inability to commit. For two people terrified to take a chance, they must risk their decade-long friendship for a shot at love.

To my daughter...

When people tell me that you'll be pretty, I agree:
Pretty smart
Pretty strong
Pretty passionate
Pretty kind
Pretty curious
Pretty outspoken
Pretty weird

I'm so glad you're my daughter and owning your confidence will be hard. But never let the opinion of others define you.

I wrote this book as you cuddled against me and this story will forever remain one of my favorites because of our cuddles.

CHAPTER
ONE

Daniella

There were perks and downsides of having red hair. The color was beautiful, and people complimented me on it all the time. There were red-haired scholarships I'd applied for and received, and there was a small amount of the world's population that had natural red hair. That was cool. I liked being unique. Especially in the beauty pageant world my dear mother grew up in and *never* let me forget.

The downside was the inability to hide my blush whenever I felt any emotion. It didn't matter if it was embarrassment, sadness, or guilt. My cheeks turned redder than a fire engine, and it didn't stop there. Pink covered my neck, shoulders, and chest to the point it looked like I had an allergic reaction. My face flamed worse than a candle, and I tried to force a tight smile as my teammate narrowed her eyes at me.

"Stop worrying so much," I said.

"Almost everyone I know is excited to go home for a few days. Family, food, football. Your knuckles are white on your bag strap, Dani." Cami Simpson jutted her chin toward my hands and clicked her tongue. "What's going on?"

We stood outside the recreation center, right next to the football stadium. It was a central point of campus and the easiest spot I could come up with for Van to pick me up. Cami insisted on walking with me and waiting for my ride. Something about girl code.

I'd once thought Cami Simpson was a self-centered drama queen, and I'd been so incredibly wrong. Through a weird twist of dramatic events, we were named co-captains, and she was now one of my best friends and my fierce protector. For someone who never had a sibling growing up, it was how I'd always envisioned one. She had claws that came out when I was upset, and as much as I loved her for it, it felt stupid to share my insecurity with her: my mom. I was in college... I shouldn't have *mother* issues.

I rolled my shoulders back, and unease rooted me to the spot as I lied. "I'm just looking forward to being away from campus for a bit, yeah."

"Is it Van Helsing?" She eyed the street outside the stadium where he would be arriving in a few minutes. Cami hung around until he arrived, like a hovering parent, but I would've preferred to wait in peace. It was the Wednesday before Thanksgiving, and most of the students had already left town. Since Cami's dad and boyfriend lived here, she'd be staying.

It was wild how quiet everything was with so many students going home. I liked it that way. Less crowds. Less pressure to fit in and be someone.

"Van? No." I frowned. Van was by far the best part about going home. Well, seeing his sister, my best friend Elle, and their family was my favorite. They were the siblings I had always wanted—which caused the same roller coaster of guilt to spin around my stomach. "I'm excited to hang out with him for a few hours."

"Then, for real. I've seen you face a linebacker head-on during a drinking game without a speck of fear, but now you look nervous. I'm really persistent if you didn't know. I refuse to call myself annoying, so unless you tell me—"

"It's my mom, alright?" God, my face burned hotter than a midwestern sun in July. "She's... we're... problematic."

"Girl. If you want to swap stories of difficult mothers, you should've asked." She laughed and squeezed my forearm, her bright orange nails sticking out against my pale, freckle-covered skin. "I haven't seen mine in six months, and she lives in town. She has two twin toddlers now, which I'm sure is wild, but seriously." She paused, her tone lowering into a more thoughtful one. "If you're worried about seeming weird or immature for having issues with your parents, don't. Relationships are hard as fuck, and it's okay to be complicated."

My eyes prickled with emotion, and I yanked Cami into a hug. She smelled like vanilla and cookies, and I didn't care that she wasn't used to my embraces yet. I was a hugger. A toucher. Sure, my mom wasn't in the slightest, but my dad? Yeah. We embraced like it was an Olympic sport. Even though my parents were still together, we somehow never talked about my mom. It was the elephant in the room.

Cami groaned as I squeezed around her middle, but I didn't let go. "I love you," I said, my voice muffled into her shirt.

"Well, shit." She laughed against me, pulling back a bit, and a slight pink dusted her cheeks. "I feel like I should tell you things are intense with Freddie."

I rolled my eyes and shoved her away, not-so-discreetly wiping under my eyes. Much to my mom's dismay, I also showed my feelings. A lot. Good, bad, happy, sad. I was a walking emotion thesaurus, and I knew the second I stepped foot in our house, I'd have to pretend to be someone I wasn't. I was an embarrassment to her—single, not in her realm of beauty, and not the daughter she wanted.

My mom prided herself on her looks and ability to get an M.R.S. degree in college—by landing my super-successful dad. Yeah, I grew up constantly being asked about why I wasn't dating the most popular, driven, handsome boy in school. She'd scope out guys *good enough* for her and set me up on these horrible dates as bribery. If I wanted a car at sixteen, I'd agree to go out with her rich doctor friend's son while my dad laughed it off. It annoyed me that he always sided with her, so to survive, I lowered my expectations of him, even though it made my insides twinge. He was a good father...he just loved his wife more than me. Why else would he never speak up?

The string of dates was endless embarrassment, my mom pushing me to be someone I wasn't. Every date made me feel worse, and here I was, twenty years old and having fun at school while worrying myself sick about going home for a weekend. A freaking *weekend.*

God, I hated myself sometimes.

"Hey." Cami squinted down the road where a large black truck shone its headlights at us and brought me back to the present. The wind had a chill, and my nose stung from the temperature. No other reason.

"I love you too, okay? We're friends to the end, and when you get back, we'll get wine and cry—well, you can cry. I'll pat your back or something. We can talk about it, or not, but you're not alone."

"Careful, Cami," I teased, my smile stretching across my face. She had no idea what her support meant to me. None. Gratitude, love, loyalty burst through me. There was nothing I wouldn't do for her. "You're turning into a really good friend."

"Fuck off, Dani." She grinned at me just as Gabriel Van Helsing, captain of the Central State hockey team, parked his truck. She whistled. "Do the rest of the girls realize you two are close?"

"No, and for a reason."

Her eyebrows rose, but she didn't say a word. She got it. A lot of girls on the team preferred dating athletes. It was common, and while I loved being co-captain with Cami, I didn't have the same level of trust with all of the girls. I was a transfer, so I didn't know them super well. They did try to mutiny me for the first two months when I was captain. I let it go, for the most part, but them learning about my ten-year friendship with Van? No way. For two reasons—he was a player, and I couldn't handle him hurting my teammates, but the bigger one was protecting him.

A secret, never-admit-it-out-loud one would be because of my crush on him, but that lived in the back of my mind. It made me feel foolish to think anything would ever come of it, then guilt followed. I couldn't ever do anything about my crush on my best friend's brother. It was a rule.

"Call me, anytime." Cami waved at Van as he walked around the front of the truck. "Hey, Van Helsing."

"Simpson." He jutted his chin out toward her before glancing at me with the same goofy smile I'd known since I was ten. One dimple popped out on his left cheek, the only part of him that could be described as adorable. The rest of him was all thick muscles and dark hair and hard lines.

"D. You make the playlist?" His deep voice comforted me as much as it sent a ripple of awareness from my head to my toes. He was so *hot*.

I held up my fingers. "I'm good for three things, Van. Playlists, dance moves, and emergency snacks. *Of course* I made a playlist." I rolled my eyes as he picked up my suitcase and tossed it in the back with just one hand. He wore a navy dry-fit long-sleeved shirt that hugged every part of his massive arms, and I glanced once. Okay, twice.

He was fit, gorgeous, and always smelled like he'd just gotten out of the shower. Rainforest and soap. I didn't harbor an *aggressive* crush on him anymore. It was way worse in high school when I saw him all the time. Here, I could play it cool and only thought about him in my deep fantasies. So, it was safe to admire him, objectively. The dark black hair that always looked like he ran a hand through it. The jawline sharp enough to cut through the windshield of a semi. Plus, his size. All six feet of him with the muscles and the abs. Yeah, he was attractive. Gabe was hot as shit and nice. It was the kindness that had me writing Mrs. Van Helsing in my notebooks though.

"Ah shit, D. You're all red." He grinned, my damn blush one of his favorite things to tease me about. "Thinking about snacks again?"

"Shut up." I scoffed and waved goodbye to Cami one more time before getting into the passenger seat. She winked. A wave of gratitude washed over me as I watched her walk away. She was a precious and surprise gift of a friend. Transferring here as a sophomore had made me all sorts of nervous, but becoming her friend was game-changing. She hadn't had it easy, and maybe I could confide in her when I got back. Even if she told me I was a horrible daughter, it'd be better to hear it from someone else instead of my own mind.

My phone buzzed as Van pulled onto the main road. Two hours until we were in our hometown suburb of Chicago. Two hours to prepare for my mom. Ugh. Speaking of her...

Mom: I bought you two dresses that actually complement your hair and skin tone for our outing tomorrow. Set up manis and pedis after lunch, so don't make plans. Elle can come if she wants.

The beauty regime of Lily Lea Laughlin, former beauty queen and trophy wife, took hours. A blowout, a spray tan, nails, makeup. I was a fucking dancer and loved getting dolled up for school spirit. It was fun with music and the right people. But with her? It was her chance to make me fit the mold she wanted.

"Chewing on your nail a little hard there. You alright?" Van asked as he turned on his signal to enter the highway. Everything was so *him* in here. All black leather and an air freshener that didn't really cover up the smell of his hockey gear in the backseat. It was honestly a miracle that he was able to drive me home with their schedule, but he didn't have to play until Friday after the holiday. So, thankfully, I was going to try and weasel a ride back with him.

But… what I hoped for—a playful car ride back to distract me from my dear mother—would be shot to hell if he picked up on my mood. The handsome bastard was too perceptive for his own good. It made sense though—he was the team captain for a reason. Always up for a good time, a great teammate, and sympathetic.

I sighed and leaned back into the seat. "Just my mom."

"Uh oh. What did the Lovely Lily Laughlin do now?"

I snorted. Elle and I started referring to her as the *Lovely Lily Laughlin* when she got all wacko with… everything. It was a way for me to cope with her passive-aggressive and straightforward insults about who I was as a person. Elle and I would laugh and talk in a British accent. "And how do you know about the Lovely Lily?"

"First, Elle is loud as fuck, and her idea of whispering is shouting instead of screaming. Second, you basically grew up in our house. I wasn't just some pretty, dumb jock. I listened to you when you were upset."

"Aw Van, if only all your lady fans knew how soft you were." I reached over and poked his side, making him yelp like a Chihuahua. "They have no idea you're not the big badass they think you are."

"Settle down there, woman. I am big and badass, never forget that. Plus, don't get me started on my *fangirls*." He sucked in a breath, and his shoulders tensed. Even his grip on the wheel tightened for a beat before he slid me a look. The half-smile didn't quite reach his eyes. "This might ruin my rep, but I'm ready to settle down all the… what did you and Elle call them? Fling flangs?"

I barked out a laugh. What a stupid yet accurate name. "We're idiots."

"Without question."

"But do you hear yourself? No more flinging? No more flanging?" A spark of hope rooted in my gut, deep and low. No more flings? He was always off-limits because of Elle, but also, I knew I wanted more than a fling. The tiny flame of *what-if* had no business being in the car, and I extinguished it. He had to be joking.

He cracked the knuckles of his left hand before shifting in his seat. "Nah, just focusing on the team right now. Some of the guys are acting like morons. Plus, we have this fucking sophomore I want to punch in the face every second of every day, and so what does coach do? Name him *alternate* captain. It's like he's trying to cause me to go gray. Look at this luscious hair? I can't go gray yet. I'll rock the salt and pepper look later, but at twenty-two? Ugh."

Van had the unique ability to be humble and ridiculous at the same time. To hear him openly admit a struggle with another player? This was huge. "Obviously you'd be the best-looking gray-haired twenty-two-year-old ever."

"Yeah, no shit. I'm aware D." He waved his hands in the air. The gesture made me laugh, and just like he and Elle had done my entire life, all negative thoughts of my mom went out the window. They were mood boosters.

"Well, I just went through a weird captain issue with the dance team, so if you wanna talk about it… for real, I'm here."

He glanced at me for second, his light brown eyes softening as the side of his mouth curved up in a genuine Van smile, the one that I knew meant he always had my back. "You text me when you need an escape from Lovely Lily and it's a date."

A date.

We both understood that word didn't mean *a date-date* like two people who had feelings for each other and were trying it out. He meant, like a scheduled meeting between two people who'd known each other for decades. It was silly and absurd how my skin tingled just a bit picturing what it would even be like to *date* Gabriel Van Helsing.

He'd totally take charge and place his large hand on the base of my back. He'd be polite and kind and damn well show me a good time in the bedroom. I was sure of it. I heard all the talk and might've fantasized about it once or a million different times. *Shit.* My blush prickled along my neck, and I shifted in my seat, cracking the window a half an inch to cool the hell down. My skin felt too tight for my body, like the heater was on super high. My thighs squeezed together as I fanned my face.

Thank God Van turned up the volume of my HOLIDAY MIX 3.0, and Megan Thee Stallion blasted through the speakers. I had no excuse thinking for even a moment what dating Van would be like. No sense at all because a guy like him and a girl like me? Well, we just didn't fit.

He was popular, handsome without trying. He could date the most eligible woman alive without issue. He didn't get laughed at on dates because his mom didn't set him up on them. But mainly, he was confident, and I was not. There were parts of myself I liked but not many. *So* yeah, Gabe would never go for a dork like me. Lovely Lily made that *incredibly* clear.

God, only two more holidays with her, then I could stay on campus forever.

CHAPTER
TWO

Gabriel

S eeing my sister's best friend rap along with Cardi B was definitely the serotonin boost I needed. Daniella Laughlin was the perfect combination of ridiculous, talented, and goofy. So damned goofy. It was hard to remain grumpy about Cal Holt, about fucking *Becca*, about Christopher who was probably sneaking steroids, or how Ty was partying a little too hard. All those thoughts went away when Daniella was so entertaining.

She wasn't kidding about her talent of creating a playlist. I never told her, but I used them when I worked out. Her, Elle, and I all shared anything we made as an unspoken rule from our teenage years, but even now, Dani was a kickass DJ. With her dance skills and rhythm, it made sense she had superior taste.

I hated how her mom gave her so much grief when Elle and I had lucked out in the best parents ever category. But we never could choose where we came from, just picked who we wanted to stay in our lives. Dani was one of those people for sure. All our kids would be best friends, guaranteed. The Van Helsings considered her one of us.

"I forgot to ask, are you heading straight to your house or ours?" Selfishly, I wasn't ready to drop her off yet. My parents and Elle would ask me about the team, about being captain, about graduation and *what's next* and *when are you going to bring home a nice partner,* and while I loved the hell out of them... I wanted to stay in the Daniella bubble a little longer. She knew me well enough that I could be myself but didn't offer the pressures of my well-meaning family. Plus, she was a little red-haired ball of sunshine. She was cute in the *little sister's best friend* kinda way because thinking anymore more would result in my sister physically harming me. I'd let her too. Dani was adorable and fun, and I *loved* her long red hair. But that was as far as I'd allow my brain to go.

She eyed her phone. "Fuuuuck. My mom invited *guests* tonight who are looking forward to seeing me." She groaned and tossed her phone onto the floor. Then she made even a louder noise as she picked it back up. "I guarantee Chad is an aspiring dentist who loves fly fishing and riding horses at sunset. Oh! And I bet Richard owns a yacht at the age of twenty-one! And wears a Rolex! And knows the pope!"

My lips twitched as her voice turned into a strange mixture of a Chicago accent and an Eastern European one, and she pursed her lips the entire time.

"So, Chad and Richard are..."

"Dates twenty-four and twenty-five of Lovely Lily's goal of marrying me off to a rich douchebag." Daniella huffed and crossed her arms over her baggy Central state sweatshirt. "Every single visit I see her, if she's in town on campus or when I'm home, she plans these dinners against my will. I swear that woman created an online profile for me or something. I don't know how she finds all these guys. Seriously. I'm so fucking sick of being set up. I don't care that I'm single. I like it, and I don't need to date to be happy. She just doesn't get it."

My chest tightened at the clear distress in her voice. Daniella rarely got mad. Sure, she blushed head to toe with every emotion she had, but anger? Fist-clenching rants? Nah, not D. "My mom's been on me too about settling down."

"Well, yeah with all your fling flangs. That makes more sense than what Lovely Lily is doing. She wants me to secure a diamond, a new last name, and a rich man, or I'm worthless. Me being *me* isn't enough."

She spoke with conviction, like Daniella actually believed her value was dependent on those items. I clenched my jaw and took a breath before responding because what the fuck, Lily? "D, you know that's bullshit."

"To normal people, yes. But not to my mom." Her brought her knees up to her chest and wrapped her arms around them. She wore black leggings and orange socks that matched the little gems in her ears. I liked bright things on her. They went with her hair and personality.

"Have you told her you don't want to date these d-bags?"

"A million times, Van. I hate coming home." She hung her head and sniffed, a telltale sign she was about to cry. I reached over and squeezed her forearm, letting my hand rest there a few beats. She was warm.

She placed hers on top of mine and squeezed back. "I love my dad, and I'm so thankful for having a privileged childhood, but this toxic BS with her? I'm over it. After New Year's this year, I'm done coming home, and I'm living at campus full-time. Then I can control when I have to hear her comments and deal with her dates because she doesn't listen to me. She ignores everything I say and still tries to change me."

She let go of my hand, hung her head on her arms, and her shoulders trembled. Goddamn it. I was a sucker for tears. Elle could get whatever she wanted growing up if she cried. I hated when she was sad, and the same feeling transferred to Daniella —*must get them to stop*. The sound of sniffles made my insides clench, and my heart raced as I thought of a solution. Help her! Solve it! No more tears!

"Use me." The words left my mouth before the thought

finished, and in the echoing silence, my brain pieced it together. *We could pretend to date.*

My stomach swooped in the same way it did before a game. Excitement.

Becca would leave me alone and put our drama in the past.

It would help Daniella survive the holidays *and* stop crying.

It'd get my mom to stop hounding me about settling down.

It'd keep the puck bunnies away.

It'd prevent distraction so I could actually focus on Cal and the team.

Sure, we'd tell Elle the truth, but what were the cons? From now until New Year's Eve? I could do six weeks of it. I liked hanging out with Daniella. She was easygoing.

"D, seriously." I pulled over the truck in a McDonald's parking lot, carefully parking and undoing my seatbelt. She eyed me like I'd grown three heads and clucked like a chicken. "Let's pretend to date until the new year."

"You and me. Dating." Her large blue eyes were the size of pizzas, and her mouth hung open. "*What?*"

"Pretending to date. Yes. Hear me out." I spun in my seat and took her hands in mine. "I hate seeing you cry. You know this, and I blurted out the first thing that came to mind, but it could work."

"You and me." She removed herself from my grip.

"Yes, in this scenario, I'm specifically talking about *you and me*." I grinned, aware of her fire-red blush spreading across her entire face and neck. "It'd get your mom off your back, right?"

"I mean… yeah." She guffawed and blinked a few times, her eyes a lighter blue from the tears. They reminded me of sapphires. The more I digested my idea, the happier I was. It was *ideal*. We could totally make this work. We understood everything about each other already. We had to add a little hand-holding here and there, but that was it.

For one hot second, I thought about what it'd be like to kiss Dani. Her full red lips, her gorgeous mouth on mine. My grip on the wheel tightened as I shoved the attraction down. She was my sister's best friend.

"Perfect. Then no more horrible dates with Kyler or Chad or Dickface."

Her lips twitched a bit, but a line still remained between her brows. "But Van, your fling flangs."

"I told you, I'm over that. I had a situation come up, and honestly—" I paused, rubbing the back of my neck and squeezing it for a second. "—This would help me out too. There's this girl, and well, it didn't end great, and this would solidify that we are over. Plus, this would give my parents something else to talk about instead of the *what are you going to do with your life* conversations that keep happening."

"Oh, no, no, no. I can't lie to your parents." She shook her head hard, biting down on her lip. "Not Helen and Patrick."

"It'll be fine." They were the least of my worries. "They know I'm too much of a player, and we'll say you ended it."

"I can't break it off! My mom would never forgive me. You're so far out of my league, and she'd refuse to talk to me again for ruining it."

"First off, you're not out of anyone's league, so never say that shit to me. And isn't that what you want? Her leaving you alone?"

She leaned back into the seat, running her hands through her ponytail and frowning. "How would this work, exactly?"

"We say we were trying things out the last month, that it was new and we waited until now to announce it."

"Elle will murder us."

"She'll know the truth, obviously." God, lying to my sister was a death wish. I shivered, just picturing what would happen if we didn't tell her. "She's the only one."

Daniella exhaled, nodded a few times, and pulled on the edge of her sweatshirt. "Do we go on dates? Kiss?"

"Dates? Sure. We've gotten dinner together before. No big deal there. And kissing? If the situation calls for it, I guess. But I think we can play it right. Trust me, D. Now... when I drop you off at home, shall I escort you inside?"

Hand-holding. That's it. No kissing.

"Van, this is wild. A terrible idea."

"Wild, yeah. Terrible? No. It helps us both solve a problem. I don't plan on dating anyone anytime soon, so this is no biggie for me. Are you interested in anyone that this could cause an issue with?"

"No, not at all. Just dance."

"See? I'm about hockey, and you're focused on dance. We're a perfect match." I flashed her a grin, my flirtatious one, and she shoved my shoulder.

"None of that nonsense. Don't you use your charm on me, real or fake." Her skin flushed, but the tension left her neck and shoulders. "Oh, hot damn. That means I can ride back with you Friday morning because obviously I'm gonna support my hunky boy toy at his game."

"For sure, but don't call me boy toy. Hunky, yeah. But boy toy?" I scrunched my nose, and she snorted.

"Gabey Baby." Her wicked smile and evil eyes made me groan. My worst fling ever from high school called me that. It became a *thing* for a minute.

"No. No."

"But it's sooooo cute."

"I regret this already." I sighed, starting up the truck again to finish the short drive to her parent's house. It was just a few minutes south of ours, and it would be a lie if I didn't have a little thrill at the idea of running into Chad and Dorkface. Maybe it was a competitive thing or possibly the fact I didn't like how these guys made Dani feel, but I was ready to flaunt our fake-tionship. "You want to hit up the drive-thru first?"

"And show up with a takeout bag and fries on my sweatshirt? Lovely Lily will shit herself."

"I'm taking that as a hell yeah then."

She ordered fries and a shake, and I asked for two

cheeseburgers. I maintained a regimented diet during the season, but that was going to hell on Thanksgiving. I ate my body weight in green beans, sweet potatoes, and turkey, so I cheated. The ride was easy until we pulled into her parents' driveway. A large white house, three car-garage, and too many windows greeted us. Lights were on everywhere, and the dull thud of a stereo carried through to my truck.

"They having a party on a Tuesday night?"

"She loves to entertain." Daniella unclicked her seatbelt and took forever to get out of the passenger's seat. Gone was her confidence and goofiness. This was a different girl. Slumped shoulders and no sparkle in her eyes—that wouldn't do. Irritation prickled my skin at the shit her mom did to her, but I had to be content with our plan. I got her stuff out of the back and walked up to her side, grabbing her hand.

"Hey." I intertwined our fingers and waited until she looked up at me. When she did, a weird pang formed in my chest. Her lashes seemed crazy long, and her freckles painted her face in the cutest way. Yes, I'd protect her at all costs. In the most confident voice I had, I said, "We got this, girl. I'll take the lead."

She chewed her bottom lip and gave a curt nod. "Things could get weird."

"I happen to like weird."

She took a deep breath, closing her eyes for a beat before she straightened her shoulders. When she stepped forward, she walked with the same grace she always had. Damn dancer body with long legs and smooth movements. I might dominate the ice, but she dominated walking. I matched her elegant stride up to the door. She hesitated and glanced back at me with worry written all over her freckled face. "Van?"

"Hm?"

"If this works out, thank you."

"It will. And you're welcome." I smiled, hoping it'd reassure her just as the door opened. In the flesh, Lily Laughlin was stunning. She could've been thirty or fifty. I had no idea. She was beautiful with her curled blonde hair and red lips. "Mrs. Laughlin, lovely to see you." I knew how to use my charm and winked at her.

The surprise on her face transformed to delight as she eyed me up and down. "Gabriel, you look well. Thank you so much for driving our dear Daniella home for us."

"Of course. We've been looking forward to this trip, haven't we, D?"

"Uh huh." She nodded too fast and stared at her socks. Her discomfort was so damn obvious I had to do something. Anything or the whole ruse would be off.

I let go of her hand and put mine on her upper back, dragging it back and forth as she tilted her head up. I cupped the back of her neck and pulled her gently toward me. Her body was stiff as a board, but I wrapped my arm around her completely before pressing her back to my chest and resting my chin on her shoulder. She smelled incredible, like flowers and laundry. I swore I felt her shiver against me, but I was so worried about the size of Lily's eyes that I didn't pay enough attention. "We're officially dating, Mrs. Laughlin."

"You and my Daniella?" she said, her voice raising three octaves. Her lips parted as she stared at me. "You're dating my...daughter?"

"She finally agreed to it." I adjusted Dani's ponytail so it wouldn't pull against her head from my weight and carefully set it on her shoulder. Dani's entire neck was red, but she didn't seem like she was going to throw up anymore. "I asked her to wait to tell everyone, so don't be upset with her, Mrs. Laughlin."

"Upset? No, I'm not upset. Daniella! Oh, baby, I'm so happy for you." Lily pulled Dani into her arms in squeeze that kind of looked like a hug, kind of like an attack. Dani kept her hands firmly at her side, and a part of me broke inside at seeing that. We hugged a lot in my family, often too much. Meeting up for dinner? Welcome hugs and leaving hugs. A holiday? A birthday? A Tuesday night hug? The reasons were endless. My family was the complete opposite of Dani's. They were supportive. Yes, my parents' constant questions about graduation annoyed me, but it was because they cared. They never tried to change me or make me feel small. Even just standing at the door of Daniella's parents' house, I felt cold. Colder than outside. Like the air was different when there wasn't enough love inside the walls.

She let go of Dani and smoothed her green dress as she glanced over her shoulder. "Please, come in Gabriel. Join us. Let me take care of something very quickly but then we must hear *everything.*"

"I'll help carry her bag to her room, and we'll be right down." I blasted her with my best smile, the one I used on puck bunnies. It was so easy and unfulfilling. Endless hookups, no strings, no worries. Not the case with Becca, but I shoved that down. Maybe this was exactly why I'd blurted out this idea. I needed something different. "Come on, baby."

Daniella walked inside and immediately went right where there was a large staircase that led to the second floor. Her house was spotless, exactly how it always was the few times I'd been here. Pictures of Lily's beauty days lined the walls, and I only saw *one* photo that contained Daniella—a family photo of the three of them from at least ten years ago.

Anger formed in my gut, growing as we approached her bedroom. She was raised in this house? With a shrine to the former beauty pageant winner? Blah. No wonder Daniella always came to our house. I'd want to escape this prison too. "Jesus Christ." I tossed her bag on the floor and shut the bedroom door. "I need a bingo card."

"Why?" Dani crossed her arms as she plopped onto the bed. "Regretting this already?"

"Not for a second. How many photos are there of your mom? Seriously, that shit is weird." I joined her on the bed, and my weight caused her to slide down so her thigh hit mine. My thigh was at least six inches longer than hers. She was so petite. It was kinda cute.

"Too goddamn many." She huffed, and a serious look entered her eyes. "Van, she's probably already talking about weddings and babies and how quickly you can be her son-in-law. It's going to be horrible."

"I can take it." I shrugged, ready to fight Daniella's demons with her. It was easier with her than with my own parents. They were real, genuine. This was like, a way to pass one over on Lily. I didn't want to talk about my real life with my parents, not when I didn't have answers. This would distract them *and* give Lily a secret middle finger.

Elle would support this; I knew without a doubt. Dani didn't have to deal with this alone. "Don't worry. There's gonna be a time in the next six weeks when I'll lean on you, so this is just my turn."

She narrowed her eyes like she didn't believe me. "I doubt you'll need *me*."

"Trust me, D. I do." My voice lowered as Becca's face swirled in my head, mixing with Cal's, and my blood pressure spiked. I forced a calm sigh and pulled the end of her hair softly.

"Wanna head down there and see if we can get a glimpse of Chode face and Dick?"

She laughed, like I wanted her to. My lips curved up, and I stood, holding out my hand for her.

She took it with an eyeroll. "I thought you'd never ask."

CHAPTER
THREE

Daniella

E lle admired the emerald dress and the purple one, pretending to be a game show host. "On my left, we have a leafy green sheer dress that would surely drive my brother bonkers. But on the right, we have a perfect plum number that would make your small titties pop. Oh, choices."

"Fuck off, Elle." I laughed, so thankful that Elle was here and on board. I spun around in the bright red desk chair in my room, counting down the seconds until I could leave this town with Van. We'd somehow survived last night, and my mom bought our story. I think she was so dazzled that someone like him—all looks, glory, popular—would be with me that she didn't ask deep enough questions. But it had been late, and he'd only stayed for thirty minutes. Tonight? My parents annual *Black Out Black Tie* dinner? He'd be my date for hours. "Are we crazy?"

"Yes, but I kinda dig it."

That caused me to face her. "Meaning...?"

She scrunched her nose and set the purple dress on the bed.

"Y'all always got along, care for each other, and I don't know. It makes sense."

"This is *fake*, Elle." My voice came out stronger as my face burned. Elle told me years ago she'd end our friendship if I ever went for Gabe. And now she was saying it *makes sense?* Anger prickled behind my eyes. "Not even a little bit real. Just to get Lovely Lily off my back."

"Girl, I understand. He gave me the whole spiel. I'm saying… it's not that unbelievable. The two of you as a couple? I'd have questions. That's all. Now, you need to wear the green dress. With these earrings." She pulled out two emerald studs my mom got me when I turned ten.

What ten-year-old was responsible enough for a precious gem?

I stood and took off my sweats and shorts. I wanted to dissect her comment with a fine-tooth comb. She'd have *concerns* if we were really dating? That was it? No knife throwing like she made it seem in high school? Why the change? I didn't ask any of the questions, too afraid of the real answer. Plus, we only had an hour to get ready before guests arrived, and Lovely Lily liked me and Elle downstairs to greet everyone. Called us her youths. "What about you? What are you wearing?"

"I'm borrowing your little black dress. Kirby is stopping by, so I want to look as hot as possible." She started stripping and slid my dress over her curvy body. It fit her so much better with her hips and boobs. She smoothed down her sides and whistled. "God, I look good."

"I admire your confidence."

She arched a brow as she eyed me. "Do you need Giselle to come out?"

Giselle—her super motivating alter ego who pretended to be a smoker. She started the gig in junior high, and the memory eased my tension.

"Maybe? This is all just so weird, and I hate feeling this way." I scrunched my eyes and made sure not to rub them because Lovely Lily spent hundreds on our hair and makeup already. I tended to avoid giving her reasons to critique me.

"Babe, look at me." Elle changed her voice to her *alter* ego, the one where she gave me pep talks. "You are beautiful and a butterfly. You'll soar and be magnificent. Look at this hair. I'd murder for your hair. And your face. So smooth, not a trace of a zit, you bitch." She squeezed my cheeks. "You will sparkle and fly and amaze and twirl and—"

"Okay, okay." I laughed and already felt better. "I know you wouldn't believe me, but I'm not like this at school. I'm... more confident in who I am there. Transferring to Central was the best decision in the world. I'm me. It's just being here that I feel stifled..."

"Hon, I do believe you and am counting down the seconds until I can move in with you in June. But your mom has always been toxic. You can still love her and be thankful without liking her, okay? Don't feel bad about that. Now, let's get ready and sneak some of your mom's vodka."

"There's a reason I kept you as my best friend."

"Future sister-in-law." She wiggled her eyebrows and started singing the wedding march. Had I envisioned what it'd be like to walk down the aisle with Van? Yeah, I was a teenager with a major hidden crush. But with Elle's jokes mentioning it, I couldn't help but imagine his smile, how he'd look in a tux. The way his brown eyes crinkled when he grinned and how something really funny made him laugh just a bit too loud. My own lips curved up, picturing him waiting for me at the end of the aisle. Elle would be there, grinning ear to ear, celebrating the fact we'd be sisters for real. Van and I would kiss and *chill out*. I righted my posture and hid my blush from Elle. I couldn't do this again, obsess over all the reasons I crushed on him *hard*. Not when we'd be spending even more time together. It was easy to do it from afar when I saw him once every few months. Now would be the worst time for the feelings to rush back.

It'd been less than twenty-four hours, and I was already picturing our wedding. I was worse than Lily. Ugh, at the thought of my mom, my smile disappeared. I had thirty-six hours until we could leave, and I could be strong until then.

Plus, Van was going to be here soon anyway, and that guy could charm a wall. I just had to avoid my mom until he got there, something I was getting better at doing.

An hour later, I was armed with a vodka Sprite that my dad snuck me with a wink. The emerald dress dipped low in the front, something I could pull off because I had a small chest. No big boobs for me. It didn't matter how many times I threw away the padded bras my mom bought me since she always gave me more. To *enhance* the features I didn't have. To bring out the curves I lacked. I smoothed my hands over my boobs, hating how they were so small, so unexciting. It meant going braless was so much easier than it was for Elle, but it was another reason for Lily to criticize me.

The band my mom hired played some acoustic version of a pop song as I scanned our foyer for my fake-boyfriend.

It didn't take long to find him. My mom had her arm looped with his as she escorted him to me. He looked *good,* wearing a black suit and gray button up and tie. His hair still had that messy feel but somehow seemed professionally styled. My heart skipped a beat at the sheer beauty of him. My lifelong crush. My breath stuttered at the split second I thought it was genuine, that he was staring at me *like that* for real. His brown eyes found mine, his gaze moving from my face to my chest, down to my legs before a smile broke out on his face. "Shit, Dani, you are gorgeous."

"Isn't she?" My mom beamed. "We spent a fortune taming that long hair, but with the right amount of product, and dedication, it can really shine." She reached out and picked up a curl, pinching her lips as she eyed a split hair.

My stomach twisted. I thought I put enough product in to hide the split ends. Of *course* she found one I'd missed. I wished I'd cut it or checked a third time for them. My eyes prickled, and I wanted to run back upstairs to ensure there wouldn't be any other reasons for her to scrutinize me.

"Look at you." Van placed a hand on my hip and carefully spun me around, his warm touch grounding me as he moved us slightly away from my mom. My skin buzzed from where he touched me through the fabric. "This is your color. I thought it'd be blue because of your eyes, but nah, green."

Gabe's words pulled me back from the mental gymnastics of trying to come up with an excuse to go upstairs. His tone was strong, self-assured. Everything I wished I was. I tried to get my mouth to smile, and he noticed, his eyes narrowing on my mouth. His fingers dug into my back, like he was projecting his confidence into me.

"I've tried telling her green was her color for years. Redheads with her complexion should only stick to certain shades. When she does, she is stunning! But does she listen to me? Of course not. She ignores the former Miss Illinois and reigning—"

"I'm stealing my girl away from a minute. I haven't seen her all day, and I can't stop staring at her." Van spoke to my mom, but his gaze was on mine. Anger lurked behind his pupils, mirroring the same irritation I had about her comments but then he placed his hand right along my collarbone, dragging his thumb along it.

I shivered head to toe as goosebumps exploded across my body from that one touch. Such a simple thing, the pad of his thumb on my skin, but I swore I felt that *everywhere.* My breath caught in my throat as he moved his hand to my lower back and guided us toward the living room currently set up with a round table. This was a fantasy come to life, him touching me, being proud to be seen with me. Even if it was fake, I let myself marvel in my fake-reality. We'd dance, kiss, and sneak up to my room where I could take off his handsome tux. Whoa, girl. I let him lead us, a bit dazed from his touch and smell.

Soap and rainforest. It made me think about kissing in the rain and watching thunderstorms through windows.

I sat down on one of the rented chairs, and he lowered himself next to me, resting his arm behind me. "Thanks for that."

"Oh, none of that was for show. You look gorgeous." He smiled, his cute little dimple showing on his right cheek.

His words lit me up like the twinkle lights decorating our foyer. He might be playing his part too well with the deep voice, but his compliment felt sincere enough to cause butterflies in my stomach. "Thanks, but I meant escaping from her." My face flamed red, and he chuckled. "Elle was with me all of today, so Lily kept it pretty tame."

"I don't understand it. You're beautiful, so I truly need someone to explain it to me why she says those things." He spoke with such conviction that my stomach swooped. I took a sip of the drink, dribbling a bit onto my dress like a total doofus.

"Damnit." I set the glass down and grabbed a small napkin to dab at the moisture where one would normally have cleavage. "Think anyone saw that?"

He cleared his throat. "Nah, you're good."

I glanced up at him, and his gaze burned my skin. He stared right at my chest, his nostrils flaring a bit. Another zing went through me at the heat in his gaze—there was no way Gabriel Van Helsing was looking *at me* like that. Then suddenly he sat up straighter and finished my drink. "Sneaking your parents' alcohol?"

"To survive tonight, God yes. My dad hooked me up." I laughed awkwardly, aware that his face was tighter than before. Lines surrounded his lips but not from smiling. I hated knowing I put them there.

"Good man." He finished my drink before standing up. "I'll pour us more."

He didn't say anything else as he walked away, leaving me alone at the table. My nerves twisted with worry at his abrupt departure. This wasn't something I'd considered when we made the deal in the truck—what if our friendship was ruined because of this? We'd known each other a decade. We went to each other's graduation, sporting events, and his grandparents' funerals. Sure, I secretly wanted his babies, but it was a fantasy. Not even in the realm of possibilities. I saw countless girls try to befriend Elle to get to her brother, so I'd never cross that line. *Even* if he was my ideal guy.

This fake dating thing was stupid if we'd risk our easy friendship. God, I'd see Elle the rest of my life. Did I want each get-together to be uncomfortable where Van and I avoided each other because of this well-intended but horrible idea?

I wouldn't have it.

I could survive my mom on my own if it meant keeping our friendship intact. Nodding to myself, I stood up in search of him so we could talk privately. I didn't get far though. A handsome guy wearing way too much cologne approached me.

"Daniella? Hi, it's wonderful to meet you. Your mother spoke so highly of you. I'm Brayden McCarl." He held out his hand, a shy smile crossing his face. While he looked humbler than all the others, it was the same setup as usual.

My mom pushing me toward another guy who wanted a trophy wife.

"Uh, look, my mom—"

"There you are, baby." Van's voice had an edge to it as he interrupted my mom's latest tryout for son-in-law. The protectiveness to his tone made my heart race a little faster, but that didn't prepare me for the kiss.

It wasn't on my mouth. No. Somehow, this was worse. It was *right* on the edge of where my lips met my cheek, and the touch singed me. The roughness of his day-old scruff tickled my sensitive skin, and his minty breath washed over me. Suddenly, Mc-what's-his-face disappeared, and it was just me and Van. His eyes darkened as he watched me, his face void of expression as I touched right where his lips were a second ago.

My pulse pounded at the base of my neck, and I could feel each heartbeat in the tips of my fingers. All from a simple kiss. I stared up at him, my fake boyfriend, unsure why I wanted him to do it again. Just to see if it was a fluke. No innocent kiss like that had any business turning my insides to fire.

"Right, uh well, I'm heading out. Nice to meet you."

I waved my hand in the air, not even caring that I'd forgotten about my mom's setup. Van still stood right next to me, so close his breath hit my face, and his body heat radiated off him. Attraction wasn't foreign to me. I'd done the one-night stand thing a few times with the right mood, but I'd been so focused on dance that it had been *so* long since I'd felt this. This lightning bolt of lust.

"Here. Figured you might need this." He grinned, handing me the new drink and losing all traces of heat I swore I saw on his face.

"Thank you." I exhaled, willing my pulse to settle as we sat back down. It was hard not to take the loss of interest in his eyes personally, but Van scooted his chair an inch away from me so our legs didn't touch. That stung. I might've imagined the chemistry between us, but even so, I knew I had to call this off.

But liquid courage never hurt anyone.

I took two large swigs, enjoying the burn of my mouth and throat. It didn't erase the tingle still remaining on my face from his lips, but it did get me in the right headspace. "Gabe, we need to talk."

He sat up straighter and leaned onto his elbows. A deep wrinkle formed on his forehead as he faced me. "Gabe? Am I in trouble?"

That made me smile. "Not yet."

"There's still time then." The bastard winked and relaxed, confusing me even more. He was so easygoing. He would definitely try and convince me this was no big deal, but I couldn't do it. Not after two awkward moments.

I swallowed the weird ball of emotion in my throat, almost like regret, and scooted closer. He tensed but didn't move as I leaned toward him. "I'm not sure we should do this," I whispered, careful that no one overheard us.

"Because of the kiss?" he whispered back, his lips almost brushing the shell of my ear.

"What? No. That was… no." I had to regroup. Between his kiss, his mouth, and his cologne, my brain was having a tough time sorting out words. "Ten years."

"Is a decade?" he answered, his tone slightly amused.

"Shut up." I snorted, thankful for a break in lust. I met his eyes and said, "I can't ruin our friendship." *What if I fall for you even more?* "What if… something could change and make things awkward between us. I love your family and—"

"Nothing weird will happen, D." He placed one large hand on my bare knee and squeezed. "I swear, okay? Nothing will change between us."

"I still think we should call it off," I mumbled, not confident in my words but needing to say them. His grip on my knee tightened for a second before he shook his head.

"No."

"After this weekend, we can end it. No drama. No harm."

"No." He said it more firmly this time, his eyes clouding with annoyance. "We agreed until New Year's, Daniella. That guy? There will be more of them. Who else will save you, hm? You have a whole other day and all of Christmas break."

He was right. I knew that, but the awkward zing from earlier still remained fresh in my mind. "Pinky promise right now that nothing changes."

He rolled his eyes but held out his hand, pinky outward. "I promise."

I interlocked our fingers and kissed my fist, waiting for him to do the same. He did, but while we said the words, my gut still felt like it was a lie.

Fake dating Gabriel Van Helsing was going to change *everything*.

CHAPTER
FOUR

Gabriel

By some miracle, not only did the Bears win their game, but things were back to normal with Daniella. She hung out at our house on the holiday like all the years before—wearing sweats and chatting with Elle nonstop. When it was the three of us, shit was easy. I wasn't thinking about the newfound attraction that had gripped me the night before, stealing my common sense and confusing the hell out of me.

Daniella was beautiful. That was my objective opinion, but seeing her all dressed up in that low-cut outfit? Made a man forget that we had a *fake* deal going on. But my head was screwed on right as I said goodbye to my parents. I was picking Dani up before returning to campus so I could get back before we needed to be at the rink. My bag was loaded, and both my parents *and* Elle stood at the edge of the garage watching me. This was the farewell team. They did this every time I left.

"Okay, let the hug train start."

My dad pulled me in first, his thick arms enclosing around me with his familiar scent of cigars. "It was nice seeing you, kid. Play well tonight. We'll stream it."

"Always try my best."

I broke the hug and went to my mom. I was at least six inches taller than her, but that never mattered. She ran the house and did it with love and a terrifying voice when she was pissed. She cupped my face and gave me the same look she had when I told her about Daniella. Her eyes got all soft, and her mouth had a sly smile.

"Mom, no emotional stuff."

"I'm just so happy you and Dani are together. It's perfect. My baby boy has settled down and found a wonderful woman to be his partner. This is all I've wanted for you."

Guilt ate at me, knowing it was a lie. I hated keeping something from my mom. If she found out, she'd be so hurt. Best way to avoid feelings though, use humor.

"To have a girlfriend? Wow, dream big, Mom." My voice came out normal, thank god.

She swatted at my shoulder. "No, idiot. To find someone who totally gets you and doesn't give a shit about your stick."

Elle snorted into her fist. *That's what she said.*

"Don't be weird." I tried pulling away, a dull ache of shame edging itself into my gut. I didn't love lying to my mom, especially when she was this fucking happy, but we were in it. Six weeks of it.

I still couldn't believe Dani had tried to end it. I'd deal with that on the drive back.

"Love you, Mom."

She yanked me tighter against her into a real hug for a full ten seconds before I moved onto Elle. She made sure to meet my eyes before clapping real dramatically. "I've always wanted her to be family, and maybe she'll be my sister-in-law someday!"

"Oh, that would be *amazing.*" my mom added.

I mouthed *fuck you* to my dear sister before hopping into my truck and getting the heck out of my hometown. Dani's emotions had worn off on me, and I wanted to return to campus where I didn't have all guilty feelings. I waved at my family, still standing and watching me leave, and finally took a breath.

No more touching Daniella and accidentally thinking about her lips. No more holding her hand or breathing in her floral perfume that enticed me more than it should. We could be friends again who kept up the farce as needed.

The brief moment of happiness dulled at thinking about the after-party later that night. Becca would be there, and having Dani by my side would be helpful...but then, we could use some distance. We'd survive tonight and then we'd schedule dinner next week. Send a photo to the family and all that.

Content with my plan, I drove to her house and parked on the side of the road. I didn't even get two steps out of my car before she bolted out of the front door with her bag and flushed cheeks.

She wore ripped black jeans and a tight white shirt with the school logo on it, and her hair was down, covering half of her face. It didn't hide the anger though.

"Yo, you alright?"

"Gabey Baby, put your cute ass back in the truck and drive."

"Yes, ma'am."

I wasn't a fool, I obeyed. Dani straight up threw her bag into the back and slammed the door, buckling her seatbelt and crossing one leg over the over with a loud huff leaving her mouth.

"Want to put on my anger playlist?" I asked, sort of kidding but also serious if she was into it.

She looked at me, her large blue eyes crinkling at the sides as she threw her head back and smiled. "You are the best fake boyfriend, ever. Fuck yes, put on the anger playlist."

"You got it."

Three songs later, we were on the highway, and it was like a switch went off in Dani. Her smile was back to normal, and she stopped sitting straight as a board. "Have you ever had a girlfriend before?"

"Mm, random question, but girlfriend? With a label?" I shook my head, picturing all the girls I had *things* with but never committed to. I was always so focused on hockey, and honestly, no one had ever clicked enough to put in the effort. The idea wasn't terrible to me, but after years of putting hockey first, it was easy to keep everything shallow. Surface level. "No, don't think so."

"Great, me neither. So, not one of us knows what the hell we're doing." She laughed and texted someone on her phone. "It's Cami. There's a party tonight the girls are going to, and honestly, a fun outing is what I want. A night out where I can wear whatever I want and be myself."

She never had a boyfriend? Was that what she said? Huh. I thought back to high school and all the times I visited home. She always came by herself. I guess I assumed she would've dated at the community college last year, but it felt weird to picture her with someone now. There wasn't a soul good enough for her.

I cleared my throat to refocus. "Ah, so I had a favor to ask about tonight." I hated to take her away from her friends and a night she clearly needed to wash away her toxic mom, but *Becca.* "As my girlfriend, I might need you at a party running defense. I'm sorry."

"After the stunt you pulled with my mom, you could ask me to dive into a brick wall for you, and I would. Yeah, I'll head to a party with you." She spoke way too fast and a little too loudly, a clear sign of her enthusiasm. "Where?"

"It's at the hockey house. We can make an appearance and then I'll take you to your other party so you can hang out with your girls." I snuck a glance at her, and she looked at me with so much appreciation that my chest felt all weird again. "Or... we get a little drunk so you can forget this weekend."

"Either option sounds great, Van." She shook her head, her cheeks reddening as she stared out the window. While she seemed better than when she'd gotten into the car, it was evident something was on her mind. "Are we... how is this going to work on campus? At first, I figured we'd pretend for our family's sake and get a lunch here and there, but if I'm with you tonight, people will talk."

"Yeah." I rubbed my jawline, irritated that she was right. I hadn't planned all the details, just knew that I liked the idea. How *would* it work on campus? I needed her around me to keep Becca away, but that meant the lie would spread beyond our close circle. "I mean, we'll say we're together. That shouldn't be a big deal. You said you're focusing on your team, and I'm busy with the season. I don't imagine it'll be too complicated."

She didn't answer immediately. In fact, she remained silent so long I got worried. "Right?"

"Without us ever having a significant other, are we sure we should—"

"You're not breaking us up, D. Not now."

"Fr-aking us up, you mean."

"Come again?"

She laughed at herself and held out her hands, swirling them around. "Fake breaking up. Fr-aking up. It's the perfect smash up of words."

"Jesus." I snorted. "Still not happening. We'll figure things out as we go. It can't be that difficult. We're smart, capable people. Hell, we're both leading teams, so there has to be something in our minds that works well."

So, the rest of the drive we made a plan. An easy one. A *safe* one. She'd attend the party with me tonight but then weekly dinners, some planned selfies, and bam. We'd survive the holidays with our families and then *end* it after the New Year because we were better off as friends. Mission accomplished. Couldn't be *that* hard.

We lost the game because of one fucking person. I'd never say that to the team, but I knew it—Cal Holt. Hotshot and already drafted to the NHL, the kid played like we were all lucky to breathe the same air as him, and it took all my effort not to shove him as I walked toward the showers. His attitude and demeanor were the worst on the team, and it was amazing any organization wanted him. He had talent, sure, but he was an asshole. *And the alt captain.*

There was no laughter or banter in the locker room from me. Not this time. Not when the loss could've been prevented if Cal had stuck to the plays instead of getting fancy and veering off to be a lone wolf. If I were Coach, I'd rip him a new one, but I couldn't. That wasn't my role.

Ty and Jenkins goofed off though, laughing and talking about how drunk they'd be that night. They should be quiet, focusing on the game. Not acting like everything was fine. We didn't win to the easiest team in the division. Did they not fucking care? Was it a joke to them? I studied the players' reactions, my knuckles going white against my thigh. Christopher kept his back to us, his always-present *protein drink* shoved in the black duffel he always kept zipped shut. Everyone else left their stuff open but never him. I knew *why*— the dude always put stuff he shouldn't into his drinks. But my anger was too much right now, and it wasn't the time to blow up at him for using steroids.

The hot water blasted my face, and I washed away the gross feeling of the loss. I wanted my senior year to be the best, for us to make the Winter Cup and to break records. But not beating Eastern? They were a joke, and we'd *lost*. We played down to their level and fucking suffered for it. Because of Cal. And no one seemed to give a shit except me.

My muscles tensed as play after play went through my head. If *he'd* passed the puck and did what we practiced, we could've scored. If *he'd* remembered we were a team and not shadows who followed him around, we could've worked together. My fists clenched as I cussed. *Fuck* that guy.

I finished up, wrapping the towel around my waist before heading back toward my locker with the intent to settle down. Confrontation wasn't my thing, and I preferred to avoid situations that made me lose my temper—like with Becca and right now. I wanted a few beers to wash away the L and to move on to something more positive. But someone stood in my way. Assistant Coach Michael Reiner.

"Dude, what?" I barked, annoyed at his proximity to me. He was all up in my space, his eyes narrowing.

He ran a hand over his jaw, his face twisting into a grimace. "Heading somewhere fun? You alright with this? With how *everyone* played?"

"No, I'm pissed. Obviously." My blood boiled, and my fingers flexed against the towel. I tried to move past him, but he wouldn't let me. The guy was quick. "Fuck, I want to dress and get out of here."

"You're pissed? Ohhhh sweet. About damned time we found some emotion in ya, Cap. Pissed, huh? What does that mean then? You finally gonna take a stand?" Something lit up in his eyes, a spark of excitement that made me nervous.

"What are you talking about?" I was angry at Cal and Ty, not *him*, but his provoking was making my skin crawl with brewing tension. The guys liked Reiner. He was fresh off the ice after graduating the year before and had a swagger that made people follow him. He knew his shit but never flaunted it. Most of the time, I respected him, but right now? No.

"You are the coach on the ice once the puck drops, Gabriel. You. Not me, not Simpson, you. Everything we do before the game is on us. But game time? That shit is you. The captain." He poked my chest, his eyes flashing with challenge. "I've watched you the past year and a half. You're laidback. Easy. Unflustered. Unemotional."

"Your point?" I gritted out, my left eye twitching from the conversation. All my past coaches loved my demeanor and how I carried myself on the ice. I wasn't a hothead, and I never reacted with anger. I encouraged, used tactics my parents always did—positive reinforcement, focusing on the good in hopes it would foster more outcomes. It was intentional and my choice. Plus, too much emotion never helped anyone. It was messy, and I preferred my life as uncomplicated as possible on and off the ice.

Reiner crossed his arms and rocked back on his heels, his mouth curved up in a smile, like he was about to tell a joke. My body tensed, waiting for the punchline.

"Stop waiting for someone else to deal with the issues when you have more influence right now. Own it, and do something about it. This is on you." His gaze moved for a half-second toward the other side of the locker room where Cal Holt sprayed cologne on his neck and eyed himself in the mirror. Then, Reiner hit my shoulder and walked away.

Me deal with Cal? God, no. I couldn't think of anything I'd rather do less than talk with the fuckhead. Plus, why couldn't Reiner handle it? We all knew the two of them had some weird friendship outside the rink. He could deal with the man-child during their meet-ups and with their inside jokes.

I dressed fast, the locker room starting to get louder with plans for the night. We should've won the game. There should be zero chatter about post-game plans. Just a growing silence of frustration. Despite stretching and icing, my shoulders felt too stiff, and I blamed the loss for my stress. The tension hadn't left by the time I got back to my apartment to drop my shit off. The usual post-game energy surged through me, this time fueled with more than adrenaline. It was uncertainty, anger, and irritation.

Cal.

Ty.

Jenkins.

The fact the team didn't care?

I groaned, rolling my shoulder before checking my phone. A sliver of relief flowed through me, releasing part of the anxiety growing in my chest. The party. Daniella. Maybe her bubble of happiness and goofy demeanor could help pull me out of this mood. My lips curved up as I thought about whatever ridiculous thing would come out of her mouth. With a new spring in my step, I walked toward her dorm and could almost feel the stress of the game leaving my body.

Van: I'm outside.

D: Great, um, I'm having a moment.

Van: A good moment?

D: Could you come to my room please? 20A.

I pocketed my phone and frowned. With her, one never knew what was going on. Someone exited the south side of her dorm, and I snuck in. Curiosity got the best of me as I made my way to the second floor and knocked. A moment? Like, she was on her period? Or had something happened with her mom, and she was upset?

That sent an uncomfortable brick to my stomach, and I walked faster.

"D," I said, hitting the door again. Soft shuffles carried through and then a click. I wasn't sure what greeted me when she opened the door. It was a flash of bright red hair, a black lace thing, and skin. So much skin. "Um, what?"

"I need help. Get in here." She pulled on my shirt and yanked me inside with more strength than I would've imagined. She smelled like summer, and it took me a second to realize she wore a jean skirt and hardly anything else. Stickers covered her nipples.

Fuck, it was warm in her room. I adjusted the collar of my shirt and cleared my throat. "Why are you almost naked?" My voice came out hoarser than intended.

"All the cool kids are doing it," she said, sarcasm dripping from her tone. I couldn't see her face due to all the hair, but she stood tall and gave her bare back to me. "I'm not sure how this happened, but my crop top is stuck in my hair. Horribly. I've been trying to get it untangled for ten minutes now."

"Ah."

Yeah, I said 'Ah' like that made perfect sense as to why Daniella was shirtless in front of me. Her back was all muscles and freckles. She was a petite thing but strong. She had to be with all the dancing, but *shit*, I didn't expect my stomach to drop or my heart to beat a little faster just from seeing her bare back. Could spines be sexy? They were bones, but the curve of hers had my tongue swelling in my mouth, had me curious about what it'd be like to lick down that skin. Two delicious dimples sat above her ass, and I swallowed, hard.

Get it the fuck together, Van. It's D.

"You need me to… sort it out?" I thought of the rink, Cal's face, my mom. Anything. The mere sight of her back sent my libido into dangerous, unfamiliar territory.

"Obviously." She huffed. "Please."

I can do this. I stepped closer to her, noting the way her hair was so silky and smelled like cherries. My fingers grazed her neck a few times as I found the clasp and the large knot surrounding it. "Damn, D. This is bad."

"I know. Do you think you can save it, or do we need scissors?"

"Cut your hair?" The idea appalled me. She had beautiful hair, and to trim it? "No, we don't need them. I'll get it." So, I focused more. I found the parts that were so tangled it was a rattail, and I smoothed it out with my fingers. I ignored the line of freckles on her back and the curve of her spine *and* that every once in a while, goosebumps would cover her neck. The tension in my shoulders doubled from sheer willpower to not let my attraction to her get in the way.

I could be fascinated by my sister's best friend and my fake girlfriend. That was normal. Acting on it would *not* be.

"Almost got it." My voice sounded typical to my own ears, and for that, I was proud. She had no idea all the thoughts I had

TAKE THE LEAD   41

in my head about her skin and those damn nipple stickers? I wanted to peel them away and see what was underneath. She had perfect small tits that were so fucking perky I knew they'd bring me to my knees.

"There." I undid the lace top from her hair and set it on the bed. I should've stepped back and turned around to give her privacy. Hell, even leaving the room would've been a better choice, but no. My dumbass lifted up her hair and smoothed it over her shoulder. It was so silky and thick. Auburn hair didn't do it for me typically, but on her? It fit, so well. She let out a little sound, kind of like a moan and squeak at the same time, and I laughed. "No hair loss either."

"Thank you, Van, seriously. I almost called to cancel my girlfriend duty out of sheer embarrassment." She faced me with bright red cheeks, and my gaze dropped to her round tits again. She followed my attention and scrunched her nose. "You seem confused."

"Why are you wearing... those things?" The temperature had to rise about ten degrees at this point. At least. Casually brushing my hand over my temple, I forced an easy smile. I was calm and cool, just like I was on the ice. No emotion. No mess. Chill.

"Had a nipple situation last year, never again." She shrugged, laughing at herself with an ease I admired. She cupped her boobs and squeezed them together, not at all noticing how my body went rigid.

My cock twitched.

I was a statue of lust.

What the *fuck* was she doing?

"I know they're small," she said, holding them in her hands. "But I gotta hide the girls when I wear that thing."

"What thing?" I croaked, sounding like I'd spent six weeks in the desert without water. Why was she still touching them? Cupping them like how I now wanted to? Was she always naked like this?

"The culprit of this whole mess." She picked up the black lace garment and brought it over her head, adjusting it to cover her boobs. The half-shirt rested inches above her trim stomach and teased all her skin with the lace. "See? Great look, but a nip could sneak out."

God, I'd love to see that.

She looked at me expectantly, and for a second, I wondered if I'd said that out loud. I shuffled my feet. "Right, can't... can't have that. No nip slips."

"You see my point then." She went to her closet and pulled out an extra-large green coat that hung around her and paired it with black Vans. I couldn't stop watching her get ready with her pink lipstick and large hoop earrings. She was so damn pretty, and when she was done, she smiled at me. A real, genuine Daniella grin that made my insides get all uncomfortable. "Thank you for helping. I am ready to be your clingy girlfriend, Van. You tell me what you need, and I'll do it."

Show me your tits. Let me taste you. I said neither of those. I held out my hand and jutted my chin toward the door. "Let's go then."

CHAPTER
FIVE

Daniella

Hockey boys partied a little differently than what I was used to. It wasn't anything bad, I drank with football guys and the girls a lot, but it was certainly... rougher. It wasn't abnormal for two guys to wrestle around for a few minutes before picking themselves off the floor to laugh about it. If that happened at a post-football game party, there'd be black eyes and a full battle.

I didn't dislike it though, the vibe here. The house was taken care of with a slight smell of gear and lemon cleaner. It wasn't intentional that I'd never been to this hockey house before, just that I didn't often find myself hanging with hockey players. Van and I would see each other on campus and always say hey, but attending a party *with* him was news. Big news.

Like, everyone who walked by us did a double take.

Leaning toward him, I whispered, "People are staring."

"Good." He moved his arm around my shoulders and pulled me closer to him. We hadn't touched since he let go of my hand outside the porch, and now, the heat of his palm spread from my upper arm to between my thighs. Three different girls approached him on the way in, wanting autographs and photos. He obliged but gave them his fake smile. And as soon as the photo was done, his arm was back around me.

It was wild to see how popular he really was. Girls buzzed around him constantly in the short time we were there. When one got bold and approached him for a dance, he pointed to me and grunted *girlfriend*.

Never thought there'd be a downside to being Van, but I understood it more. If he wanted to relax and just hang out, he'd never be able to without a decoy. Even now, we were a drink in, and he couldn't sit still.

He clenched his jaw as his gaze moved toward the front of the house, right when two beautiful bombshells walked in. It was like a movie scene—heads turned, and the girls ate it up.

Rightfully so, they were clearly hot and knew it.

Like effortlessly beautiful and stacked. Holy boobs, their tits were huge and perky. A flash of envy went through me, and I forced it down. I was okay with who I was despite my mom's words my entire life, but it didn't stop the insecurity when I saw people who looked like them.

Van's grip tightened on me, and his entire demeanor changed, pulling me from my own self-pitying thoughts. He wasn't just tense anymore—he was *pissed*. Like, eye twitching a bit and neck muscle bulging out. One of the girls stared directly at him, her red lips curving into an 'o' shape as she eyed me head to toe, slowly and without holding back her disdain.

"Gabriel," she said, almost like a purr. "You played so well tonight. I missed you."

Shit. I never even asked about the game. I was an asshole. I scooted closer to him so there was no space between our thighs, and he tucked me into his body more. His warmth embraced me like an old friend, my face reddening on its own accord.

"Thanks, Becca." His voice was strained and lacked the usual warmth I was so used to—Van rarely acted on anger.

Sure, he'd flex his muscles and have all the signs, but yelling? Never. That wasn't him.

"Do you have a few minutes to talk? I'm sure she can spare you." She pursed her lips and gave me a fake smile, one that sent ice in my veins. This wasn't just some mean girl bullshit that I grew up with in Lovely Lily's pageant world. She was intentionally wanting me to feel small and unnecessary. But why? Who was she to Van?

Was this part of the reason he asked for his fake-tionship? Not just to fend of interest but *her* in particular? She seemed more aggressive than the rest. I narrowed my eyes at Becca and refused to be intimidated by her beauty. Van stood up to my mom for me so the least I could do was be strong for him.

"Pretty sure my girlfriend prefers I stick by her side." Van moved his hand to my waist, picked me up, and placed me right on his lap. His fingers dug into my hip, sending a ripple of tingles down my legs and to my toes.

I was consumed by the clean smell surrounding me, his warmth, the way his voice vibrated through his chest and into my back pressing up against him. His thick and strong thighs tensed beneath me. All my senses went into overdrive while Becca's face tightened.

She sucked in a breath, her lips curling up in a sneer. "I thought you didn't do commitment. *Girlfriend?*"

"I didn't stutter." His tone was firmer than I had ever heard, and I knew, deep in my soul, I never wanted to be on the receiving end.

She didn't take a hint. She pouted and jutted out her hip. "Babe, come on. We hadn't defined anything, and that's on me. We can talk it out."

"Leave us alone, Becca." Van's voice was colder than ice, piercing the air between us. Nothing but a chilled awkwardness remained. Becca blinked twice, her eyes growing misty.

Her posture stiffened before she spun around like a villain.

All she was missing was the cape. She joined her friend, and the two of them moved onto a different room.

I had so many questions, but my poor brain couldn't handle thinking when Van's fingers were below my belly button. He hadn't repositioned them. Not even a little.

Why did I wear a crop top? I shuddered, and his rough fingers moved from just beneath my belly button to my side. A much safer location. Thank *god* the room was dark or everyone would be able to see my full-body blush.

He leaned onto the couch more, taking me with him so I was straight up snuggling against him now. Me. Awkward, redheaded Daniella Laughlin cuddling up with the handsome hockey captain at a party. My thoughts became clearer now that Becca left, and unease crept in. He needed me for some reason, but this *touching* was almost too much.

"*What* are we doing?" I managed to ask, my damn face redder than the Solo cups throughout the party.

He forced a laugh, but it didn't sound like the easy chuckle I grew up hearing. "I'm relaxing, D. Well, trying to. You could put more effort into it instead of acting like a damn board. You're so stiff."

"Rude." I pinched his side, making him laugh for real. The genuine humor put me at ease. This banter was normal, was us. My momentary shield of insecurity crashed down, and my unfiltered words flowed out. "It's not every day I lay on a couch with a big muscly guy. Remember? Never had a boyfriend before."

"I haven't forgotten." His eyes darkened for a second before he finally moved his hand around from my stomach and placed it on my neck. His gaze dropped to my mouth, and *fuck. Shit.* He was gonna kiss me.

I wouldn't survive it. I'd combust into a pile.

My legs clenched together as heat ignited my insides. His breath hit my face, and I held onto him for dear life... ready for the moment our lips met. It might've been a secret fantasy, wondering how he'd taste and kiss all these years, but to experience it? I held my breath, desperate to finally know how his lips felt. My nerves were on edge, tingling with anticipation, but the kiss never came. He just looked at me and leaned closer, his eyes bouncing back and forth between mine.

"Hm?" I said, wired and so aware of how hard his body was.

He gave me a sheepish smile. "Becca was staring at us. Sorry I turned up the charm there."

"God, no kidding." I forced a laugh, needing to downplay the aggressive attraction I had for him. Embarrassment melted through me like butter, and I cleared my throat. *Be chill.* "That was a panty-melting move there, Van. The eye contact, the leaning. Fuck. No wonder you have so many fling-flangs."

Distance. Put distance between us.

"Yeah?" He arched a brow and gave me a filthy smirk, one that I had no business receiving.

"Shut up. You know what I meant." I tried to push off him, but he held on tighter, his fingers going behind my jacket and onto my bare back. A wicked gleam was in his eye, on the edge of playful. This was new territory. "Are you trying to fluster me right now, Gabriel?"

"Mm, my full name. Do I *fluster* you?"

Was it me or was his voice gravellier? Deeper, somehow? Was this fake-flirting because Becca was at the party, or was this... no. *No.* It was a show. He said girlfriend duties. *He admitted she was watching, dumbass.*

Feeling a little stupid, my skin prickled with shame at how far I'd let my thoughts go without supervision. If he wanted a show, I could play along. After everything he did for me with my mom, I owed him this.

I turned around to straddle him, my skirt riding up in the process. I never wore a skirt without my spandex underneath, but Van's gaze zoned it between my legs as my thighs covered his. "Think she's watching?" I asked, just above a whisper.

He nodded, his gaze never leaving mine as he slowly brought his fingers up my spine. The other hand moved to my jaw, tilting my head to the left as he traced where my pulse went haywire. This was dangerous. A new line between us. Even if it was clearly for show, my body felt alive, wanted even. His nostrils flared as he traced my throat, down to my chest where the crop top stopped.

His fingers trembled a little bit, so unlike the confident Van I knew, and I sucked in air as he moved toward my ribs. I'd let him go as far as he pushed, damn well acknowledging this would never happen again. It was the showdown with Becca, the party atmosphere, or something. I was channeling my inner Cami, just being wild and free and enjoying myself with my fake boyfriend. I'd replay this moment in my head over and over, pretending I really was his girlfriend later.

Then, something crashed.

I bolted out of his lap, my adrenaline spiking as fight or flight took over. A large armoire or something hit the ground right in the center hall, and glass shattered everywhere. "Oh no," I said, clutching my chest as everyone stilled around us.

"My bad." A deep, slurred voice came from Cal Holt as the guy shrugged and gave a lazy smile. "Didn't see it there."

Cal stumbled a bit to the left, knocking into a girl and causing her to spill her drink all over herself, which pissed off her boyfriend, a beefy guy with a mustache. "What the *fuck,* man?"

"S'my bad, bruh." He grinned, clearly sloshed, and the large guy grabbed him by the collar.

"Get the fuck outta this house." He tossed him toward the door, but Cal had no balance or skills. He fell hard onto the ground in a loud thud. No one spared him a second glance as he groaned on the floor. Van stood, his hand sliding off my hip as he shook his head. If daggers could fly out of his eyes, they would right now and go straight into Cal. Everyone knew the hotshot hockey player was a bit of a dick, but a sloppy drunk too?

"He's a fucking mess." Van gritted his teeth, and his eyes darkened.

"We should help him," I said, my stomach souring at something similar that happened to me a few months ago. A low moment of my captainship when I overheard girls talking about how I wasn't pretty enough or talented enough to be captain. I'd gotten too drunk, and Cami had taken care of me. The girl who hated me for stealing her dream. Van snorted, an amused look crossing his face.

"Um, no. He can deal with his own shit." He huffed, like my suggestion was hilarious. A flash of anger got me tense.

"Gabe." My voice went low, and he stilled. "*You're* the captain of the hockey team. He is on the team. You have to do something."

Gabe raised a hand in the air, clearly annoyed. "He's the reason we lost the game, Daniella. He's an asshole with an ego to match it. He doesn't deserve shit." Red splotches covered Van's cheeks, and I took a deep breath, really thinking about my words before pushing back on him. This was the most fired up I'd seen him, and I wasn't sure I liked it.

"When people act like that, sometimes it's because they are rotten. But more often than not… it's because they're hurting." I squeezed his forearm, the tendons flexing against my fingers. His brown eyes got darker as we stared at each other. I wasn't backing down. "You're not the person I thought you were if you leave him on the floor."

His gaze never left my face, his jaw tensing with every breath. A myriad of emotions danced across his eyes, some harsher than others.

Then he ground his teeth together before marching to Cal. His movements were jerky, and it was obvious with the stiffness that he hated every second of it, but at least he was being a leader. It was the biggest lesson I'd learned from Cami earlier that year. Being a leader was hard and wasn't defined by the title or the badge. It was the little things that not everyone saw. Like when she took care of me and walked me home. Or how she helped me cover up my hangover the next day. I was forever grateful and would be that type of leader the rest of my life.

"Get up. Come on." He kneeled next to Cal and shoved his arm. "Pick your ass up now."

"Chill, man." Cal groaned as Van pulled him up by his arm. "Hop off my dick."

"You're a mess and causing a scene." Van helped him stand and half-shoved, half-guided him to the door. "Where do you live?"

"Not going home."

"Yes, you are. You're plastered."

Cal stumbled down the porch steps and rolled onto the grass, staring up at the sky with a dazed look. There was an achingly familiar glint in his eyes, like he was lost and sad and confused. My heart hurt for him. "Cal?"

"What up, gingy? Carpet match the drapes, eh?"

"Don't speak to her, you son of a bitch." Van kicked his foot before glaring at me. "Still think this is a good idea, *Daniella*?"

"It's the right thing to do, *Gabriel*." I crossed my arms over my chest, suddenly chilled. There was a bite to his tone, and while I knew Cal pissed Gabe off, I didn't like it being directed at me.

"Where do you live? Do I need to call Reiner?" Van asked, pinching the bridge of his nose and rolling his shoulders.

"Nah, he'll bitch at me."

"As he should. You're an embarrassment to yourself, to the team, and to this school. You boast about being drafted, but you'll last two seconds in the NHL. You're a team of one, and a douchebag no one wants to play next to. Tonight's game? That was on you. You're the reason we lost. You might know this, and you might not care, but I hope you felt every ounce of disappointment in the locker room. I wish it kept you up at night because you are the problem on the ice, Cal Holt. Now, give me your fucking address, or I'm calling Coach. Babysitting you off the ice is *not* my job."

Not once did Van's voice shake. He spoke with conviction and a calm that made every insult worse. No overt displays of rage or emotion. Never that. Just harsh words that cut deep. My eyes prickled with the anger in his tone and even the truth. He felt everything he said.

It shocked the hell out of me to see this side of him. I thought I knew everything about Gabe but maybe I didn't. The perfect guy I assumed he was would never consider leaving a teammate on the ground.

"A couple blocks from here." Cal pushed himself up, wincing as he wobbled a few times. His entire expression seemed off, like the lights went out behind his eyes. "I can walk alone."

"We'll make sure you get there safe." Van met my eyes, and I glanced at the ground. I wasn't sure I liked this version of him.

"I can head home, call a car or something," I said, taking a step back from the situation. It was tense, and distance from Van seemed like the right move.

"No." He ran a hand over his jaw. "I'll walk you back."

"It's fine, you should handle Cal."

"Please, D."

His tone changed, and his eyes went all soft. I was a sucker for puppy-dog eyes, big and brown and sad. He held out his hand, worry lines stretching across his face as I stared at it for a few seconds.

Did I take it? Did that mean I accepted how he treated Cal? No. We could talk about it later, but there was a magnetic pull to him I couldn't explain. With a resigned sigh, I grabbed his hand and tried not to think about the twist in my gut.

There was so much to deal with. The attraction, the touches, the fact that I'd wanted him to kiss me before the crash. Then, with him not wanting to help a teammate? Sure, I'd heard about Cal's reputation of being a total asshole, but could the rumors be exaggerated?

I kept my thoughts to myself as the three of us walked the short distance to an old-bricked building with a bar nearby. Cal stumbled twice, and Van steadied him, but no one spoke. The silence was horrible and thick, heavy with emotions between the two of them. Every few seconds, Van would change his grip on my fingers like he couldn't get comfortable.

"I'll walk him up, and you stay here, okay?" Van waited for me to glance up at him before he nodded. He helped Cal with his keys and disappeared through the glass door. Not two minutes went by before he returned, letting out a long whistle. "Jesus. Sorry about that."

"Never apologize for helping someone who needs it." I held my coat tighter around my middle as the night chilled. I wanted to sleep, to put distance between my family, Van, this night. "I think I'll head home now. We accomplished your mission, right?"

I stared at the empty street where laughter and sounds of music echoed. Crickets chirped like mad as fall surrounded us, and there was a faint smell of a bonfire somewhere in the distance.

"Sure, yeah." He pocketed his hands, rocking back on his feet and looking unsure of himself. "You did great."

"Good."

Shit, this was awkward.

"I'll walk you home." He cleared his throat and frowned at me for a beat before tilting his head to the side. "Are you upset with me?"

"You were an asshole to him. I've never seen that side of you, and it... doesn't look good."

"Daniella, Cal is a poison to this team." He shook his head hard, flashing his teeth. "I might've been an ass, sure, but he deserved it. You wouldn't get it."

"I wouldn't understand? Me? The girl who grew up with the ultimate mean girl as my mom? The girl whose dance team tried to stage a mutiny on me? Yeah. Got it." My temples throbbed with annoyance, and I took off in the direction of my dorm. It was a ten-minute walk, but I moved fast. Desperate to get away from Van, to just think, I quickened my pace. He wasn't far behind me, but he was a smart guy and kept his distance, not saying a word.

I slid my keycard into my dorm building, and once it unlocked, then I glanced back at him. "Text me where to meet next week for lunch or whatever."

"D, come on." He ran a hand through his hair, the ends sticking up in a very cute way. *Not* cute enough for me to prolong this night though.

"I'm tired. Thank you again for everything and the ride back. We'll talk soon." I didn't wait for a response. I went inside and didn't look back once. Not only was I battling an attraction to Van that I'd been able to hide all these years, but I was learning different sides of him. It was a reality check of sorts to see Gabe act that way. It was cruel. Different than anything I'd witnessed from him before, and I hated it. My version of Gabe was kind and helpful and gentle with words. That guy? I didn't know him.

I chewed my lip, my fantasy about Gabe crashing down with reality. Maybe this was a good thing? Helped me see more of a picture of him? I rubbed my temples, exhausted and annoyed.

Regardless of how much I didn't want things to get weird between us, it was already happening.

CHAPTER
SIX

Gabriel

I planned on watching football all Sunday with the hopes of ignoring the pang in my chest that hadn't left since Friday night. Some of the guys were coming over for the Bears game, but that wasn't for another few hours.

I'd already done the little schoolwork I needed, worked out, and I *still* had a restless energy. My knee bounced up and down as I tried finishing my resume. I didn't know what my skills were or what I had to offer the working world. I didn't have the passion for anything the way others did. My sister knew exactly what she wanted to do for the rest of her life, and I was envious. It had always been hockey for me, but that was winding down. To have that focus aimed at something else would be great. Instead, I stared at a word document with my name, email, and phone number.

Quotes movies well. Loves hockey. Uses jokes when confronted.

I was pathetic. I attempted flipping through channels to find an old movie but nada.

Deep down, I knew I needed to talk to Daniella but couldn't bring myself to do it. A part of me was guilty, but another part felt justified. Cal needed an ass kicking, and verbal was about the only kind I'd ever do. No quick punches to fight it out. Wasn't my style.

But for her to call me an asshole? Maybe I was. I ran my hand through my hair, pulling the ends in frustration.

I shouldn't have told her she didn't get it. Of course, she'd understand That was on me, and I twirled my phone in my hand, staring at the messages I'd typed in my notes.

I'm sorry, could we get coffee?

Could I buy you cheesecake as an 'I'm sorry' gesture?

The girl loved cheesecake, so the bribe might work. I sent the second message and set my phone on the coffee table out of reach. That would help me to not check it every three seconds like a fucking lunatic.

But then someone knocked on my door.

Daniella! I bolted up and swung it open without checking who it was. That was my mistake. Cal Holt stood outside my door, hands in his pockets and his face pale. Nothing could've shocked me more. I rocked back on my heels, blinking to give myself a second. Then I took in his appearance. Disheveled was putting it nicely. "You look like hell."

He cleared his throat. "Can I come in?"

"Fine." I moved aside, completely confused by the turn of events. Cal showing up here? How did he even know where I lived? Why was he at my place?

"Reiner gave me your address."

Ah. "And you're stopping by because…?"

He shifted his weight back and forth, clearly uncomfortable. "Thank you for Friday night. I'm sorry for insulting your girlfriend."

"She's not—" I paused, mentally slapping myself. "It's done. No big deal."

"It *is* a big deal." He looked at the ground, his shoulders hunched, and something Dani said came into my mind.

People who act like that are often hurting. And like an ass, I'd told her she didn't understand. It didn't sit right with me.

He met my gaze, his eyes wide as he spoke slowly. "Everything you said that night, I remember."

The clarity on his face, the timbre of his voice—this seemed serious.

"Look." Discomfort lodged in my throat at how direct and awkward this situation was. I was the happy-go-lucky guy, the one you could count on for a good time. This *emotional*, heavy conversation was the last thing I wanted to have...ever. But he stared at me expectantly, like I could absolve him of whatever was going on in his head, and I forced the words out. "I was pissed about the loss—which you did contribute to with your shit. You were making an ass of yourself and our team, and I let it boil up."

"No. Own it, Van Helsing." Something flared behind his eyes, his body coming to life. "You meant what you said, so admit it."

Bold little dick. I took a breath, fought every urge to make a joke or lighten the mood, and rocked back on my heels again. "Fine. I meant every word."

He barked out a laugh. "You know, everyone talks all sorts of shit about me. I hear it. On the ice, off the ice, on campus. But never to my face. You're the second person here to say it to me." He gestured to the air. "Reiner being the first."

I nodded. No surprise there. "You're different with him."

"Because we have an... agreement." He glanced at my TV before looking at me again. "Self-destruction seems to be a forte of mine. I'm as good at it as I am hockey."

"I'm not going to disagree there. But why?"

"Easier." He shrugged, and the brief emotion on his face disappeared. "Anyway, I wanted to thank you and apologize to your girlfriend. That was all." He ducked his head and shuffled toward the door.

The entire situation was so surreal, him being in my

apartment, him thanking me that I wasn't thinking right. The urge to pacify the situation gripped me by my throat. I was the peacemaker, the fun one, the conflict-avoider. That was the *only* reason why I asked, "Want to stay for the Bears game? Some of the guys are coming over."

He stopped in his tracks. "Would I even be welcome?"

"Gotta start somewhere, man. You want my unsolicited advice? Show a glimpse of the guy I just saw. Be humble. Be real. Not this fake-ass persona we all dislike."

Cal slowly turned around, his cheeks a little red as he blinked. "Uh, I can't today. Another time though."

"Sure, alright." I shrugged, a little annoyed that he'd passed on the invite. But it was fine. I at least did *my* part in extending the invitation. That was captain material. My jaw stopped tensing, and I breathed a little easier, but nothing was *solved*. Not really.

"I have a thing." He rubbed the back of his neck and bolted out of my place without a backward glance. It was the most we had talked one-on-one in the last two years, and my spine prickled with regret. It didn't matter how many excuses I had, this was my fault.

The senior on the team. The captain. He was just a punk sophomore who needed someone to guide him, and I'd blamed his actions rather than getting involved. Convinced myself I tried easing the tension by not yelling at him, allowing his behavior go because it messed with the locker room vibes. If I let myself think hard about it…this was on me. My refusal to take a stance and possibly upset people. The scene from the postgame locker room still ate at me, distracting me from doing anything. The way the guys had laughed and carried on like there was no shame in losing. My blood pressure spiked again. This was the right first step, but our team was still in a bad spot. I had to be a better leader if I wanted things to change. It wouldn't be Coach Simpson or Reiner and certainly not Cal. I had the influence to make a difference.

Fuck. Dani was right.

Dani.

I ran to my phone, ignoring the texts from my family about coming to the game that week, and frowned at her lack of response. No cheesecake for her was a sign shit was bad. Epically bad. I eyed my watch and calculated. I had two hours before three of the guys—not Ty, Christopher, or Jenkins— would show up for the football game. Plenty of time to get a dessert and to grovel. Fake girlfriend or not, her opinion of me mattered. She saw every side of me, and for her to be disappointed with me? That hurt. We had too much history for me to disappoint her. I liked her thinking I was the goofy guy who got her to smile. Who could cheer her up and get her to laugh. I didn't want to let her down...that was like making Santa upset.

I knew what to do.

There was a pastry place outside the quad that had the best croissants *and* cheesecake cups. Found it freshmen year after my buddy's girlfriend broke up with him and he had a craving for sweets. He got over it, but secretly, I was glad we ended up there. I bought three desserts and headed to her dorm, trying to come up with the right things to say. Sure, I had no way of entering the place, but if she was ignoring me for being an ass, I could wait until someone exited the building.

Boom. Not thirty seconds after I arrived, a guy left and held the door for me. "Thanks, man."

20A, here I come.

My palms sweated, and my stomach felt like I ate too many tacos too fast. It wasn't a great combination, and I attributed it on the confrontation with Cal. For the guy who liked to keep things easy and even, the conversation had rocked me. The honesty on his side and the reality that I was partly to blame was a lot to digest. Throw in the thing with Dani and seeing Becca Friday? Yeah, my stomach was in knots. I knocked on her door and got no answer.

Damn. I didn't think that she'd be gone. But she had a huge social circle. She had the team and Cami and her friends...her own life. I couldn't assume she'd be here. *Fuck.*

I could leave the desserts outside her door and send a text? One of the other dorms had a marker pinned to the outside, and I took it and wrote a brief apology on the bag. It'd have to do for now, but right as I set them on the floor, a soft click of a door shutting came from down the hall.

"Van?"

"Dani." I stood up straight, my lips curving up at seeing her again. Relief flooded my veins until I noted what she was wearing—a pink towel. Just a towel and purple flip-flops. It rested a foot above her knee, and it was like someone removed my vocal cords.

Her hair was in a knot on the top of her head and her face clear of any makeup, but my god, she looked adorable. All her freckles were amplified with the light, and her skin looked so damn smooth. Smooth enough my finger twitched at my side. I wanted to touch the spot where her neck met her collarbone just to feel how soft it was.

Dude, settle. I cleared my throat and focused on why I was there—to apologize. I held up the bag and gave her my best *life's good* smile. It was forced and a little awkward. I needed to use words. Not act like a caveman.

She gripped the edge of the fluffy pink towel tighter, her blue eyes widening. "What are you—are those treats?"

I nodded and almost threw them at her. "Cheesecake."

"Ah, you want something then." She grinned, scrunching her nose as she eyed me. "Definitely the right move."

"Can we talk?" My voice came out normal despite the turmoil crashing inside like continual waves. *Why* did she have to be in a damn towel? Why were her eyelashes longer than normal? And that damn skin...did she lotion? She smelled delicious. "After you... change. Clothes. Put clothes on, first, obviously, for reasons."

She fought a smile, a light blush creeping down her neck. "Sure." She unlocked her room just as another girl came down the hall wearing workout clothes. She looked vaguely familiar, and her eyes lit up when she recognized me. A fan, maybe?

"Shit, get in here."

Dani grabbed my shirt and pulled me into her room where it was just the two of us, the cheesecake, and the towel. "Maria saw us at the party and knows we're together. Asked me all about you in the bathroom this morning. It'd be weird if you waited outside while I got dressed."

I nodded, admiring how her freckles stood out more as she blushed all along her chest, neck, and face. When I'd pulled her onto my lap at the party and felt her against me, I forgot about what was pretend and real and focused on her. I ran my hand through my hair, pulling it until it stung to derail my thoughts. "I'll just turn around."

Something like a snort escaped her, and I stared at the photos she had on the wall. A bunch of pictures of her and Elle, her and dance teams, and hey— I was in one. Bending closer, it was a snap of me, her, and Elle at one of her parents' New Year's parties. We all were decked out and grinning so big. I laughed. "I forgot about this night." I touched the frame and smiled. "We had fun."

"Elle snuck three shots of whiskey, threw up in my boot, and my dad had to discreetly give us a sports drink so my mom wouldn't find out. You stole cigars, and we smoked them out my window. Definitely a fun party." A drawer closed, something shuffled, and she moved next to me. "Wasn't that the night you wanted to hang out with us to avoid some lady friend but she showed up anyway?"

Jesus.

"Or wait, that was a different time. This was another instance...some chick was hunting you down. An older one who wanted a second round, hmm?" Dani teased me, but I didn't have the same amount of joy there.

Shame flooded my face at the continual pattern of my life. Me hiding, taking the easy way out, not confronting people because it was uncomfortable. Becca had a pregnancy scare and told me she wanted more with me besides casually hooking up. The thought terrified me. I was always safe, and what sucked was I wasn't sure I believed her. I stayed until it was negative, then I ended whatever we had. But even when I said I was out, had I been direct enough? Clearly not. I avoided the tough conversation and always had excuses.

Same with Cal.

The turmoil about the guys not acting like a real team.

All the flings in the past.

"I'm an asshole." I plopped onto the twin bed, the mattress squeaking with my weight. A light went off in my mind, the realization suddenly so clear. "Fuck."

Daniella faced me, winced, and put her small hand on my shoulder. "Look, Friday was a lot of everything, and I was hard on you."

"No, you were right." I stared up at her, her large blue eyes lined with pale lashes, and I swore she saw through my bullshit. There was no judgement there, just understanding and worry. "How many times did I use you or Elle to help me hide from some fling? All my years playing hockey, I prided myself on being chill and unruffled when the team needed me to step up and *be* a leader. I may not be a typical alphahole, but I was inadvertently one by avoiding conflict."

"Hey." Her voice was soft, and she cupped my face, her smooth skin sending flames straight to my groin. "I think there's a good balance in there where you can still be my Van, but maybe… you can be more assertive when the situation calls for it."

My Van. I liked the sound of that coming from her mouth.

"I'm sorry I went too far Friday night in front of you. I should've handled that in the locker room. These are my apology desserts." I made sure to hold her gaze when I spoke, needing her compassion to settle this anxiety.

She sucked her bottom lip into her mouth for a beat before nodding. "Thank you."

"You forgive me?" I placed my hand over hers. For comfort? I wasn't sure. But it felt right, intimate even. Her hands were so small compared to mine, and a protective surge went through me. I wanted to continue to be *her* Van, even after this weird fake-dating situation and on. I never wanted her to look at me with disappointment again.

"Of course, Van." She smiled, her cheeks bright red as she reached for the bag I set on her bed. "If we're going to see each other more than normal, I'm sure we'll learn things we don't like. The cool part about us being decade-long friends is we have wayyy to much history to let one bad night ruin it all."

She plopped down next to me, crossed her legs in her bright orange workout shorts, and pulled out a cheesecake cup. The ball of nerves untangled slowly, but something she said bothered me. *We'll learn things we don't like.* Did that mean she assumed she'd be annoyed with me again? That I had other tendencies that were unfavorable? I nudged her knee with mine right as she took a bite. "Anything else I should know about myself?"

"What do you mean?" she asked, crumbs falling out of her mouth and onto her chest. The image made me smile. I happened to like unfiltered, un-Barbie-like Daniella more than I should admit. Sure, she was stunning in her dance uniforms and hairdos and makeup, but this version? Her and I eating in her bed with casual clothes? Everything just seemed better when I was with her.

"I don't want you to see things you don't like about me." There, I said it, my ears burning from the truth of it.

"Well, that's ridiculous." She snorted, covering her mouth with her hand and glancing me with amusement dancing in her blue eyes.

"Are you saying there's more you don't like?" A twinge of vulnerability edged its way into my voice, my stomach hardening as I prepared for her answer. She wasn't my parents or sister griping about something dumb—this was Daniella, and she was...different.

She arched a brow, seeming to realize the seriousness of my question before she patted my thigh. "No, Van. You're wonderful most of the time. I mean... I've heard you fart. I've smelled you after not showering for a week—which was disgusting."

"Hey, we went camping. I showered in the lake." I playfully shoved her shoulder. "And don't think I haven't seen you in odd situations too. The braces. The dark makeup thing you tried in high school."

"God, don't remind me." She fell onto her pillow in a dramatic fashion, the thermal shirt riding up on her midriff and exposing a line of her stomach. The mere sight of her skin got me worked up, and I pushed off the bed.

It was the smarter decision to stand. I even shoved my hands in my pockets so they wouldn't get any ideas. She pushed up onto her elbows, the shirt straining against her chest and clearly showing the fact she wasn't wearing a damn bra. Her pebbled nipples poked the thin fabric, and it took more effort than it should have to meet her eyes.

"There are so many good things about you that I love, Gabe. You care so deeply about those you in your circle. Your parents, sister, team, me. You volunteered at the special Olympics every year and have the patience of a saint. You're so fun and make everyone laugh, all the time."

"I sense a but coming." I rocked back on my heels as she sat up.

She chewed on the side of her lip, a look of determination crossing her face like she had to build herself up to say the next thing. I didn't want her to fear me. I needed her to speak her mind all the time.

"Dani, spit it out."

She clasped her fingers together until her knuckles turned white. "Seeing you dislike someone so fiercely surprised me. It's not you. I know you haven't shared that much, but I can tell how you carry yourself that something with the hockey team is off, and honestly? I think you can start the fix if you work it out with Cal because even though it's hard to hear...the solution begins with the leader of the team, and that's you."

There was no disappointment in her voice, just truth, and despite the urge to disagree with her, a calm overcame me. "You're right."

"I can help." She bolted up and squeezed my forearm, her eyes wide with excitement. "I'm not an expert and am still learning how to lead myself, but I can totally go over ideas with you."

"You gonna show up at the rink?" I teased, a little bummed that she let go of my arm. Her hands were like velvet on my skin.

"If you want. Seriously, I can brainstorm ideas with you and talk you through the crazy. You could want nothing to do with me besides our forced dinners, now that I think about it." She trailed off, and that dark, unsure look crossed her face, and I didn't need a second to make a decision.

I yanked her into a hug, placing my chin on top of her head. She smelled like flowers and home—not something I cared to dive too deeply into. "Daniella?"

"Hm?"

"Thank you."

"For *what*, exactly?"

"Being you."

She tightened her hold on me, and while I knew I had to head back to my place for the game with the guys, a part of me wanted to stay with her and just be. She was uncomplicated. Easy. And...called me on my shit.

I released her, my chest tightening with the realization I

didn't have anyone else quite like her in my life. "I'd love to talk through ideas with you. You're brilliant and don't hold back."

She glanced up at me, her face an open book of joy, and she nodded. "Perfect. That way I feel like you're getting more out of this fake dating thing if I can at least help you with the captain stuff. Yes, it'd be more even then. We could chat about plans when we meet for our scheduled lunches?"

"Sure." I smiled, glad the knots in my stomach loosened and Dani was looking at me like I hung the moon again. "That sounds great."

She backed away from me, pulling out her phone from a drawer. "When should we plan our fake-dates this week? Tuesday lunch? Or Friday before your game?"

I thought about the unanswered text my mom sent. "Well, my parents are coming to the game Friday, and I have a feeling they expect you to be there."

"Good thing I actually like watching hockey then." She grinned at me. "Tuesday lunch for our staged photos and then I'll cuddle up with Elle and your mom Friday, pretending to swoon over you and how you use a big stick so well."

I rolled my eyes. "Had to mention the big stick, huh?"

"What's the point of playing a sport without the euphemisms?" She scrunched her nose, and just then, everything felt right. Balanced. How it was supposed to be.

"I gotta head back to watch the Bears game with some guys on the team, but I'll see you Tuesday, alright?" I forced my feet to point toward the door, to the exit, so I could leave her and her cute smiles and short shorts in her room.

"Sounds good, boo." She winked, and I had a huge smile on my face as I left my *fake* girlfriend in her room. Sure, she was beautiful, and I liked how she looked at me, but all feelings and inappropriate thoughts were tucked nicely in the right boxes. I didn't have time for real attachments, and plus, Elle would never forgive me.

We'd continue to pretend to date like we planned with the lunch, and she'd sit with my family at the game Friday. Her and Elle would be thrilled to hang out anyway, and our ruse would continue without issues. I might have always have great ideas, but coming up with this fake-dating? Definitely one of my best ones.

CHAPTER
SEVEN

Daniella

Mom: *Hoping you look the part—we're coming down to watch the game with the Van Helsings tonight. Shall we meet you at the arena or at your dorm?*

I stared at my phone, chewing the side of my lip as my stomach hardened. Sitting with Van's family with Elle at my side was one thing. Easy. Natural. But having *my* parents there too? That was as inviting as spending the day with a hangry Dracula. Sighing, I grabbed my brush and started going through my hair.

"If you brush hard enough, you'll lose that gorgeous red hair, babe." Cami met my gaze in the mirror and raised a brow, the question clear on her face. *Why was I combing it so damn fast?*

Why was this chick always around when I had inner turmoil about my damn mom? I smacked my lips together and forced a smile. "Just want to look good."

"More than that." She put on a coat of red lipstick and moved to my side of the dressing room. We finished practice, a longer one than usual since senior night was coming up soon and no one was rushing out for Friday afternoon classes. Most of us were able to manipulate our schedule to not have Friday classes to accommodate the football season, which let us take our time getting ready post-practice.

She removed the brush out of my hand and carefully repeated the process, only going slower and more gently. "You're stressing. I can tell. This have anything to do with your new *boyfriend* I keep hearing about? Didn't realize you and Gabe were a thing, Dani."

I swore there was a lilt of hurt in her voice, like she was upset I didn't share the truth with her. My gut tightened, and I took a deep breath. "It's not... legit." I kept my voice low so no one else on the team could hear. Shame consumed me. How much of a loser was I to have a pretend boyfriend? There was no way Gabe would be with me for real and it was obvious, but saying it out loud, in the open...it felt worse than a hangover. "We're pretending until New Year's."

She nodded once, not giving a thing away on her perfectly done face. I expected her to smile like "yeah of course it's fake he's too good for you." But she remained neutral.

God, she was goals when it came to makeup. With or without it, she was stunning, but her winged eyeliner? The lashes? I wanted to *be* her sometimes. I swallowed down the envy as a wave of gratitude went over me. I loved her and was so thankful we were co-leading the team together. After this year, she'd leave, and it'd be just me so I was soaking in everything I could from her.

"Alright then," she said.

Her lack of probing prompted me to explain. She could form her own conclusions, and I'd rather her hear it from me. "It's 'cause my mom is always shoving dates down my throat during the holidays and going on about how I'm not enough or dressed well, that kinda shit. It was his idea though. Not mine." That seemed important to mention since he was so far out of my league. "He said he has his reasons, which I'm not sure if they're legit, but we're doing this thing and have staged dates and—"

"Girl, you don't need to explain it to me. He's fine as hell. Fake-dating that hunk for a few months would be fun. Are there benefits involved?" She wiggled her eyebrows at me.

My entire body heated up something fierce, and my throat got a little too tight. Benefits with Gabe? Jesus. In my wildest dreams, sure. He was my type down to every freckle on his face, but we were friends. His sister was my best friend who was sick of people crushing on her brother. Anything more would never happen. "Um, what? No. No benefits of that sort."

"Why not?"

"Because." God, my face burned hotter than the curling iron she held in her hand. "It's Van."

"So? He's good-looking. You're hot. If you can't even sleep with other people, why fake date then?"

"Shh." I glanced around to make sure no one else heard. Van was popular, and girls were always trying to hook up with him. The truth of us being together couldn't get out. "He doesn't see me that way, Cami. He's…off-limits. Out of my league."

She clicked her tongue, shaking her head as she picked up the curling iron and started taking small chunks of my hair to style. I always loved the feeling of someone playing with my hair, and being taken care of like this? It was different than my mom doing it to pretty me up. I relaxed into the chair as Cami remained quiet, curling my hair and applying hairspray every so often. The silence helped cool me down before thoughts of hooking up with Van took over. Sure, his touch lit me up, and I could've sworn there was heat in his eyes at that party. But his ex was there, and it was very clearly for show.

I freaking heard him say his senior year of high school that I was his sister's baby-faced best friend who he viewed like family. He'd said it with his own mouth to his buddy, and while those words crushed the smallest torch I carried for him in secret all those years, they kept me sane. Fake-dating with benefits wouldn't happen.

I needed to change the topic, stat. Clearing my throat, I sipped my water and met Cami's gaze in the mirror.

"I have to go to the hockey game tonight with Gabe's family *and* my parents. I didn't know they were coming, and now I'm all anxious because of it. I love Gabe's family. His sister is my best friend, but my mom? She makes me see every flaw I've ever had. Loves pointing them out too. It's her hobby, and she excels at it."

"Ah, that explains why you were brushing your hair so hard." Cami nodded and clipped up hair my hair to curl the underside. "Confidence and appreciating yourself isn't anything anyone can do for you. It's all self-created and owned. I'm not saying it's easy or simple, but learning how to say *fuck it* to external opinions will be the best thing you can do in college."

"Is that why you're so confident?"

"It's part of it. I'm proud of who I am, regardless of rumors or what people think. Even people close to me. It's always harder when it's your family, but being related to someone doesn't give their opinion a higher value than your own. It just makes it more hurtful."

Wow. Her words resonated with me so deeply I couldn't respond. I mulled over them, replaying them as we did my makeup and dressed. Some of the other girls chatted about going to the hockey game too, hoping to hit a party after. The background noise of a happy team and chitchat made up for the fact I didn't respond to Cami. Her advice was so profound I wanted to bottle it up and drink it like a potion.

Self-created and owned. My confidence.

I could do this. Sit with my mom for a hockey game and listen to her point out my shortcomings or how Gabe was too out of my league. Hear her comment on how pretty other girls were around us. She'd always done that, and I'd taken it. Let her do it and internalize it. But that was out of my control. Owning my confidence?

I liked the sound of it.

Dressed in a tight Central State hoodie and my distressed, low-rise jeans, I added some hoop earrings and applied one more layer of mascara. My makeup was on point—thanks to Cami, and a tickle of pleasure went through me at my reflection. I liked how I looked. I just hoped the high lasted through the game.

It had been a minute since watching the Central State Hockey team, let alone Van, skate on the ice. He glided like his purpose on earth was to be on top of the ice. He was so in control when he passed the puck and went in for the goal. I didn't have to pretend to be in awe of him in front of our families as the game went on. He was mesmerizing. The way he controlled his body and moved, how he commanded his presence on the ice without being loud like some top dog players I'd seen. He directed with action and a servant type of leadership, always going the extra mile and being there for his teammates.

Even hotshot Cal Holt.

When Van held out a hand for a high-five to the temperamental alt-captain, my insides melted. The fact my words had impact on someone as popular and cool and easygoing as Gabe was a big deal to me.

"Your jaw is hanging open. Great *performance*." Elle elbowed me in the side, a smile playing on her lips as she spoke in a whisper. My muscles tensed at her insinuation, and I made an effort to relax. She assumed my ogling was fake. I could work with that rather than explain to my best friend that I was straight up thinking about Van in a non-friendly way. I couldn't admit that to her though. It'd break our code.

"He's playing well."

"Yes, he is." Elle relaxed into her chair and texted furiously on her phone. "God, why is Holt so hot?"

"You and your crush."

"He's so aggressive and angry, and I love the roughness." She shivered. "I hear he's a dick though, so Gabe says."

"He's... an asshole," I said. Some people were dicks, and Cal's reputation preceded him around campus. "Van's working with him."

"And you're working my bro, huh?" she said, raising her voice until both sets of parents looked at us. I'd lucked out, and my mom sat by Elle's mother, the two of them chatting like old friends when I knew the truth. My mom was sucking up, hoping to convince their mom I was good enough.

"Stop it." I forced a laugh. Her comments grated me because she seemed so at ease. She was teasing, obviously, but I expected a talk, a confrontation. She had to realize I had a secret crush for him all this time. I couldn't lie to save my life, and here she was, cracking jokes. It made my stomach hurt with all the real and fakeness of me and Gabe.

My feelings and attraction were legit, but us being together wasn't.

The third period only had five minutes left. They were up by three, and unless their goalie, Jenkins, totally fucked it, they'd get the W.

"Dani, is Van expecting us to wait for him by the locker rooms? We're hoping to get a quick drink all together before the partying starts." His mom reached over Elle's lap and patted my knee. "I love you two together. You already feel like family."

My smile was real this time, but the guilt bounced around my gut like a rock. "Thanks, Mrs. Van Helsing. You're so welcoming all the time. I'm sure waiting for him is perfect."

She scrunched her nose, the gesture reminding me of Elle, my best friend. My partner in life who loved every part of me. *I can't be thinking about sleeping with Van. Elle's brother.* Damn Cami and her dumb question had me all out of sorts. Fake dating with benefits. Could I even imagine it?

Yes. Those large hands, talented on the ice and off. There was a reason girls were so into him if the rumors were true about how good he was in bed. Giving and patient and wild. *Shit.* My pulse raced, and sweat pooled between my breasts…in a hockey rink, where it was freezing. Something was wrong with me. More than the list my mom surely had typed out on her phone.

Focus. I sat on my hands and let out a sigh of relief when the buzzer signaled the end of the game. Central State won, and the guys were thrilled. I jumped in the air with our families, all of us hugging and high fiving. The stands went wild—Central had the most intense hockey fans. I was so involved with football since we danced at their games that I didn't realize the hockey team was having a rough year, so I was proud they won. All wins and losses fell on the shoulders of the captain, so I smiled, knowing Gabe would be in a great mood.

The guys huddled together as applause echoed throughout the rink, and my heart stumbled in my chest when Van pulled the back of Holt's jersey, yanking him back to the team huddle.

There he is. The leader and considerate guy I knew him to be.

He hadn't taken off his helmet yet, but I swore he glanced my way, and I lifted my fingers in a little wave. He nodded briefly before celebrating with the team, and my skin tingled with pride. One of the most popular guys on campus had taken *my* advice and was helping a teammate. Me. An ordinary redheaded dancer with chicken legs and small boobs. The girl who's major was *elementary education* where we practiced addition and subtraction.

The feeling was intoxicating.

I clapped my hands harder together with the extra adrenaline, and Elle side-eyed me. "What? My hunky boyfriend won. I'm happy!"

Her eyes narrowed for a beat before she rolled them. "Alright, weirdo."

"I can't wait for you to transfer here." I leaned into her, shoving any odd thought about Van down deep to think about way later. She smelled like my childhood—flowers and laundry. She'd been the most constant source of positivity in my life for decades. Being apart from her the last two years was hard, and the fact she'd transfer to finish out her schooling?

Stoked didn't cover it.

"Me neither. We can be roomies still, right?" A momentary vulnerability flashed in her friend's eyes. "You have the dancers—"

"Elle, we're living together. Don't worry." I half-hugged her, and she sighed, another wave of guilt hitting my chest. She'd hate me if she knew the thoughts I was having about her sibling.

The crowd dispersed, and from memory, I knew it'd be about twenty minutes before the guys came out of the locker-room. Our dads chatted about the NBA and how well the Bulls were actually doing (always mentioning the 90s) while the moms shared photos on their phones. For one brief moment in time, I could see how easily it would be to blend our families. Even though the Van Helsings knew all about Lovely Lily, they were kind and civil to her. Gabe and Elle's mom caught me staring at her, and she winked.

She'd be the best in-law ever. Guaranteed.

"You guys want to wait here and I'll get Van?"

"Nonsense. We can all go," my mom said. "You might want to check your hair and lipstick. Here, use my mirror since you don't carry any purse. How do you ensure you're always put together, Daniella?" She pursed her lips in disappointment, and like usual, my shoulders slumped.

"I feel okay. I don't need a mirror."

"Your boyfriend will be dressed in a suit. You should look good when you greet him."

"Oh, Gabe has seen her in way worse things," Elle said, laughing. "Like the time we dressed up as zombies and chased his friends? God, you had fake blood spurting from your mouth."

"And fake vomit," I added, mainly to annoy my mom. Elle grinned more, and we both burst out laughing. "You had that crush on his friend Johnson, and he was freaked out."

"That's right. Ah, I can't wait to come here and do stupid shit with you again."

My mom's entire faced tightened like we told her I had eight warts on my lips. Seeing her so displeased kinda made me happy, which was fucked up. I could admit it was a toxic situation. I just didn't know how to fix it. How did I get her to like me for me?

We made our way toward the other side of the stadium where other families and partners waited with signs. Fans stood off to the side where security lined the perimeter. Hockey was huge at our school, and while Gabe wasn't drafted to the NHL like Cal, they all still felt larger than life sometimes.

Same with the football players. Some people just gravitated toward the talented and were hoping to hitch a ride to fame.

Cami's twin sister Naomi waved to me as she leaned on a beam with an iPad in her hand. Her dad was the head coach and her boyfriend the newest assistant. Her face lit up when the first guy walked out, and sure enough, her boyfriend Michael Reiner threw his arm around her and kissed her.

Chatter increased as the players started to leave, and my entire body tensed with the upcoming issue—did we kiss?

We hadn't planned it or talked about it, but our families were here. watching. Expecting us to be together. Shit. Damn it.

I'd thought about kissing Van for most of my life and to have it finally almost happen with an audience was some sort of prank. But worse... what if I went in for it but he stopped it? Not realizing everyone was there? Oh lord.

My breathing picked up, and my palms sweated. Everything was too loud and the hoodie too tight. Damn it. *Damn it.*

The air changed when he strutted out of the hallway, his freshly-showered hair curling around his forehead, and my stomach dropped at the sheer beauty of him. He laughed at something a teammate said and then his gaze found me.

His smile changed, and his eyes... Oh god, they warmed. Without overthinking it, I ran to him. I needed to tell him our families were there waiting, not in the distance. A warning so he wouldn't ruin it all.

I skipped right in front of him and blurted out, "Family's here–gonna kiss you."

Then, the bravest move I have ever pulled, I put my hands on his shoulders, stood on my tiptoes, and kissed him.

CHAPTER
EIGHT

Gabe

She tastes like strawberries.

Her lips touched mine for .2 seconds before she stepped back, blinking up at me with bright red cheeks and parted lips. Her eyes pleaded with me, so damn big as she stared up at me, nervous as hell. "I'm so sorry. They are all here, and it was the expectation. I couldn't blow it."

Her words didn't compute in my head. I was high on adrenaline from the win and then to have her give me that pathetic peck? No, that wouldn't do. I didn't care who watched —it was a terrible excuse for a kiss. If we were gonna do it, we would do it right.

"You call that a kiss, Dani?" I set my bag down and gripped both sides of her waist, digging my thumbs into her jeans. She shuddered at my touch, her mouth falling open as her eyes turned to liquid gold, simmering. Something primal took over at the forbidden contact of her mouth on mine. I gently guided her toward me, moving my hand up her spine to cup the back of her head. Her hair hung down in curls, and I gripped the red strands in my hand, something I'd dreamed about doing since high school.

"Baby, *this* is a kiss."

Lowering my mouth to hers sent a ripple of anticipation and lust through me, making me pull her closer and slamming my lips against hers. That little preview before wasn't nearly enough. I was eager and hungry for her, and her soft sigh about did me in. Her lips were so soft, warm, and inviting, and I lingered there for a beat or two before sliding my tongue into her mouth. Mint and strawberries.

Goddamn. She kissed me back, hard, gripping the collar of my shirt and letting out a little moan. Daniella breathed me in, our teeth clashing as she went harder. So hard, I forgot the whole point. The whole reason this was happening.

Us pretending to date.

Instead, I wanted to suck her tongue until she trembled and move down her jaw. Lick every part of her until she whimpered. I tilted her neck back, deepening the kiss and feeling every stroke of her tongue. We couldn't kiss hard or fast enough, and I pressed my body closer to her. My neck hurt from the angle, but I didn't give a flying fuck. *More.*

"Damn, Van." The voice of one of the guys pulled me out of the moment, a cold reminder of where we were and who was around us. She stilled, and I slowly broke apart the kiss.

Dani stared up at me with her large brown eyes and long lashes, her bottom lip wet and pouty, and I couldn't get over how fucking beautiful she looked like that. Every part of my body was attuned to her, how her chest heaved and her tongue kept darting out to the side of her lip. I wanted to do the same, savor how she felt on me and tasted.

"Whoa." She touched her face and stepped back. "That was quite a performance kiss, Van."

My gaze darkened, the urge to pick her up and prove to her it wasn't an act dominating my mind. There was no way that kiss was an act, not with her greedy hands and hurried tongue.

I opened my mouth to say just that, but her mom appeared right there.

"Oh, Gabriel, you played wonderfully tonight." Lovely Lily moved past Daniella and pulled me into an awkward hug, where her very large and fake boobs pressed against me. She wasn't a cougar, by any means, but she had her own definition of personal space, that was for sure.

"Thank you." I cleared my throat and adjusted the collar of my dress-shirt. Coach demanded we looked nice for games, showing we were professional and dedicated to our sport. I loved it while some of the guys bitched. Hell, I liked how I looked in a suit, and it seemed Dani did too. Her gaze traveled from my face to my chest, her audible swallow making me grin as her blush traveled to her neck.

We weren't alone for more than two seconds before Elle and the rest of the parents joined me in a hug. My dad clapped my back, and my mom kissed my cheek, both gushing over how well I'd played. Sure, it felt great to hear, but my attention kept moving back to Daniella and that fucking kiss.

Had she always had a mouth like that, all soft and dangerous? Or was it new?

"Broseph, you didn't suck." Elle held out her fist, our continual joke staying strong. She refused to compliment me since she thought it went to my head at a young age, so she insisted on giving ten percent compliments.

I dished them right back.

"You don't smell like a sewer rat stuck in a rainstorm in middle of the summer."

"Aw, you're so sweet. Gosh, Dani, your *boyfriend* is a modern-day wizard with kind words." She faked a smile and hooked her arm with Daniella. "You're *so* lucky."

"Hey, your taste in friends is pretty good," I said, winking at my fake-girlfriend who kissed like a goddess.

"Blah, stop." Elle stuck her tongue out. "Mom promised food if I came. Let's go eat."

A typical Van Helsing dinner often included a teammate or two. But an idea struck, inspired by Daniella.

"Hold on a second." I held up a finger and scanned the guys coming out of the room. One particular annoying face came to view, his shoulders slumped and his phone two inches from his eyes. "Holt."

He glanced up, confusion swirling in his eyes. "What? I said good game."

My lips quirked at his automatic defensive tone. Sure, we'd made two strides, but we weren't friends. Hell, we were whatever was the step past enemies. "Join us for a post-game meal and drink."

A deep scowl crossed his face before he eyed the people standing behind me. We were a lot, I knew that. My parents wearing matching jerseys and Elle with her worn hat from when I'd signed to attend Central State. Even Dani's mom had on a bright orange sequined thing. We screamed annoying but dedicated, but almost everyone on the team had someone to go celebrate with before we met up at the house to get drunk.

He paused and stood up straighter when his attention moved to Elle, and I cleared my throat. That wasn't gonna happen. "Nope. Don't linger on her unless you want a skate to the face."

"I wasn't... fuck, Van." He shook his head. "Thanks for the invite but no."

"Oh, join us, Cal." My mom moved toward him. "We've watched you play the last two years, and you're so gifted. Please, dinner and drinks are on us."

Cal struggled—it was clear. He shifted his weight, and a light blush appeared high on his cheeks before he nodded. "I'll stay for a quick drink."

"Perfect. Now, let's head to T-Bones."

The best BBQ place in central Illinois. And they paired beer with every dinner combo on the menu. This college town really was the shit.

We put our bags in the back of my parents' car, and when we all stood there, ready to get in, there was an awkward pause. Who rode with whom?

I wanted to stay with Dani, but the way Cal kept checking out my sister was enough to start a dull throbbing in my temple. *Be a leader.* I exhaled, forced a smile, and put a hand on his shoulder, digging my nails into him. "You go ahead and ride with my parents, and Elle, I'm going with Dani."

"Sure."

If I wasn't mistaken, there was a bounce to his step that I wanted to destroy immediately.

Elle flashed me a look like *thank you baby Jesus,* and she quickly opened the door for him while batting her damn eyelashes. If she thought... or he thought... fuck, if anyone thought the two of them would flirt or exchange a look, they were wrong. So wrong.

"Thank you." Dani came up and intertwined our fingers.

"For?" I squeezed her hand, and just like that, the tension oozed out of me from her touch. That was...interesting.

"Being a good guy even though I can see the daggers shooting out of your eyeballs at Cal. Elle's crush is innocent, so don't even worry about it."

"Crush? What?" My voice went an octave too high, but Dani just laughed. "This isn't funny, Daniella."

"Oh, full name again." She chuckled. "Come on, let's get in my parents' car. With you there, they'll leave me alone."

Shoving all thoughts of Elle and Cal from my mind—which took a lot of effort, thank you very much—I focused on the whole reason this night was happening. Helping Daniella around her mom.

We slid into the backseat of their Lexus, and when the doors closed, Daniella's entire body tensed. She sat up so straight it looked like it actually hurt. Any trace of joy or heat from earlier disappeared from her face, and her hands were in fists.

My chest tightened at her expression: utter misery. I hated

seeing her lips flat, void of the smile I was so accustomed to. The sparkle dulled in her eyes, and I reached over, taking her clenched fingers into my hand, and opened them up. I traced lines over her palm, going down each finger slowly until she relaxed. She took a shuddering breath, and I intertwined our hands.

An odd sense of calm settled over me at holding her like this. I fought a smile as I forced myself to look out the window and not at our joined hands. It meant nothing, just a friendly show of support. *Sure, right.*

"Gabriel, have I told you how handsome you are in your suit and jacket? Doesn't he look so wonderful, Daniella? Do you feel foolish in your hoodie and jeans now?"

The disappointment in her mom's voice was thick enough to cut through the cool November air. My jaw tensed, and my gaze immediately went to Daniella. Her expression was pinched.

"It's a hockey rink. It's *cold*." Her tone was chillier than the ice. "What would you suggest I wear, Mother, a ball gown?"

"Nonsense." Lovely Lily missed the sarcasm. Or chose to ignore it. "You own a number of items of fashionable clothing that fit your hair and pale skin."

"Enough talk of clothes, ladies," her dad said, his voice too high to be natural. "Let's chat about hockey, the whole reason we made the drive down here."

"Of course, of course. Just can't help that I want my daughter to be presentable to her friends and boyfriend. I love a pet project, babe, you know this. You admire my artistic and critical eye." Her mom reached over the center console and stroked his arm. Daniella met my eye and gagged.

Squeezing her hand again, I smiled and hoped to convey a confident *I got your back* look. It must've worked because she relaxed. Good. That was the whole reason for me being here, and it irked me to imagine the car ride without me. Would they berate her, or would her dad jump in? Why didn't he say anything sooner or more direct to Lovely Lily?

Was Daniella's entire life like this, just being ridiculed and beaten down with comments? God, that sucked. My parents never made me feel like shit. Sure, they'd point out real situations that needed work, like my lack of direction for the future, but they weren't dicks to my confidence.

My mood soured as I pretended to give a shit about Lovely Lily's questions about the season. Yes, we had a great record. No, we didn't have anyone else drafted except Cal Holt right now.

Just fifteen minutes with her in the car was enough for me, and I bolted out of the backseat the second we parked at the restaurant. It stifled me, Lily's negativity. I was a pretty happy dude and felt down, so I couldn't imagine how Daniella dealt with it. Seeking her out immediately, I went to the other side of the car and put my arm around her. "I love your hoodie with the Central State hockey logo and your jeans. Shows off your long legs and ass."

"I don't have an ass," she replied, her tone a little down. "But thanks for attempting to ease the tension."

"Not trying anything, D. Speaking the truth."

Her parents waited at the door for us just as my parents, sister and Cal walked up from a few spots over. I chanced a quick look at the two of them, breathing a sigh of relief when Elle had her arms crossed and *glared* at my teammate. *Thank fucking god.* There was no sign of spark or a crush or an anything between them.

"I'll get us a table," Lily said, swaying her hips as she walked inside, and with her absence, the air seemed lighter.

"Ignore your mom, honey. You know how she is." Daniella's dad shrugged, like Lily's words were just the way it was. That didn't sit right with me. Not at all. How could he let this happen? Couldn't he see what it did to Dani?

I squeezed Dani's hand and hated how the light in her eyes dimmed. All because of the comments. Anger boiled under my skin, making it feel too tight. Too much. I wanted to say something, anything, but what? How? I'd ruin the mood.

Dani relaxed just as Lily came outside, and no one said a word about what happened. Sure, we knew about Dani's mom being kind of a dick, but Dani always downplayed it or made a joke out of it. Being around it was different. It was the group's secret that we all disliked her, and the woman was either a dope ass actress or she didn't care.

Dinner was exhausting, mainly because everyone, especially Dani, did their best to seem jovial. We talked about the game, the season, Dani and Elle's majors, and what everyone wanted to do for the holidays. Cal smiled twice, not a real one, but two baby ones at my mom which was nice. My mom was awesome.

But I did catch him staring at Elle multiple times, his dark gaze almost…worried. She paid him no attention, so my world was right. Just had to cheer up Daniella for real and the night would really be a win.

My parents knew better than to have a long dinner and ushered everyone out the soon as we were done. They blamed not wanting to drive late into the night, but my mom winked and whispered to have fun at the party.

God, I was lucky with them.

Everyone said goodbyes and got into their cars, leaving Cal, Daniella, and me standing outside the restaurant.

"Can you disown your parents at twenty-one?"

"Why would you say that?" Cal hissed, snapping his attention to Daniella. "You're lucky."

"Lucky?"

"Yeah, you have actual fucking parents who took you out to dinner and love you. Why would you want to get rid of that?" Cal tilted his head, a flicker of anger in his tone that I didn't like.

"What's with the attitude, Holt?" I barked, moving to stand closer to Daniella.

He shook his head, his jaw tensing. "Nothing. I knew I

shouldn't have come to this. Fuck. I'm leaving." He ran a hand over his face and took off in the opposite direction of campus, leaving us a very confused pair.

"That was weird, right?" Daniella frowned, watching his retreating back.

"He's a dick. Don't worry about it." I too, wondered what had happened, but mainly, I wanted to talk about that damn kiss. "So—"

"Take me to the hockey party, Van. I need a fucking drink."

CHAPTER
NINE

Daniella

I t was a night for bad decisions, and I didn't know which one to make first. Did I do shots? Dance on a table? Do a beer bong? Try and kiss Van again because holy shit balls, my mouth still tingled from his.

Yikes, yeah, maybe not the last one. My brain went to mush, and my insides melted into a puddle of horny lust. It'd be best to not resort to that again. Not sure what I'd do given another chance. It was Gabriel Van Helsing. The hottest guy at school. Elle's brother.

My lifelong crush.

Best if I started with something small, like a beer. Way safer that way. Especially if Van was going to keep touching me like he had been, always keeping a hand on me. Right now, it was on my lower back, and I swore I could feel his radiating heat through my damn sweatshirt. The entire walk here, even though no one was around us and it was dark and nighttime, he never removed it.

It charmed and annoyed me. Charmed me because he'd always been a gentleman since I'd known him. It was his character. Holding doors, being polite, ma'ams and thank yous, and hands on backs. God, I'd see him do that a thousand times with girls in high school. It didn't make me special...which annoyed me. Yeah, beer wouldn't cut it.

Vodka sprite, here I come.

I pushed through the crowd of people standing on the porch outside the hockey house. Van chatted with guys on the team while I smiled, playing the girlfriend part. Athletes all mingled together at Central State, so I knew most of them enough to small talk. Space. I needed space from my fake boyfriend and his incredible kissing and large, talented hands.

Stepping away from his grip, I waved a hand over my shoulder at him. "Getting a drink."

"I'll join you."

So much for distance. I understood though. He'd been approached by two girls already, taking selfies and pushing their tatas onto his arm. Instead of jealousy, I felt bad for him. He was clearly uncomfortable with it—something he used to love. I wasn't sure when it had changed but it seemed Van really did want to end his fling-flangs.

Like my junior high fantasies, Van put a finger in my belt loop and held on. My entire body fluttered with butterflies, my skin tingling and my heart racing at the gesture. This was straight out of my late-night dreams, him holding onto me and following me and showing me how good he was in the bedroom. I'd heard all the rumors about it, and hell, Elle and I had witnessed him making out with a girl before.

Thank god there was only five more weeks of this plan because my horny ass couldn't handle it. I was itching for a mistake to distract myself from my mom, and he was getting closer and closer to being it.

"You in a hurry, D?" He laughed under his breath as I went to the kitchen and picked up a red cup and put it between my teeth. I got a Sprite and a bottle of vodka and made one very strong drink.

"To the Lovely Lily." I held it up and didn't wait for a response before taking a long swig. It burned my throat like fire, causing me to cough, but I welcomed the pain. Just thinking of my mom and her comments reminded me of my dad. How he never stopped her. Another bout of anger rushed through me.

"Not gonna wait for me to join you?"

"This brief pity party is for one, good sir." I held up my finger. "Three more sips and I'll get over it."

He watched me with his dark brown eyes and lashes that were unfairly long for his handsome face, the intensity swirling around in them causing my breath to catch in my throat. Van didn't half-ass anything, and I licked my lips when his gaze dropped to my mouth. His nostrils flared, and he took a step toward me, his hand stretched out. "Dani—"

"There's our captain! Heyooo!" Members of the hockey team stormed into the kitchen as the music got louder. Bass echoed off the walls in the house, the mood shifting. It was almost midnight, and the air changed; it made me smile. I wasn't a huge partier, but I'd been around enough to know what the shift meant.

Bad decisions all around.

The guys were trashed. Sloppy and messy and smelling like whiskey.

I grinned like a damn Cheshire Cat and took another drink. This one didn't burn as badly, and after the third, fourth, my insides warmed, and my mom's face and comments left my mind.

I loved my sweatshirt and jeans. They were cute and comfy and me. That was Lily's biggest issue, that I wasn't her. Or the daughter she pictured having. I'd never be that girl, and she'd have to get over it or else. Yeah!

Feeling bolder, I had another swig and made a fist in the air, standing off to the side in the kitchen. I'd give her a piece of my mind next time I saw her. Maybe I should text her how I felt. Fumbling with my phone, I started to write in my notes app.

Never type a message TO the actual person. Too easy to accidentally hit send.

"Is there a reason you're chewing that lip to death and staring at your phone?" Van joined me again, his teammates gone, which left the two of us in the kitchen. His brow was lined with stress, but I blamed that on my parents. The dinner from hell.

I'd moved to the chair at some point, and he sat next to me, pulling it close so his leg rested against mine. Good lord, his legs were long, like a foot more than mine.

That had me thinking about what else was long on him...

"Now you're blushing." He grinned, his dimples blessing his face and making me rearrange my bad decision list. Kissing him again jumped to the top. Just once more. Elle didn't have to know it was real for me. I'd blame our farce. The act.

"What are you thinking?" he asked.

His voice was a little breathless, kind of how I felt inside, and I set my phone down. Somehow, he moved so his face was inches from mine, and his perfect, delicious lips were right there.

"Rearranging my bad decision list," I whispered, afraid to move or do the wrong thing to ruin the mood. Because this was a total moment. Just us, his breath hitting my face and his hand now resting on my knee. His palm covered it entirely, and a bolt of awareness spread from my kneecap to my toes, all the way to my fingertips. A warm, wonderful tingle that had me whimpering.

"Oh yeah?"

Ungh. His voice dropped low, sending any self-restraint I had into a tizzy. All I could do was nod.

"What's at the top?"

"It was," I started, pausing to swallow the lust in my throat. My voice was too raspy, too deep, and too horny. "It *was* to text my mom how I felt. That I was done."

He studied me for a beat, his chest moving too fast for just sitting down. Then, he took the phone from my hands and set it on the table. "What is it now?"

I licked my lip, every cell of my body primed and ready to pounce on him. But foolish, naïve not pretty Daniella still lived inside me after years of believing it, and how could I even think about starting something with Van that wasn't prompted by our ruse? What if I tried kissing him, and he turned his head, or worse, laughed? I wasn't his type at all. He could turn me down with pity in his eyes.

Knowing him for all my life was a blessing and a curse because right now, when our mouths were inches apart, I could only see the girls he'd been with. The gorgeous, perfect girls that Lovely Lily would've preferred as daughters. I was the awkward, small-chested, skinny redhead with too many freckles, not a bombshell that should be on Van's arm. He always dated tens, and I wasn't one.

"Where'd you go just then?" He cupped my face with his hand, his eyes swirling with concern. "Your expression changed."

"It... doesn't matter." I closed my eyes, sighed, and counted to three.

"Don't hide from me, Dani."

There was a plea to his tone, one that had me opening my eyes to find him even closer. His thumb traced along the edges of my jaw, his skin causing goosebumps to explode down my body. I took a shaky breath, needing to push him away and pull him closer at the same time.

But then, a miracle happened. A gift from the earth. One of his former flings walked into the kitchen, and I used her as an excuse, anything to kiss him again. The negative thoughts disappeared on my mission to be the best fake girlfriend ever, and I grinned. "Give me that mouth, loverboy."

Van's intake of breath was his only reaction before he closed the distance between our mouths. I felt that kiss everywhere, from deep in my soul to between my thighs and all the way down to my feet that tingled. God, his mouth was perfection. His soft lips contrasted with the roughness of his jaw, and his tongue slid against mine in a slow rhythm, enticing me and teasing me to kiss him harder.

This wasn't the time for small, gentle kisses. No, we had a show to put on. I wrapped my arms around his neck, digging my fingers into his hair. He had thick, gorgeous curls, and he moaned when I tugged on them.

"Dani, Christ," he said into my mouth, pulling me onto his lap and wrapping my legs around his waist. Without meaning to, I rocked against him. He shuddered and sucked my bottom lip into his mouth, tilting his head back and staring at me right in the eyes.

My world flipped in that moment, Van's hands on my ass and teeth on my lips. I ground more, moving my hips in a slow beat, my own gasp coming out at his arousal.

I gave Gabriel a boner.

It was stupid to feel smug, but I did, and my lips curved up.

"Enjoying yourself on me?" He kissed down my jawline, nipping at my sensitive skin until he got to my ear. He took my lobe in his mouth, bit down, and chuckled. "Fuck, your skin tastes so good."

His hands moved under my sweatshirt, his palms resting on my lower back as he moved them up. Then up some more as he returned to my mouth. The music blasted in the background, the sounds of partying becoming the perfect noise to drown my thoughts out. Not even the smell of weed or stale beer ruined the moment as Van trailed his fingertips from my back to just beneath my ribs.

Holy shit.

Our tongues clashed as the kiss deepened. I couldn't stop moving on top of him, the need to feel more of him aggressively taking over my mind. His chest, neck, back muscles were divine. I gripped his broad shoulders as his fingers teased the underside of my breasts. "Shit," I whispered, jumping at the touch.

"Dani," he said, his tone hoarse and rough and a walking dream. "Can I?"

Hearing him say my name with that tone? I'd died. That was the only explanation. Because asking for permission was proof he was the best guy in the world. He broke apart our kiss to ask, meaning I was looking at his swollen lips and heated gaze. It was all *for* me.

I nodded.

"Say it for me, please." He kissed my lips again slowly, without tongue before teasing my ribs with his fingers. "Can I keep going? Be clear."

"Yes."

His answering grin made my insides squirm, and I clenched my thighs around him. He didn't wait more than a second to cover both of my breasts with his hands, my pebbled nipples pressing against his palms as he touched them. "Jesus, Dani," he grumbled, kissing down the other side of my neck.

He pinched each nipple once, twice, before cupping them again. "They are fucking perfect."

"They're small."

Damnit. Self-doubt was creeping back in, ruining the best moment of my love life ever. It clouded the way I moved and kissed him, and he pulled back, a line between his eyebrows. "Did I go too far?"

"No, no." My throat hurt from the ball of emotion swelling inside. Fuck. *Fuck.* Why did I have to say that and ruin the moment? Real or fake, it felt good kissing Van. I focused on the blue backsplash of the kitchen instead of his face, needing to put some distance between him, me, the kiss, and my own issues.

"Hey." He tilted my chin to force me to look at him. "I'm sorry."

"Wait, why are you sorry?" I couldn't handle it if he

regretted this already. He probably did. That would just kill me. "You know, don't tell me. I don't want to know." I put my weight on my left leg, hoping to get off him when he wrapped his arm around my hips and kept me right there on top of him.

"Daniella." His tone was tight, like he struggled for words, and it made me sit up straighter. It almost sounded like anger, and I had no idea why? I didn't do anything to offend him.

"Vannnn!" A loud voice burst our bubble, the sheer volume of it making me jump off Van's lap.

Three guys from the team huddled in the kitchen, chanting about the game as girls followed. One held a bottle of whiskey and poured it into everyone's mouths, and oh boy. It was rowdy time.

"Get in here, Cap. Take a shot! Take a shot!" Jenkins, the wide-shouldered and tall goalie with long hair pulled back into a manbun, egged him on. "You gotta, man."

I chewed on my bottom lip, the sensation stinging from how hard Van had kissed me, and I stepped back to let him get up. He hadn't stopped staring at me though. His brows were drawn and his jaw tight as he opened his mouth only to close it again.

He didn't need my permission, but I gave it anyway. "Go celebrate with your team."

"This isn't over, you and me and this conversation." He pulled the edge of my sweatshirt until I stood a few inches from him. "We're finishing what we started."

And with that, he plastered on a smile and took the shot glass from Jenkins. He played the part of the captain celebrating the win well, but he kept those dark, intense eyes on me the entire time.

I couldn't stop thinking about his words though. *What* were we going to finish, exactly? That conversation or that kiss?

CHAPTER
TEN

Gabriel

Well, I hated Jenkins now. The bastard got me drunk. I knew I should talk to him about partying too much, drinking too often. It was becoming a real thing, but I couldn't bring myself to mention it. Not while I was too intoxicated *and* thinking about Dani.

I hated drinking that much, but he kept cheering and starting chants, and Cal stopped by and smiled once with the guys. Plus, no one punched him or yelled at him. Jenkins even pulled him in for a one-armed hug.

It was weird and bonding and fuck, my tongue felt like a slip n' slide, and nothing made sense. The team getting along for a brief second, even though all our issues were just swept under the table. We won a game, and no one was yelling.

Daniella fucking Laughlin's tits with her perky nipples that I wanted to suck until she came. Her lips. Why did they taste so good, like a magical combination of everything I loved in women? Soft, fruity, intense. Awareness prickled beneath my waist, my gaze seeking her out in the crowd. I wanted another kiss.

And to see her tits. God, I wanted that more than I needed oxygen. I took a step, lost my balance a bit, and laughed it off. I might be smooth on the ice, but four shots of whiskey made me worse than a toddler walking for the first time. That reminded me of a viral video I saw. Dani would think it was funny. For sure. Maybe I should find it for her to get her to laugh again. Yeah, I liked her laugh a lot.

My ears rang as I heard it, her laugh. It was deep, a little throaty, and I grinned hard, searching for her. She was just a ray of sunshine in my life. Except for the frown in the kitchen and around her mom. I could help her with her mom, but I needed to get to the bottom of the mystery scowl. Perhaps my touching went too far?

She wasn't a virgin, I knew that. But was she experienced?

Okay, that didn't help. Her with another dude made my chest feel like I took another shot without a chaser. It got all burny and acidic. *Fucking Jenkins.* I hit the center of my chest a few times and went on a mission: find Dani's laugh.

There she was, sitting on the edge of the couch with a red cup dangling from her hands. Her red hair hung down in those curls I loved, her mouth curved up in a smile as she hit someone on the shoulder.

That someone was a guy. A very handsome, tall, black guy whose face was on billboards around campus. Deandre Smith, our campus running back. He leaned closer to Dani and said something to make her howl with laughter again, and the same acidic feeling formed in my gut. Indigestion. I heard it happened when you were older, but I thought I still had some time.

I got my phone out and made a note: talk to Doc about heartburn.

"So then," Deandre says, putting his damn hand on Dani's knee. "Jax screams so loud and high pitched I honestly thought it was a girl."

"Did he catch the chicken?" Dani asked, leaning a little

closer to him.

"No. He called me and two other guys, and we had to chase that damn thing all over the dorm. Took two hours to corner it." He slapped his knee, his eyes watery from laughing.

I didn't like how cozy they were.

"What's so funny?" I asked, my tone more urgent than I meant.

Dani's gaze moved toward me, heat entering her eyes for a beat before she frowned. I hated that transition.

I wanted her smiles and laughs, not her sad faces. Why did I make her sad?

"Oh, Deandre was going on about a prank one of the guys did on the team. Funny as hell."

"Heard about the win tonight, brother." Deandre held out a fist, and I bumped it. We knew each other in the way any talented athlete who spent time in the gym did. Always greeted each other and were positive, but the guy could've been a model and had the reputation of being a womanizer.

Dani wouldn't go for that... right?

You're a womanizer. My brain bitch-slapped me with some reality, and I faltered in my steps.

"Whoa, Van." Dani hopped off the couch and gripped my arm. "You do too many shots?"

"Dude, been there. Take two Tylenol and chug a sports drink." Deandre stood up and gave Dani a warm look. "I'll catch ya later. Better take care of your man here."

She waved at him before looking up at me with mild amusement. I wore a goofy ass grin because he called me her man. That meant they weren't flirting. "Your man."

"Jesus, you're tanked." She wrapped an arm around my waist and moved mine over her shoulders.

"You gonna carry me, D?" The room did spin a little. Perhaps there was an earthquake. Yeah, central Illinois got those. "Is there an earthquake? Check Twitter trends."

"Oh, Van." She giggled, the magical sound I craved blessing

my drunk ass.

"There she is. That beautiful melody." I closed my eyes and pulled her close, smelling her floral perfume. "Your laugh is my favorite. All sunshine."

She snorted and guided us toward the exit. "We better get you home and follow Deandre's orders."

"Yes, sir. Ma'am. Hey, you and him? A thing? A thang of the past?" I had to know, and asking wasn't rude. We questioned each other all the time. "A thingy thang fling flang?"

"My god, you're a ridiculous drunk. How did I not realize this?"

"I don't think I like him sitting by you. He touched you." She still didn't answer my question, causing that same terrible feeling in my gut. "Which, it's your body. I know that. I appreciate that. But you touched him too, and it was weird to watch. Unpleasant."

She pushed open the front door, the freezing November air smacking me in the face like an old friend. I loved the cold. "Do you like the sun, Dani?"

"The sun? Sure." She snorted again, the unattractive sound seeming…adorable? Yes, that weird honking sound was cute on her. Oh, Dani.

"I could never live anywhere hot. The cold is so nice. I love the sting in my nose, you know? That's why I chose hockey and not swimming. I could've swum, I was the best in my fourth-grade team."

"In all the years I've known you, I never would've guessed you were a chatterbox after a few shots. This is delightful."

"You're delightful!"

We cuddled together on the way to somewhere. It wasn't the direction of the dorms. We'd have to pass the library for it to be that way so that meant we were going to my place which was great, but she'd have to walk back herself, and that was unacceptable. "Oh no. We gotta go the other direction. Gotta take you safely to your place and tuck you in, girlfriend."

"I'll order a car home or something. Getting *your* ass into bed is the priority, boyfriend."

"You will not take a car. If you insist on being all stoic and responsible about this, then you stay over. No exceptions. I will keep you hostage, so my dear, the dorms or my prison?"

"Seriously, what did you drink tonight?"

"Jenkins supplied it all, and I have no idea. Whiskey was one of them. I hate drinking to get drunk. I have regerts already. Big regerts. Like that GIF of the guy with the tattoo on his chest with regrets spelled wrong?"

"Why did you keep doing shots if you hate this feeling?"

"Because of your frown and our kiss. It messed me up."

"Because you regret it?" Her voice got small again, too small for my girl Dani. She should speak with purpose because she was amazing.

"No! The opposite of regret, which is… hm. I can't recall but how could I regret kissing you and touching you? Gets me hot thinking about it. Mm. But then you frowned, and it bothered me."

She didn't respond, but she swallowed so loudly it clicked. Interesting. Very interesting.

"Did you enjoy it?" I asked, desperate to hear her say it. I needed the validation or at least to know it wasn't just me.

"Yes. You're a good kisser for a fake boyfriend."

Hm, she could've gone without that last part. "Have you had a lot of experience kissing fake boyfriends? Or fake girlfriends? Or fake partners?"

She sighed like I irritated her, but that made me laugh. We rounded the corner and came to the bricked unit where my humble apartment stood. I lived with Fraser Arlington who I lovingly referred to as Farlington, but he was gone this weekend. His girlfriend lived out of state, and it was actual the perfect roommate situation 'cause I had the weekends alone most of the time.

"Your silence is deafening. First, you avoid the Deandre

question and now this. You're slowly killing me like a Taylor Swift song."

She laughed. Boom. I high-fived myself and explained when she arched a brow. "I got you to laugh, so I rewarded my talent with the highest of fives."

"Where are your keys, goofball?"

"Back pocket. Feel free to get them and cop a feel."

She reached into my pants but sadly did not grab a handful. Oh well. I shrugged at no one in particular and counted the stars visible through the clouds. There were at least ten.

"Are you able to walk up the stairs, or shall I try carrying you?"

"Toddler legs! Oh, I gotta show you this video!" I tried grabbing my phone out to hand it to her, but so many messages popped up from women. Saying good job on the win, telling me they missed me. A couple were some sexy photos, but I quickly deleted those. They were exciting when I'd first gotten to college because I was semi-famous, but they were old now.

Daniella sucked in a breath, and the laugh lines around her eyes disappeared. Oh no. I took her hands in mine and waited until she looked at me. "Oi, those don't mean shit, alright? I get them all the time."

She gave a tight-lipped smile that I wanted to kiss off her freckled face. "I'm sure you do."

"Hey." I shoved my phone in my pocket, took the keys from her hands, and cupped her face. She had the best face, honestly. Round and cute with a little nose and expressive eyes. "You're my fake girlfriend. I'm not messing around on you or anything, I swear it. I'd never do that to anyone I made a promise to."

"I know, Van, it's just—" She exhaled, a small cloud of condensation forming in the chilled night air. "Stupid. Never mind."

"Whatever has you frowning on a glorious night like this isn't stupid. Please, tell me so I can fix it. I hate when you frown. Elle too. People I care about who are sad gut me. So, tell me so I can help." I pressed my thumb on her bottom lip, a burst of lust making my breath shake because, fuck, I wanted to taste her again.

But not until I got to the bottom of her frown. And, when my legs weren't like a toddler.

"It's me being caught up in my own insecurities, that's all." She placed one hand over mine, her skin soft, and she removed my touch. "I'm tired. Let's move you upstairs."

"I hate your mom." It was the only reason Daniella didn't view herself highly because the girl was amazing. We went through the entrance of the building and toward the elevator. There was no way on God's green Earth I was gonna try the stairs. Dani didn't respond, and guilt ate at me. "Not like for real hate-hate but hate in the sense she hurts you over and over. Her words matter to you, and I wish I could take that away."

"Yeah, me too."

She twisted her fingers together on the short ride up, her nerves always tangible. My chest ached for her. I wanted to help. "You're perfect, you know."

Her gaze found mine, and she snorted. "No, but thanks for trying."

"Perfectly *you*. Perfect is boring as hell and not realistic but you're everything you're supposed to be. I swear it." I held up my hand like I was saying the pledge, and I earned another smile.

"I think I like intoxicated Van."

"Well, intoxicated Van really likes his fake girlfriend so." I shrugged and held her hand. "Now, come. We'll eat some food and go to bed."

"Are you sure? I can find a ride back."

"Daniella Grace. It is two a.m. You're not leaving when I have a bed."

"I'm not sleeping with you, Gabe!" she blurted out, her cheeks going a fiery red. Oh, I loved when she blushed.

"I'm a gentleman, so I will take the couch."

"But you need rest, you played tonight."

The doors opened, and my unit was the first to the right. I narrowed my eyes at her and held up two fingers. Oh good. I wasn't seeing double. Maybe the walk had sobered me up a bit. "Listen, ma'am, we can share the bed, or I can sleep out there. End of discussion, no more comments, microphone is turned off."

It took three tries, but I did get the key in the hole—that's what she said—and I grinned like I shot a winning goal. "After you."

"You are something else right now," she mumbled, but she smiled again.

I locked up and frowned at the sad music. Really sad. Like James Blunt throwback sad. And it was loud.

"Uh, are you having a party here?" Dani asked.

I followed her gaze, and there was Farlington and three other dudes I didn't know, all surrounded by beer cans and passed out on the couch. "Shit. He was supposed to be in another city."

"This looks like a drunken heartbreak party." She chewed the side of her lip and pointed to the door. "I can—"

"If you suggest leaving one more goddamn time, I will go caveman on your ass."

She blinked a few times, pressing her lips together before nodding. "Okay then."

"Good girl. Now, let's get some snacks, water, and Tylenol and have a party in my room."

Dani stilled, so I patted her butt. "Chop, chop, baby."

It wasn't until we got the materials and were inside my room that I realized the mistake I made. The grave mistake. She'd be sleeping in my bed, next to me, and all I wanted to do was get her naked.

Which I shouldn't do because... of reasons. Right?

CHAPTER
ELEVEN

Daniella

Thank god Van had his personal bathroom because I was having a freak-out. One of his shirts sat on the sink, the one he'd let me wear to bed, and I couldn't text Elle about it. When I'd wanted to make bad decisions that night, it wasn't *this*.

Think. What should I do? Make a line of pillows in the middle? Sneak off to the floor? I washed my face and used my finger to try and brush my teeth, and still, my heart raced, and my stomach somersaulted at the situation. Fourteen-year-old me would be jumping up and down and screaming with joy that her crush gave her a shirt.

I picked it up and smelled it, all fresh laundry and evergreen. Fuck, this wasn't good.

I needed advice, stat.

Dani: Sorry if you're sleeping, but long story short, I'm at Van's, and we kissed a lot and are now sharing a bed as friends. WHAT DO I DO?

Cami: Stop overthinking. I've shared a bed with legit friends before, no big deal.

Cami: UNLESS *you want something to happen.*

Cami: *How was the fake kiss?*

Dani: *Not fake. Amazing. Got to second base before we were interrupted, and now I can't stop thinking about it.*

Cami: **wiggling cat GIF**

Cami: *What's your fear? You're not this innocent butterfly, babe (not shaming you at all) so why are you freaking out?*

Dani: *He seemed into us kissing, but it was a performance, I'm sure. I'm not his usual type.*

Cami: *Ah, so self-doubt. I've been there. It's hard, okay? To see yourself without all the bias and beliefs you've heard externally. This guy has been in your life forever, right? He's not gonna hurt you. Talk to him.*

Dani: *And say hey, I wanna get naked with you but can't because I'm afraid of ruining my friendship with your sister?*

Cami: *That might be some of it, but don't fall back on that excuse when you're avoiding the real shit.*

Dani: *Damn, I wanted a sympathetic friend.*

Cami: *I'm a bitch, but I love you, so it's the hard truth, babe. Since its clear you need advice—legit, go to sleep. It's late, you're stressing. If y'all do hook up, you don't wanna be in your head or you won't enjoy it. Sleep, then do what comes naturally in the morning.*

Dani: *you're the best.*

Cami: *I know. Talk tomorrow.*

Cami was right. Her words settled me down, and with a new resolve, I washed my face and removed all my clothing except my panties. *That* felt like crossing a line. Dressed in just an old Blackhawks shirt, I tiptoed out of the bathroom. The lights were still on, but Van was out cold.

Flat on his back, shirt off and loose gray shorts hanging from his hips, he was a fucking sight. His muscles were hard-earned, the definition clear even while he slept. And his stomach. *Ungh.* He always was toned, but it had been a while since I saw him shirtless and he'd only gotten bigger, stronger. My tongue felt too large for my mouth the longer I stared at him, and I had no choice but to just get in his bed.

Each step was increasingly harder to manage. My feet were weighed down by nerves and guilt—nerves about my growing attraction to him and guilt at how I knew this could never be more than a fake-tionship. Throw in my lingering self-doubt and I had a real cocktail of emotions that would surely keep me up all night, listening to Van breathe as he lay right next to me.

Get in the bed. Just do it.

I'd survive this. I shut off the light, held my phone like a sword, and carefully scooted under his covers. I immediately turned to my side, keeping as far away as possible. There could be no accidental touches tonight. Nope. My libido couldn't handle any skin-to-skin contact. Soon enough, Van's snores filled the room, and I matched my breathing with his. The amount of times I'd imagined this happening was in the hundreds. What it'd feel like to be on the end of his intensity? To feel his lips against mine? It was happening. Fake, sure, but god, this was a dream come true.

He kissed the way he played hockey, all-in and focused. My body still tingled from kissing him twice now. Being able to kiss him anytime I wanted was a fantasy come to life. Holding hands, touching him. This was more than I'd ever dreamed. Being in his bed next to him...my stomach flipflopped. I wanted this moment, although temporary, to last forever.

Eventually, all thoughts of the night drifted away, and I fell asleep next to the one guy I'd always had a crush on.

"Dani, baby?" a deep, soft voice woke me. I smiled into the pillow, breathing in scents of spice and detergent. A gentle touch rubbed my shoulder, creating small circles on my skin.

"Mm, that's nice." My eyelids were twice as heavy as normal. The drinking and late night combined with my emotional battle had twisted into a wicked headache. My temples throbbed, and the blankets were so warm and fuzzy. I should live in this hobbit hole.

Wait.

My eyes flew open to find Van leaning on one hand, his elbow resting on the bed as he stared at me with a small grin toying his lips. Sleep lines covered his face, making his features more adorable and innocent. Instead of handsome, he looked cuddly. His eyes crinkled on the sides, and his hair was a mess.

I loved it.

"Hi." My raspy voice sounded off, groggy and sleepy. Clearing my throat, I tried again. "Hello."

"Are you always so formal in bed?" he teased, the damn dimples coming out in full force.

It wasn't even fair to look this good in the morning, especially after a night like he had. "What time is it?"

"Seven."

"And why are you talking to me? There is sleep to be had." I pulled the blankets over my head, hoping to buy myself an extra second of peace. My damn heart sped up around him before this, and now? It galloped.

"Dani." He gently pulled the blanket down, somehow moving closer to me in the process. He scrunched his nose and grinned down at me, no sign of a hangover. "You're a grump in the morning. I don't remember that from all the nights you crashed at my parents."

"Because Elle is normal and let me sleep in until at least nine. You're a monster." I gripped the sheets to cover my face again, but he stopped me. "This is bullshit. You were wildly drunk last night. There is no justice that you're this awake and not kneeling over a toilet."

He shrugged. "I burn through it fast. Always have. And I wasn't *that* drunk."

"Uh, yes, you were. Toddler legs, counting stars, changing the conversation every five seconds. You were a damn handful."

"Nah, I was fun." He reached over and trailed a finger along the neckline of his shirt, the tip just grazing my skin. "I like my shirt on you."

My breath caught in my throat, my hormones going bonkers. An aggressive, embarrassingly red blush covered me from head to toe, and there was nothing I could do to stop it. "You say that to all the ladies."

He arched an eyebrow, repeating the motion and moving his finger along my jawline to my ear. "I don't give *all the ladies* my clothes, Daniella."

Was that sentence loaded or was it my imagination? I couldn't be sure. "I'll return it, don't worry."

"Keep it, but first, I want to see you in it fully, especially those long legs I felt wrapped around me last night."

"Van." I covered my face with my hands, the moment finally coming to head. We had to have *the talk.* Defining our fake-tionship. My attraction to him. "What's happening?"

He sighed softly, moving my hands from my face and scooting closer so his side pressed against me. He smelled so damn good, like sleep and mint. Damn. The bastard had used mouthwash already, and I had morning breath.

"Wait, be right back. I, uh, have to pee."

Wow, that was even worse. I bolted out of his bed and ran toward the bathroom, turning on the faucet and sitting on the toilet in despair. *Breathe in, breathe out.* After a few minutes, I rinsed my mouth and faced myself in the mirror. My hair still held curls, and my makeup hadn't smeared too much. If anything, I looked okay. Decent, maybe.

Now, to figure out what the fuck was happening with Van and his comment. I twisted the handle and held my head high as I walked back to his bed. His gaze zeroed in on my feet, moving up slowly toward my legs and hips. The temperature in the room rose fifteen degrees at least with that gaze alone. His eyes burned, and there was no way that was fake.

There was no one here to know.

If I wanted to act on this sexual tension, I could. He made that clear. But could I do it and live with the consequences?

"Yeah." His tongue wet his bottom lip. "You can keep that shirt. Your legs look a mile long, goddamn, Dani."

"Van." I tried so hard to voice all the worries in my head, but nothing came out. In all the years I'd fantasized about this happening, I never thought it would be this hard. My mind wouldn't shut off about what happened after: what did it mean for our ruse? Did I keep this from Elle? Was it just once or twice or... more?

"Hey, hey." Concern laced his features, and he got off the bed, moving to sit on the end right in front of me. "Please talk to me."

"Do we have sex just once to get it out of our systems? Is this because we've been celibate for the last two weeks and we're just horny? Do we do it three times? Or just oral? What does this mean for our friendship? I'm never leaving Elle's life, and god, she'd kill me. But is this just for convenience, or are you attracted to me? When did that happen?" I couldn't catch my breath, embarrassed I'd said all of that unfiltered, desperate to hear his answer. My insides were overworked, about to catch fire.

He blinked a few times before opening his mouth and shutting it. Then, he chuckled and pulled me to stand between his legs. With his hands on my hips, he kneaded my thighs with his thumbs. The sensation was like a firework of pleasure.

"That was a lot of questions to get through. So, let's break them down." He moved his touch to my bare thighs, slowly moving up my legs until his fingers danced on the edge of my panties.

"S-sure." My body trembled from his featherlight teases in anticipation of where his fingers would go next. He traced the fabric toward my ass, then back again, his attention never leaving my face.

"This isn't because we've been doing this for two weeks. It is humanly possible to go that long without sex, despite what you're assuming about me." He dipped his finger into the waistband just a centimeter, making me suck in a breath.

He smiled and ran his finger back and forth, causing my pulse to skyrocket. My heart beat so hard my neck throbbed.

"Let's not plan a certain number and enjoy each other. I'm attracted to you if that wasn't clear. You felt it yesterday, and I'm explicitly telling you now—you are fucking beautiful." He moved that damn hand up my stomach and between my breasts. "Nothing will change our friendship. That's a promise."

He said I was beautiful. It was like a geyser of joy flowed through me, spreading from my heart to my fingertips. I *felt* beautiful under his gaze. He wouldn't lie to me. That wasn't him. His words made my body hum.

"A-and Elle?"

"I'd rather not talk about my sister, but that's entirely your call." He pulled me closer, so close his breath hit my face. He grabbed the end of the shirt and tugged. "Can I take this off?"

I nodded, completely breathless and transfixed by the way he touched me. I'd been with guys, some great, some not so much, but no one had looked at me the way he did. Like he was starved for me. Van's entire face lit up at my answer, and he slowly lifted the fabric up, exposing my stomach, then my chest, then damn. I stood between his thick thighs in just my forest-green lace panties.

"Mm." He studied me, licking his lips and breathing heavier. He traced up and down my sides, dipping into the waistband again before moving up to circle my nipples. They were beaded and tingled when he grazed a pad over one of them.

My legs shook with need, but Van took his time staring and teasing.

"Please," I panted, dying from the torture of just his touch.

He gave me a wicked grin and bent forward, capturing one tip in his mouth and biting down. I arched my back, desperately craving more, and he obliged. He sucked my nipple hard, swirling his tongue around it before pushing both breasts together and switching between them.

Watching him with his face between my boobs was almost too much. I was wet as hell, shaking with need at this point, and all I could do was stand there. "Jesus." I panted, closing my eyes and loving how his scruff prickled the sensitive skin.

"Perfect." He squeezed them again, pressing a soft kiss on each one before moving his hands toward my panties. "May I?"

I nodded, again, unable to form coherent words because I was a horny mess being seduced by her crush. He slid the material down my legs and helped me step out of them. Instead of being embarrassed or worried how I looked, I felt... powerful.

Van stared at me with a deep hunger that had my stomach swirling in the most addictive way. He sucked in a breath before dragging one lone finger to my pussy, dipping it between my legs and hissing. "Fuck, you're so wet."

"I know. I'm dying."

"We can't have that, can we?" He grinned, his teeth clamping down on his bottom lip before picking me up and setting me on the edge of the bed. He did it so easily it made me breathless. He spread my legs wide, placing one on each of his shoulders, and before I could get a word in, he licked me. I shuddered. Gabriel Van Helsing was going down on me. It felt amazing, an out of body experience.

He flicked his tongue along my clit once, twice, three times before groaning. "Daniella, Christ." He brought a finger and slid inside me, wetting it before adding another. He sucked and teased and changed pace every few seconds. He flicked his tongue against my swollen nerve, driving me wild. He ate me hard and soft at the same time.

I dug my fingers in his hair, something I'd secretly imagined doing. I rocked my hips against his mouth, needing him closer to me. He hummed against me, pulling back for a second. "You're fucking perfect."

I shuddered, hearing those words from him did something to me. Made me feel drunk almost. The sounds of my body sliding across the sheets and his tongue on my pussy overtook the room. I couldn't believe this was happening. Gabe getting me off. It was a dream come true.

He thrusted his fingers faster as he flattened his tongue against my clit. It was an explosion of sorts.

My back arched, my stomach tensed, and my thighs tightened around his head. The orgasm was building at an aggressive pace, stealing my senses and mind. He thrusted his fingers hard, curling to get me right where I needed him as he increased the pressure of his tongue. It was a magical trio of sensations, and time lost meaning.

He moaned into me, sucking on my clit and fingering me like he'd been doing it forever. My spine tingled, and when he flattened the whole of his tongue on me, I came apart.

It wasn't a pretty or delicate orgasm. It was a monster of one —my head lashing back and forth and my ankles crossing behind his head, holding him hostage between my thighs. "Van, fuck, *shit!*" I cried out, the pleasure blinding me for a few moments.

The aftereffects lingered, my legs shaking and my limbs a little tingly, but Van never left his spot. He stilled and kissed the inside of each thigh, running his nose along my sensitive skin, and my god, I couldn't want him more.

"Hottest." He kissed my stomach. "Sound." Then my thigh. "Ever." Then he was back, slowly massaging my pussy with soft strokes of his tongue. He stopped the vigorous pace and instead took his time teasing me with his mouth.

"Hey, I'm not sure," I started, my throat dry. "I usually only come once."

He didn't stop licking, but his eyes met mine and lit up. I knew that face. I'd seen it a thousand times. *Bet I can.* Competitive asshole.

A shiver of hope danced down my spine at the challenge in

his eyes, and I gulped, pushing myself up on my elbows to watch him lick me. He was an artist on the ice and off it too. He moved his hands to spread my ass apart, digging his fingers into the flesh as he continued to taste every inch of me. There was something insanely erotic to watch him between my thighs —his dark messy hair all over the place, and his bedroom eyes blissed out in pleasure. It went on for minutes, the sensations so fucking good but no sign of a second orgasm.

"Van, I promise—"

"You're coming a second time for me." He stopped licking, stood up with a raging hard on in his shorts, and flipped me onto my back. "Ass up, Dani."

"Wh-what?"

"I'm not eating your ass, don't worry. Not today. But I'm earning a second orgasm from you. Call me a greedy, selfish bastard, but I need it." He sounded nothing like the guy I knew. Instead, his voice was filthy and rough and sexy as fuck. Him taking charge and flipping me like I weighed nothing sent all sorts of signals to my body. Like, fuck *this guy is hot* signals.

"There we go, good girl." He gripped my ass again, my face pressing into his sheets when he slid his fingers lower to thrust inside me. "Rock your hips a bit, baby."

I did, and he groaned, kissing my lower back twice before removing his fingers and licking my pussy from behind. My lord, this was a first. He reached around to play with my clit and dug his palm into it, matching the rhythm of my hips, and *oh my god*. His entire face was pressed against me, probing and tasting, and the flicker of an orgasm started in my spine. "Yes, Van. Yes," I moaned, rocking harder and fisting the sheets in my hands. I needed a base, something to hold onto because the pleasure was coming fast and hard.

He hummed into me, stimulating my clit with his hand and matching it with his tongue and oh my god, holy shit. I came fucking apart at the seams when the orgasm hit me like a truck.

A scream ripped from my throat, everything going black for a second as the pleasure weaved its way to every cell in my body.

Sweat dripped down my back and chest, and my fingers were so white from my death grip on the sheets, but damn, my body was a puddle of ecstasy. He laughed softly as I came to, helping me roll back over with a gentle touch. I let myself lay there for a second or two, needing to catch my breath, and when I opened my eyes, he stared at me with the tenderest expression.

But then he said, "Does that answer your question about oral?"

I laughed hard, needing a momentary break from the intense emotions going around my head. Sex didn't equate to feelings, and I had to remember that.

Gabriel Van Helsing might've eaten me out hard, making me come twice, but I had to be sure to protect my heart. He never fell for girls, and when he did, there was no way I'd be the first one. He was out of my league, and we both knew it.

CHAPTER
TWELVE

Gabe

Daniella looked up at me, her eyes dazed and her entire body flushed. Pride filled my chest at getting her to fall apart twice. But mainly, an overwhelming impulse to be closer to her struck me. It was the oddest sensation. Instead of the aggressive urge to slide inside her and get my own release, I needed to make sure she was okay. That what we did didn't upset her or push her too far. I kissed her stomach and studied her face, one I'd known for years but was really just learning.

Like the different ways she blushed. There was the embarrassed flush, the turned-on redness, and the uncertainty one. Right now, her body was like a noodle, sprawled out and content. I adored her like this, without her mind overthinking about every little detail and her lips slightly curved up on the sides. "What's going on in that beautiful head of yours, Dani?"

"Floating."

Her one-word answer made me laugh. I kissed the center of her chest and then her throat. "What was that you were saying about only coming once?"

She snorted and finally opened her eyes. "Do I sense a tone, Van Helsing? A smug competitive edge to your voice?"

"I like being the best."

"I never said you were the *best*," she fired back.

I narrowed my eyes, pretending to glare before she cracked a smile. She placed an arm over face, letting out a groan. "Fine. Yes, you are the best. Congrats."

I might've puffed my chest out a little.

She pushed up onto her elbows, the playful glint leaving her gaze as she nervously chewed on the side of her lip. The post-orgasm glow was evaporating, and my chest tightened at what would come out of her mouth.

Please don't say we couldn't do it again.

I kept my expression neutral, not letting her know I was dying inside because my god, one taste of her wasn't enough. Not even a little bit. Creating game plans was my specialty, making sure the right people made the right moves to secure a win, and right now, I had to do the same thing.

"Before you open up that delicious mouth of yours, Dani, I have an idea. A proposal of sorts."

"Your last one got us into this mess."

"Two mind-blowing orgasms is a mess?"

She grinned briefly. "It complicated things, that's for sure."

I rolled my eyes and lay next to her, our chests facing each other. "Here's my idea. Hear me out. Assuming you enjoyed my mouth on your pussy—"

"Van, god!" She shoved my shoulder and sat up, glancing down and yanking the blanket to cover herself. "I can't be the only one naked to have this conversation. Wait. What about you? Holy shit. You had me so discombobulated I forgot what year it was." She eyed the bulge in my shorts and gave me a worried glance. "I can return the favor. Please."

"Sure, but not today." I shook my head, somehow needing her to realize she meant more to me than just a hookup. Was my dick hard as steel? Yes. Was I horny as fuck? Also, yes. But could I go deal with it in the shower after taking my time to convince her to do this again? You got it—another yes.

"But your dick…"

"I'll survive, mostly." I ran my fingers over her bare arm and sighed. "Seriously, this was about you. I wanted you to feel good."

"I don't think anyone has ever said those words to me before," she said, her voice almost a whisper. The air shifted between us, almost like the molecules got heavier.

"So, back to my genius idea." I cleared my throat, easing the tension that had worked its way into the moment.

"Of course. Genius."

"We have a few more weeks until Christmas, another until New Years. We said our breakup was what… January?"

"Uh huh." Her teeth came down on her bottom lip again. "So, five more weeks of pretending?"

"Exactly. But… did you enjoy what just happened? This is a pity question because I already know the answer, but please, did you?"

"Your ego need another stroke?"

"Something on me needs a stroke right now, yes." I wiggled my eyebrows, and again, Daniella's face relaxed. Joking around and teasing were her safe space. Noted.

"Fine. Yes, I thoroughly had a great time, and they were the best orgasms I've ever had. Now, what's your idea, Van?"

"If you want, we can enjoy each other for the remainder of our time. Hell, I want to eat you up again, and it's barely been ten minutes. I'm so in if you are." I tensed, waiting to see her reaction, but none came.

She studied me, her brown eyes narrowing as she glanced from me to the wall, then back to me. "Enjoy each other, nakedly?"

"If you want. We could keep clothes on too. Wouldn't stop me."

She huffed out a laugh. "Fake dating with secret benefits."

"Yup. Hell, everyone besides Elle thinks it's genuine, and baby, if we were real, I'd certainly be getting you naked every chance I got."

A flustered blush covered her face, and she swallowed, hard. "Are you sure this is a good idea?"

"What's there to lose?"

"Our friendship."

"Daniella." I sat up and took her hands in mine. "Two decades of being friends with a person can't be ruined with five weeks of sleeping together. We care for each other, and this helps us both out. Plus, we have a timeline to prevent it from getting weird, you know?"

I truly didn't understand the holdup, but I kept my impatience in check. She had to be comfortable and into it because the last thing I wanted to do was hurt her. "Nothing will change for me, okay? You'll still be my sister's best friend, and yeah, I'll know what your tits look like, but it'll be a great memory in a few years. Our little secret."

"How would it work?" She played with the end of one curl, slipping it through her fingers over and over. "Scheduled days like Wednesdays are for oral and Fridays for banging?"

I cackled. "You are ridiculous. Wednesdays are for oral. That'd be great on a T-shirt."

A smile cracked her face, and she nodded really hard. "You know what? Yes. I'm in. Five weeks of hooking up then we do the big breakup. Fuck it. I deserve this."

"Thank Christ." Pleasure rippled through my body at her acceptance, and I moved over her, caging her under me. My elbows were on either side of her face, my cock resting between her thighs with only my shorts preventing me from fucking her. The urge to kiss her had a chokehold on me, like my lungs wouldn't work unless my mouth was on hers.

So, I lowered my lips tentatively, waiting for her to make the connection, and my soul fucking sang when she did. She nibbled my bottom lip, hesitant and shy, like it was her first time with me, and I shuddered.

Her hands came around to my back, dragging her nails down my skin and cupping my ass. "I have a confession," she said, really holding onto my glutes.

"Oh yeah?" I kissed her collarbone, grinding into her more. I knew I said I'd go to the shower, but I needed just three more seconds of this.

"I've been obsessed with your ass for years."

I laughed, sucking the base of her neck real quick before peeling myself off her. It physically hurt to walk away, but it felt important. Plus, we had five whole weeks of doing all sorts of stuff together. "That's good to know. Want me to strip for you before I shower?"

"Wait, we're not...?" She made a circle with two fingers and slid her pointer finger through it fast. "Gonna do it?"

"We have weeks, baby. I'm keeping my word. I'm gonna go jack off in the shower and then take you to breakfast." I patted her tummy and took one last look at her nipples.

"Oh, I can head out. You don't need to get me breakfast."

"Fine, you can buy." I winked, pushing off my shorts and giving her a glimpse of my ass. She stared hard, making my own face heat up. It was wonderfully *not weird* to see her openly check me out. "We need to post some photos online anyway. Our regularly scheduled fake-tionship status."

"Right. Of course. Duh." She slapped her forehead.

"Can you be ready in ten minutes?"

"I don't have anything to wear except my hoodie."

"That's clothes, isn't it?"

"Yeah, but the photos are for my mom, and she'll comment on it or something. I don't know. I'm still bitter about last night and want to avoid provoking her. I could go back and do my makeup really quick."

"I'm not going to tell you what to do because this is your hurdle to overcome, but you *could* wear one of my shirts? It'd be clear you spent the night with me, and wouldn't that be fun for everyone to talk about?"

She thought it over for a beat before smiling. "You really aren't just a pretty face. You got a nice brain in there too."

"You're so sweet with words. I'm so lucky." I walked toward my dresser and found a new team shirt with my name on the back. The long-sleeved navy shirt would look good on her. "Here ya go."

"Thank you." She smiled at me, and this time something flickered in her gaze that hadn't been there before. Warmth, gratitude, or maybe she was super hungry and excited for food. Either way, I left her there and went into my bathroom. I had a very hard cock to attend to.

"We're one hundred percent the couple that sits on the same side of the booth, D. You can't deny it." I scooted closer to her at the local diner, pressing the side of my thigh against hers. "We'd probably hold hands too."

"No, there's no way I would do this. It's so awkward. I waited tables one summer and hated those couples."

"Bitter Betty come out?"

"No, it was just weird." She tried pushing me away, but I put my arm around her shoulders. She was adorable in my extra-large shirt. She'd tied it and done this cool thing to tuck it in, and I thought she rocked the style.

She didn't need all the glam and shimmery shit her mom forced on her to look beautiful. Her smile alone lit up a room. But, if wearing it made her feel stronger, I'd never say a word. I was just glad all the worry had left her face, and instead, she rolled her eyes because of me.

"So, you're not one of those PDA couples then. Noted."

"I mean, maybe? I'm not really sure." She picked up her straw wrapper and folded it until it was the size of my thumbnail. Then, she unfolded it and ripped the lines. "Haven't really dated a lot."

"First boyfriend, go." I picked up the menu with my free hand and it took three seconds of looking at the pictures to know what I wanted—pancakes, eggs, bacon, and hashbrowns. I was easy.

"Uh, Adam, maybe? Seventh grade. We made out by the water fountain, but he dumped me over text a month later because he wanted to kiss someone else at a birthday party."

"Hey, at least he didn't cheat?"

"Yes, way to be positive about it." She snorted and leaned into me a little. She smelled like lavender, and I wanted to bottle it up. Her warmth spread into me, and my stomach got a weird tingly feeling.

Oh, that reminded me of last night and how I needed to look into indigestion. Before I could ask more about her horrible junior high boyfriend, our waitress came and took our order. Daniella got the exact same thing as me, and that made me grin like a fool.

"Oh my god, we're becoming the couple that turns into each other," I teased, poking her side. She yelped and returned the pinch.

"You're too much for me right now, god." She laughed and rested her face in her hands. "How do you have energy?"

"I'm just happy. I dunno." I shrugged, trying to figure out how I did have this much energy. Normally after a game and partying, I was tired, but this morning I felt...invigorated. "Anyway, this Adam fellow. Did he get to second base?"

"I hate you." She smiled while she said it though. "He did, not that there were bases to really get, you know?"

"Oh, I'm sure he didn't care and was excited to touch a boob."

She laughed and turned a bit, arching one of her brows. "Enough about me. Tell me your first girlfriend."

Damnit. I should've expected this, but the guilt still took me by surprise. I hated knowing my answer would disappoint Daniella. "Ah, see, the thing is, I never committed myself to anyone."

"Ever?"

"Nope." I picked up my own straw wrapper and tore it to pieces. "I'd agree to fool around with girls for a set amount of time and then it was over. I just never clicked with anyone, so it was easier to keep it short, uncomplicated."

"Oh."

That one syllable felt like a ten-pound weight crashing on my ribcage, stifling down any rebuttals. There was no issue with what I did because everyone was fine with it. There were no upset feelings, but that *oh* was laced with hurt.

Yet, I still needed to fill the silence to get that blank look off her face, but what did I say after that? Any joking felt off, and going back to her dating life wasn't the right move. My guts twisted, and I felt defensive. "There's nothing wrong with having casual flings when both parties agree to it."

"I know." She recoiled, red splotches covering her neck. She chugged half the glass of water in front of her. "Definitely nothing wrong with it."

"Then why do I feel like you're judging me?"

"I'm not, I swear." She forced a smile, pointing to her temple. "Sorry, got a hangover, I think. I need hashbrowns and more coffee."

Thankfully, the waitress brought over our food on cue and saved the mood. But as I ate, I couldn't stop thinking about why that *oh* bothered me. Having expiration dates on hooking up was the best route. It prevented people from getting hurt and from confronting others when they wanted to hang on longer. Like what we'd agreed to an hour ago naked in my bed.

So why was Daniella upset about it?

CHAPTER
THIRTEEN

Daniella

I'm like all the others.

The sobering thought was a reality bitch-slap to the face in the middle of winter. Ice flooded my heated veins, reminding me to protect my heart. I was afraid it was too late, but the realization I was like the rest allowed me to put up some thinly built walls again. Gabriel always had a deadline on anyone he was with. Not even a girlfriend, but a fling.

Elle would be so disappointed to find out I was another notch on his fling-flang list. He knew something was wrong when we said goodbye, but I needed space and time to build myself back up. We were friends. He was Elle's brother. We weren't real. He clearly separated feelings from sex, and I had too in the past. I'd never had a lifelong crush of any other hookup though, so I had to *get it together.*

Bundled up in my hoodie, I walked back to my dorm with my face pointed down. The wind was a real bitch, but it fit my mood. The morning had started out on a high and crashed like a wave by lunch. I needed to shower off the night and the gross feeling that I was nothing special.

God, I hated when I got down on myself, but it was easy after seeing a lifetime of Gabe's women. A revolving door. Yes, it was all consensual, and he always was up front, and fuck, after getting those orgasms, I'd be a fool not to agree to it. They were an out-of-body experience. Yet...it hurt.

That was the truth. I wanted to be different, but I was just like the others.

My phone buzzed, and I knew deep in my gut it was my mom. When it rained, it poured, and sure enough, a lengthy text greeted me.

Mom: Your post is broadcasting that you're sleeping with Gabriel. I hope you realize he's popular and getting attention, so you're going to be seen by a lot of people. Your makeup was smeared, Daniella, and you know how important presentation is.

Mom: Do you need me to mail you more products? Gabriel is a catch, honey, and you must make sure you do everything you can to keep his interest. Men like him are rare. He comes from a good family and is incredibly handsome and athletic. Don't ruin this by being lazy.

My eyes prickled with tears, something I vowed not to do because of my mom, and they spilled over onto my cheeks. The cold almost froze them, and I walked faster, needing to get to the safety of my room. There were a few students out and about, all bundled up in coats with gloves, and I regretted not getting a car ride back. Van had insisted on walking me, but I'd begged him not to. Space was good, and I was pretty sure he needed it too.

After what felt like ten years, I got into my dorm and plopped on my bed. It wasn't nearly as comfortable as Van's and smelled like generic detergent. Not his spicy scent. "Fuuck."

Bailey, my roommate, took off her headphones and eyed me. "There you are."

"Do you ever want to curl up into a ball and hide under your covers?"

"Sure do. Especially right now. This physics final is going to murder me dead." She pushed up her large black glasses and tapped her pencil against her teeth. "You crash at one of the girls' places?"

"Ha, no. At my boyfriend's." Even the words felt weird. "I'm dating Gabriel Van Helsing, the hockey captain."

"He's a handsome devil, I'll give you that. Definitely a little wild from the reputation that precedes him, but good for you." She studied me for a beat before pointing to super big book. "I'm here if you need to talk, but if you're going to cocoon, I'm focusing on this sexy problem."

"You're a real weirdo, B, but I love you."

She smiled and shoved her bangs out of her face before putting her headphones on. I lucked out on a dormmate honestly. She hated all things athletic, was smart as a whip, and never judged me for a single thing I did. Came home drunk? She offered me a water. Threw up on my pillow? Gave me a large bowl. She was a gem and a total nerd. I loved her. She was a transfer herself but had already found a few close friends.

Plus, we were friendly, but our social lives didn't cross, so it kept a healthy distance between us to always be polite. She returned to her book, and I went back to brooding. I hated being in a funk and needed to snap out of it.

The best way? Work out. Sweat. Push myself.

Excited to actual do something about my mood, I dressed in pink yoga pants and a cropped tank and my winter coat. The rec center was a mile from the dorm, but I could do a light run on the way there.

I even texted Cami if she wanted to meet me. She agreed.

An hour later, the two of us jogged laps at a healthy pace. We kept in shape, so the run didn't wind us, but I definitely felt myself pushing the alcohol and emotions out of my body.

It felt good.

"Going faster than normal today. Gabriel do something dumb already?"

I snorted. "No." I winced. "Kind of?"

"Might as well tell me."

She was right. She'd pull it out of my eventually, and it was a shame she didn't want to be a therapist or lawyer. She could get me to spill my guts. I filled her in on everything that happened, how I was just one of the many, and she remained quiet the whole time. "No opinion?"

"I'm thinking. Freddie is trying to work out now, and my god, do you see how awkward he is?" She jutted her chin toward a bench press where her giant boyfriend lifted a bar. Michael Reiner, the assistant hockey coach, was there with him too.

"Slightly awkward?" I laughed. "Hey, at least he's trying."

"I don't want him to hurt himself." She slowed to a walk. "Anyway, you have a choice here. You agreed to fake date him and to fool around. You can take both back any time. If it's too much, then end it."

"What if he breaks my heart?"

She scrunched her nose. "Is it worth the risk? You need to answer that for yourself. It could be a dope ass five weeks getting some from the best you've had—your words, babe. Or you could keep it casual. It sounds like you're already in love with the guy, so really... how much more could it hurt?"

"Fuck." I rubbed my temples just as a familiar voice said my name. *Gabriel.* The hairs on the back of my neck tingled with nerves as I turned and found him filling up his water bottle. He wore black shorts and a cutoff shirt, his biceps and forearms on full display. My god. It was illegal. The corded muscles, the sweat dripping from his olive skin. The curve of his mouth and warmth in his eyes, like he was pleasantly happy to see me. It was too much.

I lifted my hand in a quick wave, heat flooding my body at remembering his face had been between my legs just hours ago. What were the chances of this? Us being here at the same time? Ugh.

"I didn't know you were heading to the gym baby." He

stalked toward me and gestured his chin toward the treadmills. Three women worked out hard, but one caught my eye. Becca. His latest fling who wouldn't go away. That little reminder of *why* we were doing this dampened the flame burning inside my gut.

"I'm checking on my boo. See you later." Cami nodded at Gabe before joining Freddie at the bench, and that left me and my fake boyfriend.

He leaned down to kiss my cheek, his lips salty. He even reached around with his free hand and patted my ass. "You know how you told me you had a secret longing for my booty?"

"Gabe." I blushed, even if it was pretend, and swatted him.

"I've had one for yours too. Dancer's asses are thick." He grinned and eyed my bare stomach. He teased the waistband with his fingers. "You look good."

"Uh, thanks." I played with my ponytail and hate, hate, hated how uncomfortable this was. My feelings I'd buried all these years broke free, combining with the worry he'd break me into a million pieces. Focusing on our deal, us putting on a show, was important. "Should we uh, kiss for you know, her?"

"Absolutely." He licked his lips before leaning forward, gently pressing them against mine in a warm, soft peck. He hummed before pulling back, his smile covering his whole face. "Hi."

He was being cute, and despite the paper walls I tried building around my heart, I felt myself dethawing in my hurt. "Seriously, you have too much energy today."

"Had a great morning. Woke up to someone in bed." He shrugged, winked, and glanced over his shoulder.

That little gesture was another reminder this playfulness was fake. It hurt to admit, but Cami was right. I'd agreed to this and instead of focusing on all the ways it could go wrong, I should try and enjoy it. Feeling brave, I fisted his shirt and pulled him closer to me. He sucked in a breath when my fingers grazed his stomach, and I didn't have to fake my smile this time. "Lucky you."

He laughed, and I got a little thrill. I might be in a long line of hookups, but Van was fun, flirty, and talented.

"Hey, do you have plans tonight?"

"Maybe." The girls hadn't texted the group chat yet, but we tended to party on Saturdays. "Why?"

"I've come up with ideas for every day of the week. Seduction Saturday is tonight."

"One could argue it already happened this morning." I let go of his shirt and stepped back. Distance would be great to let me get my head on again and figure out how to be chill about this whole thing. "The girls are hanging, so I'll be with them."

"Damn. I guess I'll allow it."

"*Allow* it?" I arched my eyebrows. "Are you one of those type of partners? Can't say I'm a fan, Van."

He gave a sheepish smile and shrugged. "Obviously I'm teasing."

"Good, good." I traced a pattern on the floor with my right foot, my anxiety spiking with the same feeling I'd get around my mom where I didn't know what to say. My thoughts spiraled with ideas—did I talk about dancing or Seduction Saturday or working out?

"I should finish my reps before I get lazy. Plus, Coach wants us all to meet up this afternoon to talk about the game. I was for real joking, Dani, go out, have fun, do you, okay?" He cupped my face and pulled the end of my hair as his dimples appeared. "It's supposed to snow tomorrow, so how about we go see a movie?"

"Oh." I blinked, tickled that he was asking me on a date— fake or not, I hadn't been asked to see a movie, ever. "Wow."

"Shit, that was lame, wasn't it?" He ran a hand over his face. "It's a secret thing I do alone. I love going to movies and getting popcorn, sitting in the dark theatre without worrying about hockey or what I'm doing after graduation or if I'm pissing someone off. The drama from the team disappears, and I can escape for two hours. I even keep the ticket stubs—" He stilled, the tops of his cheeks getting pink.

"Oh my god, that's cute. How did I not know this?" My stomach fluttered at his admission. It was like a special secret just for me. "What movies do you like?"

"All of them." He shrugged and lifted the end of his shirt to wipe his face, exposing his toned stomach.

My mouth watered, but I could maybe blame that on being dehydrated from the run. "Gabe, I love this about you. How often do you do this?"

"Twice a month at least. I have a rewards card at the local theater and everything." He rocked back on his heels, and an uncertain, bashful look crossed his eyes. Like the hotshot captain wasn't sure of me...which was utterly ridiculous. "So, you in?"

"Hell yeah, but only if you show me your ticket stubs."

His answering smile sent a dangerous thrill though me, blowing over one side of the shield around my heart. "I'll think about it. It's personal, and I can't believe I even told you. If I do... you gotta tell me something at the same level."

"I don't have anything like that." I chewed my lip, wishing I had a fun hobby. "God, this is so cute."

"I'm not cute."

"No, this is adorable. What movie do you want to see?"

"You choose." He ran his fingers down my arm and squeezed my hands. "I like the midday, afternoon features. I tell my roommate or teammates I'm going to study, and no one questions it."

I was sick, a glutton for punishment and hated that I couldn't stop myself from asking it. "So, you never took your fling-flangs to movies?"

He scoffed. "No. Never. It's my thing."

My heart fucking soared, and despite all the reasons it was dangerous, I stood on my tiptoes and kissed him. It wasn't for show, for me at least. It was gratitude for him sharing something personal with me. "Well, thank you for telling me. I'll look when I get back and text you."

"Can't wait, D. Just keep in mind," he lowered his voice. "I don't share popcorn, so you'll need to buy your own bucket."

"Noted."

My smile almost hurt it was so big, and it stayed on my face as he went back to working out. I was a moron; I knew I was. The fact he never took all his other hookups to movies had to mean something. Even if I was just one in a long line, this was big. Huge, even. I knew I wasn't his type. He never committed and throw in the complication of Elle...it would *never* happen.

Yet, I got a piece of him no one else did. Now, the question was, what happened at the end of our relationship when I had even more parts of him? Surely I'd just fall even harder. I was living my fantasy with him and while I knew it would end, I was worried my heart was already too invested in him. How could I enjoy this time *and* survive heartbreak?

CHAPTER
FOURTEEN

Gabriel

I t wasn't a date. Not a real one.

I ran my hands through my hair twice and stared at the text from my sister, unsure how to respond.

Elle: you're bringing her to the movies?? Damn, you're taking this fake dating thing FOR REAL. Never thought I'd see you ask a girl on a date.

A date was a nice dinner wearing something fancy. Not wearing a gray sweatsuit with the hockey logo, unshaved without a shower. I put on deodorant and cologne because I wasn't a monster, but a date? Psh. No. *Real* dates weren't worth the risk.

Gabe: Not a date, Ellie. It's an action flick.

Elle: Have you ever brought a girl to a movie????? HAVE YOU?

Gabe: Why are you yelling at me?

Elle: Because I don't like the thought of my BEST GODDAMN friend dating you, even if it's fake. Plus, a part of me is jealous? I wanna hang out with you both.

Gabe: lmao, you'll be here next year

Elle: Not funny.

Gabe: you have nothing to worry about.

Elle: I fucking know that, but it's DANIELLA. Remember that, Broseph.

Gabe: I'm muting this thread.

Elle: Middle finger emoji

My jaw tensed, and I rubbed it to ease some tension. Her question caused an uncomfortable lump in the back of my throat, making it hard to swallow. Had I ever brought a girl to a movie? No. Never in high school or since I'd been to college. It was too personal, but Dani didn't count. She knew almost everything about me, so this wasn't that big of a deal.

Also, what did she mean *it's DANIELLA?* Was that a warning or something I should understand? A slight burning formed right beneath my ribs, and I rubbed it. If I pulled a muscle, I was gonna be livid. I was in the best shape of my hockey career and worked hard to stretch, do yoga, and be flexible to *not* injure myself. My phone buzzed with multiple texts, all from Becca, and I didn't even read them. Without thinking about it, I blocked her number.

I didn't care what she had to say. I caught her messing with a condom, and that was it. Too far. Crossing a line. She refused to accept we were done—even though I told her just until the season started, she had to keep digging.

Thank God for Dani.

I scrolled through my photos and found one we'd taken during the summer. Her and Elle had joined me and some of my high school buds for a pick-up softball game, and she was so proud she hit a double that she'd done cartwheels all the way around the field. It was nothing but pure joy, and all of us had laughed and cheered her on. I'd snapped a pic because it was so *her* to celebrate a hit like that. No one even attempted to actually tag her out—which we totally could've.

I cross-posted the photo on my socials with a sun emoji. That was it.

Not two seconds later, Dani texted me.

D: *How have I never seen this before?*

Gabe: *Forgot to show you.*

D: *Why did you take that? I was acting like an idiot.*

Gabe: *You were so happy, I had to capture it. I love this photo.*

D: *I look deranged.*

Gabe: *You couldn't stop smiling after that double. It made my night.*

D: *I did feel pretty proud… but what caused you to post it??*

Gabe: *Becca won't stop texting me.*

D: *Got it.*

I eyed the time, and a flicker of annoyance went through me that the movie didn't start for two hours. My roommate was out for a boozy brunch with his friends, hoping to use bacon and carbs to ease his heartache. I wished him well, I really did, but that was why I had limits. I didn't have the time, energy, or emotional support to go through something like that. I had hockey, my guys, my friends, Elle, my parents… even Daniella. I cringed at the thought of being so distraught I had to get blackout drunk and shove carbs in my face. No thank you.

Too many guys let that shit effect their game, and headcases were the last things teams needed. No one ever seemed worth the distraction or effort, to be honest. Why risk messing with the only consistent part of my life?

To pass time, I could work on the resume my parents were getting on me about. Maybe look at some jobs after graduation? But I had no idea where I wanted to apply. My degree was in business, and all I wanted was a job to make money—didn't have a preference. There were some small places in town that needed account managers, and I loved people, talking, chatting. I could apply for some of those.

I loved our college town, but up north was closer to home. Hockey had always determined my next steps, but once the season was over, that was it. No team, no playing competitively. Sure, there were rec leagues, but I couldn't do that. I'd play too hard and forget it was for fun. I'd thought about coaching, maybe giving back in a few years or so like Reiner. Hockey had been a part of me my entire life, and it was going to be done? Every memory involved hockey, the good and bad ones. Each holiday was scheduled around practice or games, every high or low I experienced was on the ice. And after this season, it was *done*. How did I move on from closing a book of my entire life? How did athletes just... not be athletes anymore?

Returning home would mean I'd be away from the guys on the team, Elle since she was coming here next year, and definitely Dani. She already had an apartment lined up for the end of May so she didn't have to go up north the summer. Hell, with parents like hers, I'd never go home either.

So that meant I'd rarely see her and Elle unless I stayed here.

Fuck. I stretched my arms over my head and paced my room. I didn't have to worry about that yet. It was December. I had months until graduation, and there had to be more account manager jobs for me somewhere.

Content with avoiding anything to do with *the future*, I pulled up footage of the last game and studied different plays that had worked. Ty's shots were sloppy, and he didn't have his normal speed—which I knew I needed to talk to him about the drinking, but how could I when I partied too hard myself? I rubbed my forehead, watching Christopher. He'd bulked up a lot the past month. More than he should've. The younger freshmen was twice his size, and sure, his playing time was becoming less and less, but bulking up wasn't going to make him move smoother on the ice nor play better.

God, I needed to have a chat with him about safe ways to gain muscle. But, throughout my observations, I had one small win.

Cal's minor shift of attitude made a difference. He did ten more passes than the last game, and three of those led to shots on goal. He even got an assist, something I did all the time but rarely him. An assist meant you passed the puck for another guy to get the glory.

He'd improved.

Gabe: You played better Friday. Passed more and let the others have more shots on goal.

Cal: Who is this?

Gabe: Fucking idiot. Van Helsing. How do you not have your captain's number?

Cal: Why would I ever need it?

And there went the attempt at being nice. I tossed my phone on my bed, scowling at it, before picking it up back again. I had to be the better person, the better leader. Daniella's words still resonated with me, fueling me to push past the attitude.

Gabe: Just in case there was an emergency. You need someone to show you how to do a slapshot. I don't know, a million fucking reasons. Take the compliment. You played like a good teammate.

Cal: I don't need help on my slapshot, dick.

Cal: Thanks.

That "thanks" was enough of a win for me, and I called it a success. Couldn't wait to tell Dani about it.

I learned three things while sitting next to Daniella at a movie theater. The first: she looked adorable in navy joggers and a navy sweatshirt. The second: I really liked having someone come with me. The third, and the most problematic: she asked so many damn questions.

Is that supposed to happen? What does that mean? Is he a bad guy? Does the dog live?

"Van, I swear to god, if the dog doesn't survive, I'm gonna bawl my eyes out and cause a real scene." She leaned closer to me, pulling her knees up to her chest and wrapping her arms around them. The movement caused her perfume to waft toward me, and I breathed it in. Made me a bit ravenous, to be honest. Had me wanting to run my nose from her neck to her thighs, wrapping myself in her scent.

I tilted my head so my lips grazed her ear. "You asking all these questions is already causing a scene."

"No one is around us, so they can't hear me." She shivered when I nipped her earlobe.

"I can hear you."

"Are you saying I'm talking too much?" A twinge of hurt laced her voice, making me place a hand on her forearm.

I squeezed it, staring at her until she looked at me. "Yes. Way too fucking much."

We held our gaze, neither one of us backing down until she snorted. "Okay, fair, you might be right. I just have so many questions."

"That you seem to say unfiltered without stopping," I added, unable to fight my grin anymore. Sure, the constant talking was annoying, but she was fucking cute. "What makes you think I have the answers? I haven't seen the movie."

"I don't know. You're a dude. You have a secret longing for movies. You can predict the future? Any of the above?" She sucked her bottom lip into her mouth, her eyes going wide as the action picked up on the film. Wrinkles formed on her forehead when the dog came into the scene.

I slid my phone out of my pocket, researching quickly if the dog survived in the film. "He lives, don't worry."

"You don't know. You haven't seen it!"

"Baby, I just looked it up." Seriously, she was adorable with her worry. I held my phone closer to her, and she squinted as she read the article I did. I knew immediately when she got to the part ensuring the dog lived because her entire body sagged with relief.

"Oh, thank the lord. For future reference, Van, make sure the dog lives before you ever force me to come to a movie with you."

"Forced you? Really?"

She tilted head in my direction, her lips curving up on each side in a pure, Dani-sunshine smile, and she snorted. "No lie, I was excited to come. Forced might've been too strong of a word."

"Shh!" A man ten rows up whipped his head at us, holding his finger against his mouth. "Shut up!"

"Oh my god." Dani sank into her chair, pulling the neckline of her sweatshirt above her face. "I got yelled at. How embarrassing."

"Eh, don't worry about it." I lowered my voice to a whisper because we were talking a bit loud. But I didn't really give a shit. I was having too much fun. Her questions and talking should've driven me crazy, but now, I wanted to know every thought going through her head.

Did she like superhero movies? Rom-coms? Thrillers? Horror? I could picture her jumping out of her seat at scary movies and totally gushing at a love story. I enjoyed all genres, my favorite being rom-coms and action flicks. They were similar in the sense you knew there'd be a happy ending, but you just didn't know how they'd get there.

Dani kept the sweatshirt up almost like a muzzle for the rest of the movie, and when it ended, she made no moves to get up. If anything, she sank lower. "Uh, whatcha doing?"

I stood and stretched as hard as I could, the tingles in my left foot starting to wake up. I leaned closer to her the entire time, and it was mildly uncomfortable but totally worth it.

"That guy who yelled at us needs to leave first. What if he says something? I'm mortified."

"You worry too much, Dani." I held out my hand and had the empty popcorn bucket in the other. She stared ahead of us for a beat before she took her sweet ass time standing up. "Stop stalling. Part two of the date—er, movie experience is waiting for us."

This is not a date. NOT A DATE. The word had slipped out on accident, Elle's damn text in my mind. Daniella didn't show any reaction to my word choice but her eyes going wide.

"Part two?"

"Yup."

"Is this another super-secret Van thing that only I get to experience?"

I nodded, really loving how her eyes sparkled with joy. "Sure is."

"Okay, let's go then." She placed her hand in mine, her petite one fitting perfectly inside my larger fingers. I used my thumb to trace circles on the back of hers, and it was the most natural thing in the world. Just holding her hand. She swung our arms back and forth, her lips teasing a grin as we exited the theater. We barely got outside before she stopped. "Wait."

"What is it?" I glanced around, looking for a dropped phone or a threat near us.

"We need to snap a photo so I can post on mine." She got her phone out of her pocket and held it up for a selfie. "Smile, Van!"

I did, pressing my cheek to hers and giving a goofy grin. It was over the top, but I would bet money Dani would legit take selfies for every day if she ever had a boyfriend. The thought of her being happy and chatty with someone else at a movie gave me pause, but it didn't last long.

Snow fell from the sky, and Dani's eyes turned to saucers. She broke our embrace and spun in circles, her tongue sticking out. "Fuck yes. Snow is my favorite season."

"Pretty sure you mean winter."

"No, spring is my favorite season, but snow? I love it. The way it's soft and hard at the same time. How it silences everything around you when it covers the ground. The way your nose gets cold when you're outside. Plus, sledding and snowmen and crunches with boots. Maybe that's my secret. I'm a slut for snow."

"God, Dani." I stared at her with fascination. She was incredible. "Oral Wednesdays, and I'm a Slut for Snow. You could start your own T-shirt company at this rate."

"Not a bad idea." She spun around again, not opening her

eyes as snow fell on her sweatshirt and hair. Her red locks stood out in the dreary grays of the sky, and despite the cold, my insides were all warm. It was wild how I'd known her my whole life and had always found her entertaining but getting to see these other sides of her too were special. "What's part two?"

"I didn't want to interrupt your twirling. Please, don't stop on my account."

She spun around two more times, her cheeks rosy and her eyes lit up with life. In that moment, I couldn't recall someone more beautiful than her. "Okay, I'm ready. I can stare at the snow out my window and masturbate later."

I choked on my spin, my answering howl of laughter causing multiple people to look at me. "My god, Dani."

She wiggled her eyebrows, clearly amused. "I'm joking, mostly."

Needing to touch her, I put my arm around her and walked us toward my car. It was an old Mazda with tons of miles on it, but it was perfect for my movie days and running errands. I let my roomie use it to when needed since I got the only free parking space for our unit.

Dani leaned her head on me as we walked, wrapping her arm around my hips and squeezing my waist. "Thank you for letting me crash your secret movie dates."

"Thank you for coming." I tightened my grip. "Despite your chatter and almost getting us beat up, I had fun with you here."

She snickered, and I opened the passenger door for her. Because it was the right thing to do, not because it was a date. I watched her get in and buckled before going to my side. My afternoon was one of the best in a while, hell, since the win Friday night until now had been the happiest I'd been, and I couldn't wait to show Dani the next part.

She was gonna love it.

CHAPTER
FIFTEEN

Daniella

I was in some deep shit. The worst, slow-sinking kind where I knew I was in trouble but there was nothing I could do to stop it. Gabe just kept giving me more reasons to fall for him. The movie dates alone.

The teasing.

The laughter.

The opening doors and always having a hand on me.

I was done for. Completely.

"Part two, huh? Do you do this after every movie?" I asked, trying to guess where we were going. He wouldn't say, and I wasn't familiar with the downtown area enough to know what was around here. People were outside walking, enjoying the snow like I was. Early December snow was the best because the winter hadn't gotten too brutal yet, so it was pretty. Plus, the holiday decorations were up, and people's moods were just better between Thanksgiving and Christmas. How could I be worried about heartbreak when it was snowing and I had the best date ever?

"I do, yes." He hummed and tapped his fingers on the wheel

to an alternative pop song. He reached over to grip my knee, sneaking a glance at me at the stoplight. "The rule is though, you can't tell anyone about it. It's my thing, well, it can be our thing until we're done, but then it's mine again. Elle doesn't even know. Got it?"

I was so desperate to learn what *his thing* was that I didn't even wince at the reminder that this was temporary and Van wasn't my dreamy, kind boyfriend. "Totally got it. Will keep my lips sealed."

"Good. Ah, almost here." He licked his bottom lip as he pulled onto a side street, and the gesture had me zeroing in on his mouth.

We hadn't kissed since he picked me up for the movie, and damn, I wanted to badly. I squeezed my thighs together, already trying to come up with an excuse to touch him when he started parking the car.

He pulled into a tiny spot, backed out, trying again and again. It made no sense to find it hysterical that he was such a shitty parker. Like, the worst I'd seen. "Uh, want me to get out and direct you?"

"No, I have it. Just sit there."

I had to cover my mouth with my hand to prevent laughter from bursting out. Van sweated, and his face was red and oh my god.

"Are you *laughing* right now?"

"You're a terrible parker. It's fucking hilarious!" I let it all out, earning a scowl, but he finally got the car in between the lines after six tries. "Have you always been awful? You drove me and Elle to school, and I don't remember you needing ten minutes to park."

"Shut up."

"Dude, that was bad." I could *not* stop laughing. "You're perfect at so many things, so seeing you struggle was chef's kiss." I pinched my fingers and kissed them. "I'm texting your sister. Did she know? Do you have a license?"

"Daniella, I swear." He took the keys out of the ignition and faced me. "You're being an asshole."

"I can't help it." I snickered and forced my face to remain neutral. I had no luck. The harder I attempted to not laugh, the more I did. It was like the time I couldn't stop chuckling when our freshman class had a moment of silence for a sick student. It was the whole *don't make a sound* thing that set me off. This was no different.

Before I knew it, his lips were on mine, and his large hand cupped my face. He answered my wish, and I slid my tongue into his mouth, stroking his and melting like a snowflake. He slowed my pace, taking his time tasting me and teasing me. He nipped, bit, and sucked my lip into his mouth, the deep guttural groan from his chest lighting me on fire. I could kiss him for hours and not get bored. The combination of his soft lips and rough jawline was lethal. My stomach did a back handspring when one hand dropped to my neck, his thumb resting at the base of it. It was so possessive and *hot*.

I gripped his shoulders, pulling him toward me when he paused the kiss too soon. A moan of protest escaped me before I could stop it. "Hey!"

He chuckled and leaned back into his seat, his eyes simmering when I met his gaze. "I had to kiss you to get you to stop fucking laughing. You deserve to have wet panties for a few more hours."

"You damn rascal," I mumbled, taking deep breaths and fanning myself. "I guess today will be a Sexless Sunday for you."

He cackled before opening his door. I followed, and he immediately put his hand on my lower back as he guided us to a used bookshop. Oh my goodness. It was official—I was in love with Gabriel Van Helsing. Heart-eyed emoji, write his name in my journal, and name our future children in love with him. The snow dusted his dark brown hair, and he brushed a hand through it, shaking it off as he pushed open the door. A bell tinkled, and the delicious smell of paper and coffee greeted us.

"Van." I was breathless. The store was beautiful and quirky. Knickknacks lined the walls, and bookshelves went ceiling to ground. A hipster-looking dude glanced up from the counter and nodded in greeting.

Van returned it.

"Come on." He grabbed my hand and pulled me toward the back. We walked by a local author section, my greedy hands wanting to pick up every book. I loved used bookstores. They were always so safe and a way to escape reality, especially my mom. She'd sign me up for pageants, and instead of working on a talent, I'd sneak off to a bookstore instead. Plus, Elle devoured like three romance books a week and wanted to be an author. I'd read her words too when I needed a distraction

How did I not even think about looking this place up?

There was a small coffee bar in the back, a barista with hot pink hair and tattoos covering her arms standing behind the counter. She smiled when she saw Van. "Hey, Gabe. The usual?"

He has a usual? My poor heart.

"Yes, please. Dani, my treat. Get what you want, but their *Just One Bed* Latte is awesome."

"Just one bed?"

"Their drinks are named after romance tropes. Elle would die if I brought her here, which I probably will next year. I told you I'm a sucker for romcoms." He winked at me, damn near turning me into a melty puddle of feelings.

My hands shook, and my chest got tight, and I was pretty sure it was a heart attack. Probably. It had nothing to do with the fact he kept sharing pieces of himself that I wanted to hold forever and never give back.

Both he and the woman looked at me expectantly, and I cleared my throat. "Sure, yeah, that sounds great."

"Great. I need a minute." The woman smiled and took Van's card, swiping it before grabbing supplies to make the drinks.

Van pointed to a small circle table in the corner with two chairs. We sat down, our knees touching underneath, and he made no moves to shift his weight.

"Amazing, huh?" He leaned back in the chair and had a half smile on his face as he scanned the store. "Found it freshman year when I needed to get a used book for some speech class. They have a textbook trading post over there." He pointed more toward the front. "Kept coming back."

"It's amazing. I could live here." There were twinkle lights hanging along the ceiling, and soft rap played in the speakers. "I can't believe this."

"What, that I come here?" He shrugged. "I know it might be surprising that I like reading—"

"No. No, that's not what I meant. You're just so...busy and popular and working out or with the team. This entire secret of yours is just wonderful." My throat got tight. "I'm glad you have this."

"It's a nice break from my life at Central State." He leaned his elbows onto the table as our drinks arrived. He thanked her, Cassie, and then turned to me with a serious depth to his gaze. "Leadership isn't natural for me. I'm easygoing, usually, and prefer to follow rather than take charge. Hockey is in my blood, but when Coach made me captain last year, it rocked me. It still does, honestly."

"You're trying with Cal. I'm proud of you." I covered his hands with mine and wanted to hug him until that vulnerable look left his face. "It's not easy for me either. There are things going on with some of the girls, and the thought of confronting them makes me sick to my stomach."

"No, you're a natural at it, Daniella. You always have been. You were class president and an officer in National Honor Society. You led the high school team to state, twice. You're elegant and graceful, and when you dance, you transform into this...I don't know how to describe it. People follow you."

"They didn't though, not at first." I cringed at how awful

it'd been transferring here and dealing with the fallout of Cami. She'd earned the spot, and our jealous coach had taken it from her and given it to me—the newbie. "They'd follow Cami into a volcano."

"Maybe, sure, she's been here for years. But they'd follow you too." He held up his mug and clinked it against mine. "Cheers, baby."

We sipped in silence for a few beats before more questions bubbled up. "So, what do you do when you come here? Just enjoy a drink and leave?"

"I reflect on the latest game and then, don't laugh, okay?" More red spots covered his cheeks. "I write reviews of the movie on my phone in this app where I can track all my ratings and genres. It's... dorky, I know, but I like it." He took another sip and avoided my gaze.

"That's amazing. I wouldn't laugh at anything that brings you joy. How cool that you have all those stats of movies, huh?"

He narrowed his eyes. "You're not being sarcastic?"

"No, not at all." I was dying to know his favorites.

"Just my parking then?" he teased, nudging his knee against mine. "I'm not used to have people making fun of me."

"It's good for your ego, I promise." I winked, earning a dimpled grin from him. "You can't be fuckhot, talented on the ice, secretly love movies, *and* good at parking. The universe has to balance it out somehow."

"Is that so?" He leaned further onto his elbows, his face inches from mine across the table. "I'm fuckhot, huh?"

"Jesus. Of all the things I said, you would focus on that one particular comment."

His gaze moved from my eyes to my lips, his nostrils flaring before he leaned back into his own chair. My face was too hot for the temperatures outside, and I wet my lips, aware of how chapped they were. He watched the motion before picking up his mug and tilting it all the way back. "I'm done, head out."

"Whoa." I still had half of my *Only One Bed* latte, and it was hot. "What's the rush?"

"Your mouth, that's what. You keep chewing or licking your lips, and all I want to do is get you naked. So, finish up and let's go." He stood and pulled the end of his sweatshirt down below his waistline. He wasn't fast enough for me not to notice his bulge. Excitement poured through me, my skin feeling too tight for my body. It made me feel powerful as hell to see him like this. I was driving *him* wild.

"Mm, you're kinda bossy."

"Yeah? You into it?"

"Not sure." I took another sip before setting the mug down and standing up. "You this way in bed?"

"I can be. Just say the word. Now, get your cute snow-slut ass in my car."

"So bossy." I patted his butt on the way out, unable to stop my smile. "Are you sure you don't want me to drive?"

"Fuck off."

"But it could take you five, ten minutes to get out of the spot and you seem a little horny?"

"Daniella," he growled.

He literally growled my name, and I ate that sound up. Van was never extreme in anything, always pretty mild or slightly angry. A part of me wanted to rile him up, to see him go feral.

"I could always just walk home. Snow is foreplay for me anyway. It'd probably take you just as long and could meet me there?"

"Get in the fucking car." He shook his head, one of his eyes twitching.

I grinned in response but obeyed.

It only took him one try to pull out of the parking spot this time, and damn, the tension in the air was thick. "Anything on your mind, boo?"

"You'll see."

Oof, my stomach swooped, and I could feel my heartbeat in my fingers at the promise in his words. I couldn't fucking wait.

CHAPTER
SIXTEEN

Gabe

Fuck the snow. It made the road harder to drive, and all I wanted to do was speed back to my apartment and get Dani naked. Butt ass naked to lick her head to toe. It had only been a day since being between her legs, but I was a needy man. I wanted more.

"Gripping the wheel a little tight, Gabriel."

God, she was such a tease, intentionally riling me up. I shook my head, enjoying the hell out of the banter. I meant what I'd told her—I wasn't used to people making fun of me and for some sick reason, I liked it. "Wonder why?"

"Sexless Sundays got you worked up?"

"*Fuck* your Sexless Sunday bullshit. You're not leaving my place until I got my fill, girlfriend. And I'm in a mood to tease."

She shivered, and her face got bright red. She recrossed her legs, clearly uncomfortable, and that made me smile. I wasn't the only one.

What felt like an hour was only ten minutes, but I parked in the basement garage of the apartment building and kept my libido in check as we got into the elevator. Neither of one us talked, hell I barely breathed, afraid to get a whiff of her perfume and lose my control. Sharing the day with her only made my attraction to her grow. Each quirk I'd learned had me wanting to kiss her, every laugh had me needing to touch her, and that damn kiss… fuck, I was desperate to slide inside her and make her come undone.

All that red hair spread over my pillow, her smooth freckled skin sliding against mine? God. "This elevator is moving so fucking slow."

"I know." She breathed hard, her chest heaving. "It's hell."

She sucked her bottom lip into her mouth so hard it was red and wet, and when the doors dinged and opened, I almost cheered. "About fucking time."

My keys were already positioned in my hands to open the door as efficiently as possible, and without a word, I dragged her into my bedroom. I wasn't sure when Fraser was going to be home, and I didn't care.

I needed her on top of me.

I kicked the door shut, and she stood in front of me, cheeks red and eyes wide. "Take off your shirt."

She breathed so loud the sound echoed in the room, and she gripped the edge of her sweatshirt and pulled it off. She wore a long-sleeved thermal underneath, and she removed that too, leaving her in the sexiest, laciest bra I'd ever seen.

"Goddamn." My own breathing hitched, and she smirked. "Did you think about me when you put that on?"

She nodded, but that wouldn't do. I was a greedy bastard and wanted more. "Tell me."

"I thought about you," she said, her voice rough and low. "Sucking me through the material, then sliding the straps off."

I shut my eyes, inhaled, and studied her again. "Like this?" Closing the distance between us, I got onto my knees and gripped her waist before dragging my nose up her toned stomach and between her breasts. The material was silky and soft, and I sucked her pebbled nipples through it, like she'd said. She moaned and arched her back, letting me suck her more, and she brought her hands to my hair.

I bit her pebbled points, and she dug her nails into my scalp, egging me on. "Do you like it slow?" I pulled the material covering her nipple down and swirled my tongue around it like I had all the time in the world. "Or fast?"

I repeated it, going faster before taking her bare nipple into my mouth and tugging.

"Yes."

I chuckled against her skin, cupping her breasts in my hands and burying my face in them. They weren't huge, but they were perfect in my grip. She panted at this point, and I leaned back, trailing my fingers down her neck and arm. "You wanted me to slide the strap off, right?"

She nodded.

"With my hand or teeth?"

Her eyes flared. "Teeth."

"That's my good girl." I grinned like a ravenous wolf and she was my prey. I bit down on the strap on her shoulder, pulling it while my fingers played with her nipple. I did it on the other side and finally unhooked it in the back. I tossed it onto my desk and stepped away. "Now, finish stripping."

She gulped and slid her sweatpants, socks, and boots off. Her panties matched the bra, and I couldn't play the game anymore. I picked her ass up and tossed her on the bed, yanking my shirt off as I lay on top of her. Her skin felt so good against mine, her hands coming around and running up and down my back as I kissed the hell out of her.

I wanted to be her only source of breath. I ground my cock against her, still wearing my sweats, but those had to go. All the banter, the teasing, it was the best kind of foreplay, and I couldn't recall a time I was ever this aggressive, desperate even. I kissed down her jaw, her neck, all the way to the base where I bit down. "I fucking need to be inside you."

"Same. Yes." She arched her back and gripped my ass under

my waistband, a deep, satisfied sigh coming from her. "Love your ass."

I laughed against her throat. My pants had to go. I rolled to the side and whipped them off in half a second, sliding my shoes off, and leaving my black boxers. I missed her skin on mine, and I went back to my position, our chests touching, and I trembled like an innocent teenager. "You're gorgeous." I sucked her nipple again. "Perfect." Then kissed her stomach.

"Van," she said, her voice nothing but lust and want. I looked up, and she chewed her plump, swollen lip. A lip I'd just had in my mouth.

"Hm, baby?" I slid my fingers on either side of her panties and pulled the fabric down her legs. *Finally.* Her bare pussy greeted me, and I ran my nose along the seams, flicking my tongue against her, making her jump.

"I'm… please. *Fuck* me."

My heart stuttered in my chest at how much I loved hearing her say that. I tongued her clit for another three seconds before taking off my boxers and grabbing a condom from the nightstand. She lay there, bare and legs spread wide for me, and fuck if it wasn't the image I'd dreamed about.

Her curls stood out against my gray sheets, and her pink pointed nipples still glistened from my mouth. Once wouldn't be enough. I needed all night with her. I put on the condom and positioned myself over her, carefully nudging her entrance with my cock. I was so fucking swollen and thick despite jacking off the day before. I ran my hands along her hips, sides, and tilted her chin up. "Are you sure? I can go down on you all day."

"I will kill you dead if you don't put your cock in me right now."

"Talk about being bossy." I slowly slid inside her, my damn balls tightening and my spine prickling with utter pleasure. She felt amazing, my god. I closed my eyes, went in further, and waited. She was wet and tight. Really goddamn tight. I held her gaze when I started thrusting my hips, going deep and slow to fill her.

Her throaty moans were music to my ears, and she pulled my face to hers, kissing me hard. She smelled like flowers and sweat and tasted like coffee. I wanted to eat her whole. I put an arm around her neck, holding onto her tighter as I fucked her. She adjusted to me fast, and I couldn't get enough.

I sucked whatever part of her body my mouth could reach, digging my fingers into her ass. She bucked beneath me and wrapped her long legs around me, arching her back and letting me go deeper. Each thrust felt better, and she gripped my ass so hard I was sure she broke skin.

"Fuck, Dani."

"I know, don't stop, please." She breathed harder, and sweat dripped from her forehead. I licked it up, my own sweat pooling between our chests. This was fucking fire, and I was addicted.

"Come for me." I snuck a finger between her cheeks, teasing her, and she cried out. Her thighs tightened, and her voice got all deep and gooey, and *there she is.*

She orgasmed without abandon, not caring how she looked as she lost it. I pumped harder, chasing my own release at her cries. Her entire body shook as she dug her fingers into me, like she'd lose the pleasure if she let go.

I ate up her sounds and pulled out of her. I was close, but this needed to last. She stopped screaming, so I took my opportunity. "Flip over. I want this ass in my face, baby."

She rolled onto her stomach, and I hoisted her up onto her knees. "Gonna make me come twice, Van?"

"Oh, at least." I grinned even though she couldn't see me. I slid back into her, groaning because fuck, it was heaven. I bit her lower back as I reached around to play with her clit. I used two fingers and pressed down, letting the swollen nub slide between them, and she shuddered. "Like my fingers on your clit while I fuck you from behind?"

"God, yes. Go harder."

Harder. My eyes almost crossed at her bossy, desperate tone, but I obliged. I held onto her ass, dragging my tongue down her spine until I teased clit. She bounced back, burying my face in her ass, and I pounded her. My bed rocked into the wall, knocking off a picture, but I didn't give a shit. "Grab the headboard."

She lifted her arms up and held on, and I lost it. I fucked her hard and fast, and my muscles strained, and my heart was gonna beat out of my chest. I angled her hips just so and hit her deep, her moans going even lower. "Yes, that's it, baby."

"Van, I'm gonna...I'm close."

I continued my furious pace, holding onto her sweaty skin and hoping I could wait until she came. It was the hardest thing I'd done in a while, but finally, she started the same full-body tensing, head thrown back, banshee-crying scream of pleasure, and I stopped holding back. I spread her ass cheeks apart, dipping my thumb between them, and I came hard.

Harder than I ever had.

The orgasm hit me fast, like a puck to the chest, and it kept going. I thrust three more times, the pleasure blinding me. The only thing grounding me was her body and breathing.

When I stopped, I fell onto the bed next to her, absolutely winded. More than any game or practice or workout had ever winded me. My damn ears rang like I was at a concert, and my fingertips buzzed like I'd gotten electrocuted. White lights formed behind my eyelids, and damn.

We lay there, each of us panting and catching our breath, and I knew I had to throw away the condom, talk to this goddess, get up, but I couldn't. "You killed me."

She snorted but also didn't move. "Me first."

"Daniella," I started, needing her to know that this was... amazing. Intense. But nothing came out. Worry wedged its way into the moment, my mind overanalyzing how good it was.

Never in any hookups had it been like that, and it freaked me out.

I wanted more of this, her, us, but of course, how did I communicate that?

"Dani," I tried again, my voice sounding like I hadn't had a drink of water in six months.

"I know, I know," she said, sighing. "Sexless Sundays were a terrible idea."

She made me snort, and gratitude washed over me. She eased the knot in my chest, letting me push off having any conversation about it. "Sexual Sundays it is then," I said.

She laughed softly, and I forced myself up. My legs were like Jell-O, all wobbly and tingly from the orgasm. I grabbed a tissue and tossed the condom in the trash before joining her back on the bed. Her arm was over her eyes, and she had a totally satisfied smile on her face.

I glowed, knowing I put that grin there, that I got her to come twice again. I even loved the fact she gave me shit. It felt so natural. God, the next few weeks were going to be fun as hell.

"Want me to open the shades so you can watch the snow?"

She sat up, her face flushed, and she nodded. "Look at you being all sexy. I always want to watch the snow. But I should probably get back."

"Why? Do you have plans?" I slid on a new pair of sweats and tossed her a T-shirt. "We can order food and watch Christmas movies. I mean, *White Christmas* is probably porn for you."

She slid my shirt over her head, shimmying a bit until it covered her body. That little shake was so damn cute I couldn't stop smiling. She rolled her eyes hard. "I never should've told you about my snow obsession."

"I'm glad you did." I crawled onto the bed and kissed her. She gave me a shy smile, and I kissed her again. "Stay. It's cold, and I'm such a selfish asshole I don't want to walk you back in

this weather. We can watch *Ice Age*? *Penguins*? All movies with
snow if you want?"

"Ugh, you're the worst, but yes. *White Christmas* is a classic,
and I love it."

"I knew it, you little snow slut."

She laughed, and I joined her on the bed, grabbing the
remote and pulling her against me. Cuddling wasn't a thing I
did a lot, but with her, it felt right. Normal. I might make a ton
of dumb decisions, but she was one of the best. Getting to hang
out with her like this? Sleeping with her? My favorite parts of
my week. Honestly it was a win-win situation, and there'd be
no mess at the end because we knew exactly what we agreed to.
Once I gained the courage to talk to the guys on the team, my
life would be perfect.

CHAPTER
SEVENTEEN

Daniella

A few days later, I sweated ass because the gym's heat was too high. We had our final game coming up, senior night, and there was a buzz in the air. Sure, the football team hadn't made any Bowls or championships, but *we* had a lot to celebrate.

Losing a coach, getting two captains, having a ton of drama and yet we were a team. Supporting each other and working together. Cami led everyone in cooldown stretches while some upbeat techno song blasted on the speakers, and I studied how she led.

Aubrey, our former coach who resigned after taking out her issues on Cami, had named me co-captain, a sophomore transfer, which was a risk. I was nobody, and I had never wanted to go back north more. But then Cami and I became friends, buddies, and knowing her career was done had to be super difficult for her. Her final week of practice, final week being on the dance team.

I'd already collected a few hundred dollars from the younger girls to put together seniors gifts. A bedazzled jersey with their last name, a skincare box, bath bombs, lip gloss, and a signed poster of their senior photo. It wasn't enough to express how much Cami meant to me, but it was a start.

"Okay, ladies, one final lap and we'll call it a day." Cami clapped, and everyone jogged around the gym as our new coach watched with her hands on her hips and a small grin.

Jessica was young but knew her shit, and I was excited to work with her next year, even if the thought of leading on my own scared the hell out of me. My lungs burned with the high of a good workout, the text from my mom driving me to go harder. Be thinner. Be prettier. Be *better.*

One more holiday home, then that was it.

Elle and I would move into our two-bedroom apartment in the end of May. She hoped to get a job while I already had one lined up working at a summer camp and teaching dance at a local studio. My mom sent me six links to dresses that would *match my skin tone and red hair* and complement my *skinny, curve-less* figure.

Please dress appropriately. Some of your latest posts make you look washed out, the text said. My blood soured, and I squeezed my eyes shut. The last holiday with her...I could survive it.

I'd have Van with me, and he didn't seem to care my hair was a shade too red and my skin too pale. I shivered, thinking about yesterday's *Oral Wednesdays* and smiled as I finished the jog.

Yeah, Lovely Lily's days were numbered for making me feel like shit about myself. It was time to channel my inner Cami and love myself for who I was. I liked sweatshirts and joggers and having my *too* red hair down.

I'd wear the dresses I wanted to and drink and eat and dance.

"Daniella, come here a minute, would you?" Jessica jutted her chin toward a corner of the gym, and I followed. Her body language wasn't tense and her face was void of worry lines, so it couldn't be bad news. Hopefully.

I tended to assume the worst to prepare myself for something awful. It was easier to adjust to better news and be pleasantly surprised. Probably wasn't the healthiest outlook, but eh, it worked for me. "What's up, Coach?"

"There's an upcoming leadership dinner where we want to celebrate athletes who embody what it means to be a true Central State student. I know I'm new, but I talked to Cami, and she and I agreed you'd be the perfect ambassador for our team."

My face burned with pride, and my stomach did a weird swoopy thing, gratitude overwhelming me. "Oh, wow, that's nice. I'm honored."

"Good. Good." She squeezed my forearm. "We'll get to know each other in the off-season, I swear, but you have so much potential. I'll text you the details, but you also can bring a plus-one. Each coach will give a short speech about their player, and you get a certificate and something to put on your resume."

"That's awesome, for real." I squeezed my fingers together, unable to believe my luck. This was huge. Validation that I was doing okay. I couldn't wait to tell Cami, Elle, and Van.

Plus-one.

I could bring him.

"It's the weekend before finals are over. Let me know if you can't attend."

"I'll be there. I'll make sure." I grinned and pulled her into a hug. "Thank you, Coach. This means a lot."

"You're welcome." She smiled warmly at me before tending to her phone, and I used that time to search out Cami.

She waited for me, leaning against the wall with her arms crossed. She wore a victorious grin "So?"

"You little bitch. I love you." I hugged her hard, even though she hated it. It took her a beat before she hugged me back, our sweaty arms sliding against each other. "That was so nice and unexpected. Are you sure it shouldn't be you?"

"I'm a senior, and they usually pick a younger player." She

shrugged. "I'm old news where you're the future. Plus, I already have a job lined up after graduation and have a plan laid out for me. I want to set up you and the team for success."

"You're... I can't believe I hated you."

"Right back at ya, babe."

We headed to the locker room, and she went to shower. I didn't have time because I had a geology class (fuck gen eds) that was across campus. I threw on joggers, left my crop top on, and bundled up in my puffy black coat. Snow lingered from the weekend, and I didn't mind the walk one bit.

It let me cool down from the run *and* daydream about the event. Black tie? Honoring me as a leader? Free dinner and drinks? How damn exciting. Things like that didn't happen to me.

I had an extra little spring to my step when a familiar laugh caught my attention. That deep timbre belonged to Van, and my stomach swooped in delight. We had no plans to hang out today, but seeing him would be nice. More than nice—I couldn't wait to tell him about the event.

He stood at the base of the stairs outside what I thought was the education building. There were two other tall guys next to him and a group of girls. They wore cute ear covers and hats, and the one in a red coat leaned into Van. He put his arm around her in a half-hug, that laugh vibrating my soul.

One of the guys—who had to be a player on the team—made a motion with his arms, and they all laughed more. The initial excitement of hearing his chuckle dimmed the more his arm remained around the girl in red. She wasn't his ex at least, but the image hurt more than I liked to admit.

I trusted him not to cheat obviously, but why was she so close to him? My throat felt like I'd swallowed ten marshmallows, and the pep in my step sizzled to a dull flare. He was free to do whatever he wanted—flirt, hang out, whatever. We weren't real, but at the same time, I hated how much I cared.

Nodding to myself, I decided to text him later instead of telling him now. I ducked my head and continued on the path to my geology class. The wind picked up, and my hair went every direction, the air smelling like leftover fall and trees. I regretted not showering because my sweat made a chill run down my spine, and I held onto my coat tighter.

"Dani."

Shit.

He'd spotted me. Which was, fine, but then I had to face him with the group, and I wanted to be the cool fake girlfriend. The chill one. The girl who was like 'oh hey, no big deal' that her boyfriend hugged someone else. They could be besties. Buddies. Pals.

I rubbed my lips together and rolled my shoulders back. Confidence was something I created myself, and I mirrored the way I always saw Cami walk. With purpose, to draw attention, and to win every moment even if it wasn't a competition. I could do that even if my insides were like cake batter, mushy and not quite ready. Performing was what I did, and I put on my best dancer smile and turned around. "Van? Hey."

He grinned hard, those dimples I loved so much on full display. His gaze moved along my face and mouth for a beat before he bent down and kissed me right on the lips. It was just a peck and probably for show, but it sent a flurry of butterflies through me. How amazing would it be to have him as a real boyfriend, kissing me when we ran into each other?

Focus. Be cool.

"Hi," I said, totally obliterating my plan. The group he was with walked toward us, and Van moved to put his arm around my shoulders, tucking me beneath him. He definitely didn't do that with red coat girl, and that little nugget cheered me up.

"I was telling these guys about you. Are you going to be late to class or do you have two minutes?"

"I have a few." I gulped as they neared, feeling like this was a test. Not an official one but it mattered. Plus...he was talking about me? "What were you saying?"

"Oh, just how adorable you are." The girl in the red coat grinned at me and held out a gloved hand. "I'm Nat. We were dormmates freshmen year at Dean Lyon Lane. Can't believe we've stayed friends when we're all assholes."

"Speak for yourself, Nat." A skinny, tall guy with glasses smiled. "I'm Drew. This is Tanner." He pointed toward the shorter guy next to him. "We're dating."

"God, that wasn't smooth at all." Tanner rolled his eyes.

"You told me I needed to stop hiding it! What was wrong with that?" Drew said, groaning into his hand. "You're finding reasons to be annoyed with me."

"Save it for later. I want to meet Gabe's girlfriend." The other woman narrowed her eyes at me. "How do we know you're not some puck bunny?"

I choked on my spit, laughing at the thought. "Because I've known him since he was six, and I've seen him enter a farting contest at a fair. Trust me, whatever the opposite of a puck bunny is, that's me."

The woman grinned and glanced to Van. "Okay, you can keep her."

"Thanks for the permission, but I was going to anyway." Van kissed the top of my head. "Also, I won that contest, so fuck you all."

The group laughed, and I felt silly. Super silly. They were *friends* and cared about each other, and I had to get a grip. Gabe was popular and had tons of friends who were girls, and I had zero business getting jealous.

ZERO.

"I'll catch you guys later for *Around the Horn* at the bar, but I'm walking my girl to class."

"Nice meeting you, Dani."

"Yes, it was," Drew said.

Van guided me away from the group and nuzzled my neck.

A different kind of shiver went through me at the feel of his lips on my jaw, and he chuckled. "Missed you this morning."

"Please. Last night wasn't satisfying enough?" I teased, forcing the tension out of my voice. I had one rule about us hooking up—I'd only stay at his place once a week. That seemed the safest, and since I'd already done Sunday, I couldn't again. Van argued every point possible about why it was stupid, but I refused to back down.

When this was over, it'd be hard enough to get over him and move on from it, but adding morning wake-ups to the list would kill me. He was so fucking sexy with his sleepy face and long lashes.

He shrugged and tightened his arm around me. "How was practice?"

"Um, kind of awesome?" I stopped walking and grinned up at him. "You'll never guess what happened."

His eyes lit up. "Well, tell me."

"I was invited to attend an athletic leadership black-tie event. One player per team, and my coach asked me."

"Daniella, holy shit." He pulled me to him in a hug, glanced at my face, then hugged me again. "That's fucking awesome."

"Right? I can't believe it."

"Shut it, yes you can. You're incredible." He cupped my chin and kissed me softly, twice. His eyes were molten as he stared down at me, his brows drawn together with a serious look. "Don't doubt it for a goddamn second. You're a leader, you're driven, and you're passionate. I'm so proud of you."

"Thank you." My eyes prickled—from the wind—and I swallowed the emotion in my throat. "I get to take someone."

"Oh yeah?" He bit his lip, fighting a smile. "Like a plus-one?"

"Uh huh." I poked him in the stomach, my pulse racing. This felt huge, me asking him. It was a date. No way around it. Black tie? An RSVP? I couldn't convince myself it wasn't one, which made it more real, but who else would I have fun with?

"Anyone you're thinking about bringing?" He wrapped his arms around me, resting them at my lower back as I stared up at him.

We were being *that* couple. Well, that *fake* couple. All PDA and not caring.

I tilted my head to the side, unable to stop myself from testing him. "Deandre said he might be able to make it.

"Deandre, huh? Him? That guy?" His eyes flashed with fake anger. "I'm putting my foot down."

"Oh really?" I mocked him, stomping my foot and laughing. He returned my smile, and I stood on my tiptoes, kissing him with more heat than before. He leaned into the embrace and sighed. That deep contented sound gave me the confidence I needed to do this for real. "Hey Van," I whispered against his mouth. "Would you come with me?"

"Of course, baby."

His dark eyes held mine for a beat, and something passed between us. I wasn't sure what, but I felt it in my toes. We might be fake to the him, but for me, it was all real, and maybe... just maybe, it was a little real for him too.

I sure as fuck hoped so.

CHAPTER
EIGHTEEN

Gabe

For the first time in years, I wasn't as hyped about a hockey game. We had back-to-back Friday and Saturday games, both out of town, and while I was jacked to beat fucking St. Louis again, being away for two nights meant not seeing Daniella. Call me a selfish bastard, but we only had until after the New Year until we were done, and I wanted every second I could get.

If she didn't have the stupid once a week sleepover rule, then I wouldn't be as grumpy, but I had to respect her wishes. Even if I disagreed and could make a whole slides presentation explaining my point.

Coach and Reiner stood at the head of the bus, a clipboard in Reiner's hand as they checked off guys as they got on. It was a two-hour ride there, and I usually spent the time listening to music and focusing, but Daniella and the team had their final football game. I wanted to be there to see her dance.

She'd been talking about the routine all week, and I hated that I'd miss it. I could watch the videos after, but it wasn't the same. Plus, if the football team won, they'd all go out and party together. Despite her joking and how much time we spent together, the thought of her and Deandre chatting it up while drinking felt like a pound of rocks settling in my gut.

I put my headphones on and leaned against the window when Cal sat across from me. This never happened. Ever. He sat in the back and was a real dick to anyone who attempted to engage with him, and what was even weirder...he stared at me. "What?"

"I've been reading," he said, his face serious as fuck. He looked like he'd seen a ghost or was about to tell me hockey wasn't a sport anymore.

"Congrats?" I paused my music and ran through any scenario that caused this to happen. My immediate reaction was to give him shit, but Daniella's words about being a leader still resonated with me. My girl had won an award for being such a good athlete—she obviously knew some things about being a teammate. I cleared my throat and leaned toward him. "Sorry, I meant what did you read?"

"A leadership book. Ideas to build team culture." His words were sharp and awkward, plus the way he fidgeted in the seat made the whole thing even weirder. "I have an idea."

"Oh yeah?"

"We could do a team secret Santa." His entire face turned red, but he continued. Seeing him try brought me a lot of joy. Pride, even.

"It could be a party too. I don't have a lot of space, but I can rent somewhere out. I have lots of money."

"Dude, we do a team dinner every year with Coach." I grinned, already seeing how the gift exchange could go.

His shoulders slumped, and he closed his eyes, fists at his sides, and I backtracked. "No, I meant we have the time set up. Why don't you add it to that event? It's a great idea."

"Oh." He swallowed. "Cool. Yeah."

"You want to organize it?"

"They won't want to do it if it's me. You should do it. That's why I came to you."

"Bullshit. They'll do it. It's gifts."

He narrowed his eyes for a beat before sighing. "Together then. We can meet at my cousin's bar to plan. Pick a night. I don't do much, so I'm free."

"Sure, sounds good."

He got up, hit the top of the seat twice before turning back to me. "So, your sister—"

"I'll kill you."

"Noted." He went back to his seat, and I leaned against the window, smiling at whatever the hell just happened.

Cal had read about how to be a leader. That was big.

Gabe: GUESS WHO'S TRYING TO BE A LEADER. GUESS GUESS GUESS

Dani: My god, all caps? Must be Cal?

Gabe: You got it. Wants to do a gift exchange for the holidays. It's fucking adorable.

Dani: Don't tell him that. Embrace it.

Gabe: I didn't tell him he's adorable. I'm not weird. I agreed to help him.

Dani: Good. This is great, Van. He's trying to be a part of the team. Even if you want to slap him, help him out.

Gabe: He asked about Elle. If he does it again, then no promises.

Dani: Fair, fair.

Gabe: How's the pregame going? I hate that I can't watch you tonight.

She sent a selfie of her decked out in makeup and her dance gear. Her eyelashes were ten times as long, and orange jewels lined the sides of her eyes. Her white teeth and bright red lips flashed at me.

Dani: We're glammed and ready to go.

Gabe: Sure I can't see you tomorrow morning?

We'd get back too late and the leave for the next game at noon, so the window was short, but if I could, I'd try to see her.

Dani: Sorry, we have the senior brunch and a spa activity. No Seduction Saturday. Sorry bb.

Gabe: Be ready on Sunday then.

Dani: Is that a threat or?

Gabe: A promise.

Dani: Fire emoji.

Dani: Hey, good luck tonight. Can't wait to hear about a W. Gotta put my phone away now but one last pic for ya.

This one was her whole body, her grin so genuine and real it made my heart stutter. This was the Dani I'd always loved, the sunshiny goof who radiated joy. I saved the photo to my phone for when I was in a shit mood and silenced it. I might miss seeing her the next day or so, but hockey would distract me from the uneasy feeling about being away.

It was foreign to worry about someone so much. It was different than how I worried about my sister or my friends. Sure, I'd been concerned and willing to drop everything to be there for people I cared about, but this ache in my soul was new. I hated it. It made my thoughts cloud with a *what if* and had me doubting everything.

Was Daniella as into this as I was? What if someone flirted with her and caught her interest, causing her to end this before we agreed? Hell, before I was ready? I couldn't stop her. If she came to me and said she was out, I'd have to step back and agree. We weren't real.

But that *what if* was on a jumbotron in my mind, flashing and blaring music. *What if* she hooked up with someone else? It wasn't really cheating since emotions weren't involved with us, but it'd make me look like an idiot.

Oddly enough, that part didn't bother me. The other did though. I tried picturing how it'd feel to see her kiss someone else, and a wildebeest exploded in my chest, growling and ripping my heart to shreds.

Okay, maybe there were a few feelings involved, but how could they not be? I'd known and loved Dani our whole lives.

Of course I cared for her more than other women. Annoyed at my thoughts and inability to push her out of my head, I loaded up a video of our opponent and tried to find patterns in their defense. After ten minutes, I was in my zone. My normal headspace.

Now I just needed the game to start so I could stay there.

We lost, and it was my fault. My passes were sloppy and my focus scattered. Concern for Daniella lived in there, along with Ty and Christopher. I knew I needed to talk to them, but before the game wasn't a good idea—neither was after. When would be a good time? And what if something happened to Daniella when I was away? The worries combined into a huge elephant of distraction, and it made me play like shit.

It wasn't often I was the reason we didn't get a W, and the weight of that feeling dragged me down deep. Weeds of shame wrapped around my legs, yanking me further into a bad headspace.

I'd fucked up.

Jenkins wouldn't look at me. His impressive saves in the goal were meaningless because I couldn't score a goal. He'd let one puck in the net. One. And I couldn't motivate or orchestrate a play to even it out. My temples throbbed, my chest aching with the urge to fuck shit up. We'd all made errors, but this felt worse. When the team wasn't playing well, it was easier to digest. When they finally had a good game, and I didn't? It made me want to crawl into a hole.

Especially when Cal was playing like a teammate and the guys weren't avoiding him. Three of the juniors even clapped him on the back and said good game. To me, they frowned and said *bummer, Van.*

Bummer.

The disappointment from the team radiated in the locker

room air, and it suffocated me. This was my final season playing hockey. There'd never be locker room chats or pregame warm-ups or postgame conversations as a player. And I played like this? Terrible? Sloppy? It hurt. My stomach twisted in shame and embarrassment. I couldn't go out my final season without being the best I could. Hanging my head, I waited for Coach to start his post-game talk. He'd rip into me, I deserved it.

It was quiet. Too quiet. Other guys on the team had a great game and deserved to be told that.

I hated the tension and silence, like everyone was too afraid to speak because I sucked. Did a small part of me blame the new emotions I carried for Dani? Yes. But it wasn't her fault. It was my own, not being able to compartmentalize my life, and no one could solve that but me.

The team though? I could fix this awkward, horrible pause. Some of us had to have a heart to heart and I could start by being the leader Dani thought I could be.

I pushed myself up to stand, my body aching, and I scanned the room. Most of the guys glanced at me, Reiner leaning against a wall with a small smirk forming. He must've sensed I was about to do something because he nodded. That little validation was enough for me to clear my throat. "I need to say something."

Everyone looked at me. My heart hammered in my chest, and I cracked my knuckles on each hand before continuing. "I fucked up, and I'm sorry. I let you all down, especially you Jenkins. You were a fucking wall tonight. How many shots on goal did they have? Thirty? I know the loss sucks, but your stats are killer."

"Hell yeah," someone said. Another snapped their towel at our goalie.

Jenkins nodded in response.

"Cal, we all know you're God's gift on the ice and you're drafted and blah blah, but you played your heart out. You followed every play and were the teammate we all needed. Thank you."

Cal's face remained unfazed, but I swore he blushed. A couple of the other guys nodded, agreeing with me, and I let go of the shame. Yes, I'd sucked. Yes, it happened, we all had off days, but Daniella's award for being a leader, her ability to persevere when shit was tough motivated me.

"I let everyone down, and that's on me, but we played hard. We passed and executed what we practiced. Don't hang your heads, let me shoulder this loss. To quote Ted Lasso, being a goldfish is the best thing right now. Let this one go, and tomorrow, we'll come back and kick ass." My blood pumped, and a warm, satisfied feeling flowed through me. This was the right move, and it felt good. "Now, we've struggled recently. I know you all feel it. Maybe you brushed it off, but there are things we can improve on as a team. Standing up for your team can be hard, and as your co-captain... I need to have a conversation with some of you. I'm gone next year, and I want to leave you all in the best place you can be—solid as a team."

"You got it, Captain." Jenkins stood up and fist bumped me. I didn't have to force a smile this time. They had my back.

Reiner pushed off the wall and hit my shoulder. "*That's* what I've been wanting to see."

"Me suck on the ice and admit it?"

"Being a leader. That means good and bad games and all in between. Owning your leadership. Proud of you." He smiled and joined Coach in the back of the locker room. They went through their post-game spiel, but I half-listened, instead studying the guys on the team.

Owning my leadership was something I could do. Embracing it on my final season and really working with Cal on getting him ready for next year. Getting Ty to chill on the drinking. Making sure Christopher wasn't using steroids. His scholarship meant everything to him, so why risk it? I could help him. Coach him to get stronger. Having a real purpose these final months caused a burning sensation in my soul, a good one.

Once we got onto the bus to head back, I finally took my phone out of my bag. Dani had texted me five times, and as I read them, I was grinning ear to ear.

Dani: I cried after we finished our routine, how embarrassing. My mascara ran down my face like a raccoon.

The accompanying selfie showed it. I loved the image and saved it to my phone.

More texts timestamped at an hour later came back to back to back.

Dani: I bet you're kicking ass. You skate like a god.

Dani: A sexy hockey god with a nice ass. Shit. I'm drunk?/?/?

Dani: Dinnit mean to ask a quesestion. QUESTSION. Omg QUESTION.

Dani: Could use a fake boytoy RFN. Where is van when u need him???

That was timestamped around midnight. I itched my chest, wondering where she was and if she had water or who she was with. Were the girls all partying together? "Jenkins, you hear anything about the football game?"

"Hail Mary pass, huge win. Everyone's on Athlete Avenue rocking. Might try to head there for a bit." He put his headphones on, tuning me out, and my jaw tightened.

Athlete Avenue was a dumb name, but it was the street lined with all the jock houses. All teams, regardless of gender, had a house to celebrate in, but football always drew the largest and rowdiest crowds.

Gabe: Hey, where are you?

Fuck the two-hour bus ride. She needed a fake boyfriend? Why? *Deandre?*

Gabe: Are you ok?

Dani: hhhgeees

Dani: Yupppppp.

Dani: dancing but did u win

Dancing with... who? Fuck. The same sinking feeling started at my shoulders and traveled to my gut. It burned hot. I clenched my phone, hating the distance between us and the fact I couldn't do anything about it.

I trusted her but not rowdy football players on a high from a win. Daniella was fucking gorgeous, and *how fast is the bus fucking going?*

Gabe: *Hey, can you get some water?*

Dani: *worrying about me?*

Gabe: *you have no idea*

Dani: *awwwwwwwwwww*

Dani: *too many w's my b pretend I sent aww*

Gabe: *are you with the team?*

Dani: *yup, we're partying with the guys. We won!!!*

Dani: *DID U WIN*

Gabe: *No. And I sucked. Lost the game.*

Dani: *I'm sorry.*

Dani: *hey gotta go we're doing shottttts*

Gabe: *Please let me know when you get home safe. I need my fake girlfriend to be okay.*

She didn't answer, not that I expected her too. My mood soured, negativity sparking more dark thoughts, and I pinched my eyebrow, hoping it'd distract me enough to settle my pulse.

She'd be fine. She'd been doing this before we started dating, and I trusted her. But without water, she'd be in pain tomorrow... I'd head to the party when we got back just to see if she was still there.

Yeah, I'd tag along with Jenkins and use him as an excuse. It'd be easier than admitting I needed to see Dani. I fully convinced myself it was because I was worried about her drinking, but there was more to it. I just refused to dive deeper into why.

With that, I put on a song and counted down the one hundred and fifteen minutes until we'd be back on campus.

CHAPTER
NINETEEN

Daniella

I swayed my hips back and forth, the extremely loud bass vibrating through my body all the way from my head to my toes. The football house broke laws, but no one cared. What a wild concept to do whatever you wanted because you won a game, but I held up my cup of beer and cheered anyway.

We won. Our routine kicked ass. The dance season was done. The team would be mine next year. Life was good!

"Another shot?" Cami asked, leaning into me while holding four shots with one hand. The other seniors on the team were behind her, and she passed them around. Cami's eyes were hazy, the party girl letting herself get a little loose.

"Give it to me, mama," I said, taking the shot and drinking it. The alcohol burned, but at this point, I had no idea what it was. It didn't matter. I'd feel like shit anyway in the morning but could sweat it out at the spa. "I can't believe you'll be gone."

"You'll survive." She swayed on her feet, blinking a few times. "Damn. I'm drunk."

"You sound so smart though." I cringed, hearing my own

slurring words. "You're the best."

I loved everyone. Cami, the team, this school, football, hockey, Van. Oh Van. My face warmed, and my entire body exploded like a firework just thinking about him. I fumbled with my phone and squinted at the texts from him. I'd never felt my phone vibrate, but it was the music's fault.

Dani: sry the music is so LOUYD. Your figlrriend is safe as a clam!

Dani: FAKE GIRLfriend sorrrry

Dani: I know it's fake, god these shots are getting to me.

My thumbs felt heavy, and a huge wave of sleepiness hit me. My eyelids were like paperweights, and my toes ached. Damn these stupid heels.

Gabe: where are you?

Dani: I dunno some football house my feet hurt and I'm tired

Gabe: are you alone?

Dani: no cami is here and others. Why did I do shots van idk

Cami walked up to me and pulled me into a hug, humming some pop song as we swayed. "Freddie is coming to get me. He's the best and tall and hot."

"I love that you love him," I said into the crook of her neck. Affection from Cami was rare, and I hugged her back hard. "I'm so tired."

"He'll walk us back. You first then me." She yawned, her makeup still perfect despite the dancing.

She'd helped me fix my raccoon situation, but my body still sweated everywhere even though it was cold as shit outside. Snow! I walked us from the makeshift dance floor and headed for the patio door. Cold air rushed toward us, and I inhaled it in. "Better. I can breathe."

"Are you drunk like me?"

"Yes."

"Remember that time you threw up on my feet?"

"Don't remind me." I laughed and snorted and then she laughed and snorted, and we were a pair of drunk girls giggling when a massive frame found us. Dark hair, dark glasses, extra-wide shoulders. I saw him before Cami and waved. "Hello, Freddie who is excellent in beddie."

Cami spun around so fast she almost fell down. Freddie caught her, and she wrapped her entire body around him. His answering smile did things to my heart—not that I was into Freddie, but I envied how happy he was with Cami. A pang, a longing so strong overtook me, and I closed my eyes and stepped back. What would it feel like to be so much to someone else? For them to have that smile when seeing me? To find someone who liked all the bad parts of me? God, even drunk I couldn't escape my mom's comments.

I'd sent a photo of my outfit to her and my dad, and her responses were to fix my left eye shadow. Then came the usual: Did I have my setting spray on? Did I remember Vaseline on my teeth to force me to smile? Did I not eat all day so my stomach lines would stand out more? All these flaws...could anyone really see past them and look at me how Freddie looked at Cami?

I wrapped my arms around my middle, suddenly colder, and watched them embrace. He cupped Cami's face, kissing her, and wiped under her eyes. I didn't even notice she had eyeliner smeared there. God, I wished what I had with Van was real. That he'd wipe my eyes and smile and love me and whoa. *Love?*

No, no, no. Not love. Well, maybe. Yeah, I loved him, but I already did as a friend, so did this love mean something different? My drunken thoughts didn't think so. I chewed my lip and tried not to stare at the two of them talking but it was so hard. They were relationship goals. Massive ones.

I'd never had that before or anything close, and it'd be dumb to fantasize about Van that way because it would never happen. Nope. He had deadlines for his ladies, never committing, and I snorted, picturing a contract. I'm surprised he hadn't made me sign one with big red letters for the end date.

Self-pity worked its way into my drunken mood, and I wanted to be in bed. My own bed. "A-are you guys heading out soon?"

"I'm convincing him to do one dance, then we'll head back." Cami dragged him away from our spot. "I'll find you before we leave."

Disappointment weighed my legs down, and the urge to cry surprised me. I only had three weeks left with Van, Cami was done with dance, and I hated these shoes. I was the only captain of the team now, meant to lead all the girls and their ups and downs. Could I do it all alone? I sniffed and pressed my palms to my eyes. Coach nominating me for the dinner gave me more confidence than I had before in being a leader. The real root of my misery was loving someone who would never love me back. I was his little sister's best friend, the awkward skinny one with too many flaws. I had mother issues at twenty. I wasn't *enough* to permanently stay with a guy like Van. He needed someone amazing, and I simply wasn't. Life was a real bitch.

"Dani?"

I frowned, worried I'd really crossed the line. There was no way I imagined Van's voice. It was so clear and crisp like he was right there. I squeezed my eyes shut before I smelled him— spicy cologne and sweat, and I was scooped up into a bear hug.

I wrapped my arms around his broad shoulders, resting my head on him and wrapping my legs around his waist. "Van," I moaned, breathing him in and smiling into his skin. "You're here."

"I was fucking worried about you." He dug his hand into my hair, his muscles and tone tense as hell. He seemed... mad.

"Are you angry?"

"Yes, no. Maybe." He pulled back, stared down at me, and a small smile tugged at the sides of his lips. "Hi."

"Hello." I grinned, my face flushing from the drinking...not from the way it felt like home being back in his arms. Or how he gazed at me—kinda like how Freddie looked at Cami. But that was my intoxicated brain talking. "I didn't think I'd see you until Sunday."

"Needed my fill of you." He pressed his lips against mine, softly, and a dull hum came from his chest. "You taste terrible."

"Nice way to greet your fake girlfriend."

"You need water and a goddamn coat." He set me on the ground and eyed my outfit. My crop top and skirt hugged me like a glove. I'd gone sans bra since I didn't have a lot going on up there, and he sucked in a breath. "You're gonna freeze."

"It didn't seem to matter to me before I came. Now, I'm regretting it."

"Here." He slid off his sweatshirt and put it over my head, messing up my hair. I slid my arms through the sleeves, closing my eyes at how much it smelled like him. Clean, spice, cologne. It was so warm, and I wrapped my arms around myself.

"This is my favorite blanket." I swayed a bit, and he held onto my hips. "I'm keeping this."

"By all means." His voice went soft again, and I found him staring at me, his face holding a different, tender expression. "You danced amazing by the way."

"Did you see a video?"

"That's all I did on the drive back." His thumbs grazed my stomach, going under my sweatshirt and tracing a pattern on each side. "You look so happy when you're dancing."

"It makes me joyful. Probably like you on the ice." I booped his nose and remembered something he said. "Wait, you said you lost. Oh no."

His muscles tensed, and his grip tightened. "We did. Come on, let's get out of here."

"My dorm is so far. Why is it so far, Van?" I moaned, my feet protesting as the night finally caught up to me. The emotions of the last dance, the drinking, the standing for hours with these shoes, the shots… "I won't make it."

"We're going to my place."

I opened my mouth to argue, the no-sleepover rule very

important for reasons I couldn't remember, but he put his finger over my lips.

"Yell at me tomorrow about breaking your rule. Right now, we're tired, and I want to fall asleep with my face on your neck." He turned around and patted his back. "Hop on."

"You're giving me a ride? Like we're teenagers?" I smiled and couldn't believe it. "This is so cute. Fifteen-year-old me would be dying right now."

"Oh yeah?"

"God, yeah." I hoisted myself up onto his back, holding onto him tight with my arms and legs. His large hands gripped my thighs, and he weaved us out of the party. Cami saw, and I waved goodbye. Her eyes got all wide, and she grinned hard, then made an obscene gesture with her fingers.

I loved that wild lady.

"Why would fifteen-year-old Daniella be dying?"

"Well, Gabriel Van Helsing, HGTV, you might not know this, but I had a tiny little baby crush on you."

He stilled for just a beat but kept walking. "Huh."

"Not weird or a big deal so don't overthink it. You were… are… this big hockey guy with muscles, and I love your hair. Plus, I saw you shirtless all the time at Elle's house, and you always flirted with everyone and were charming. You're really nice too sometimes, and I was a dumb teenager."

Oh my god shut the fuck up. I'd said too much. My filter was gone, and my brain stopped protecting my innermost thoughts. My heart raced, and despite the freezing air, sweat pooled on my back. I had to fix this.

He never responded in thirty seconds, and I shouted, "It's not a big deal. It's not there anymore. No more crush. Don't worry. You're gross."

He laughed, his whole body vibrating with the sound, and I wanted to bottle up that deep timbre and keep it. His amusement meant I was fine. Saved. Nothing to worry about here.

"Gross? So, it's gross when I lick between your thighs?"

"Van!"

He laughed harder. "Teasing you, D. So, tell me more about this crush on me."

"No."

"Please? I had a rough game and need an ego boost."

"Will you tell me what happened if I list three things I liked?" I kissed the back of his neck, the spot oddly sexy. His skin tasted like sweat, and his hair had gotten a little long. "I hate that you had a bad game."

His grip on my slipped before he adjusted my position. "I was off. That was it. A little distracted, but that's on me. You ever have days where you can't find the rhythm you need while dancing?"

"Yes. Absolutely. Where the moves feel forced instead of natural."

"It was kinda like that. My passes were sloppy, and I couldn't get us to score a single goal. The guys… they played great too. So, it felt even worse letting them down. Especially after having so many issues all season. Things came together tonight, and I blew it."

He stopped at a corner, looked both ways, and crossed the street. His place wasn't too far away now.

"Being an athlete is hard. One of my high school coaches told us it's more mental than physical, and that's why so many people with natural talent don't make it." I rested my head on him completely now, basically becoming a useless human. He carried my entire weight and wasn't even breathing hard. "Definitely wallow in pity tonight, but you need to let it go for tomorrow's game."

"Yes, Coach."

I pinched his side, getting him to yelp, and I laughed. "Did the guys say anything to you?"

"No, but I admitted I fucked up and highlighted all the things the others did right. Even Cal Holt played great. It was weird though, when I was speaking to them all about how I effed up, they seemed okay with it?"

"When people we admire admit they messed up, it almost gives you permission to not be perfect." I kissed his neck again. "I'm proud of you for doing that. It takes a lot of guts and maturity to admit failure. I'm still working on it, but my favorite teammates, teachers, and coaches always did, and it made them stick out."

He breathed a little harder, and I tapped his shoulder. "We're almost there, buddy boy, so let me down."

"I'm good."

"You're breathing heavy which isn't great for my own ego but—"

"I like you touching me."

I fought a grin, my insights lightning up like Christmas lights. "Alrighty then."

"Now about *my poor* bruised ego. Tell me what you liked about me." He stopped outside his door and got his keys out, still maintaining his grip on me so I wouldn't fall.

"Mopey Gabe is not my favorite, but you did just carry me." I chewed my lip, not even having to think hard about my crush because let's be real here, it had never left. It intensified, which wasn't great for my heart. "Hm, you were always kind to your family and sister. I hated those guys who were dicks to their siblings for no reason. You went to a poetry reading for Elle and made a sign—that's incredible."

"Shit, I forgot about that."

We got into the elevator, and he still wouldn't put me down.

"What else, what else…" I teased, nipping at his ear. "You were always the smile of the party. Not the life, that was that one guy David Smith. He was wild, but you were happy, and people gravitated toward you for a mood-booster."

He sucked in a breath again but didn't speak.

"You showed respect to adults. I know that sounds so lame, but kids were dicks to teachers or custodians. I watched you once talking to Jett, the third shift janitor, and you joked with him about his favorite hockey team. It was a late night, and you had practice. I did too and just happened to see you two in the hall."

The elevator stopped, and the doors opened. He led us toward his apartment, and once we got inside, he placed me down. He faced me, and I wished I hadn't said all those things. It was easier to speak to the back of his head where I had no idea what his expressions were, but now, fully facing me… my nerves cartwheeled.

His eyes were intense as hell, his chest moving with each breath. He wet his lips a few times before placing a hand on the door behind me, caging me in. *Yes, kiss me you fool.*

He did not. He stared at me hard, his dark eyes simmering before he pulled back. "Come on." He picked me up and put me on the counter. "You need water and a snack. Carbs, probably."

"It's two am."

"Yes, but I don't want you to feel like crap tomorrow, so I'm feeding you." He had a hand on each thigh, and he stood between my legs. It was so…normal feeling. Us like this. Hanging out but with more touching.

"You should sleep so you're not tired for the game." I ran my fingers through his hair, and he closed his eyes in a groan. "I can pound two glasses of water and be fine."

"Doubt it. I love your mouth, but you smell like a bottle of vodka." He kissed the inside of my wrist before going toward the fridge. "Fries. I want homemade cheese fries. It'll take thirty minutes, so why don't you go shower, put on one of my shirts, and come back here and help me eat them?"

"God, it's so sexy hearing you say fries and cheese." I licked my lips. "I could almost keep you, Gabriel Van Helsing. Better be careful or that crush will return."

Never left, you lovestruck fool.

CHAPTER
TWENTY

Gabriel

Could one have a total crisis at the age of twenty-two? Probably. I pinched my nose once Dani closed the door to my room and took deep breaths. She had no idea how much her words lit me up inside. The way she saw me. The things she remembered.

She knocked the wind out of me without doing a damn thing.

The oven pre-heated, and I got the fries laid out on the cookie sheet, but my mind was all on her and the *crush* comment. I wasn't an idiot back then. I knew she thought I was cute at least. I'd see her blush every now and again, but Elle had cornered me one day.

Demanded I never think, look, act, or breathe the same air as Daniella unless I treated her like I did Elle—as a sister. I respected Elle too much to disobey her, plus I was in my prime and hooking up with older girls. Daniella wasn't even on the radar in *that* way. And after training my mind to never think of her more than Elle's best friend, it became second nature.

And besides an occasional blush, Dani had never hinted that

there was something more going on. The girl could blush on command and a part of me wondered what I would've done if I'd acted on it.

No, I doubted it. Elle would've killed me, and I was too into riding the high of being recruited to come to Central State. Flirting with my younger sister's best friend wasn't the move. But now?

I wasn't sure. She said there wasn't a crush anymore, but her words and observations meant there had to be something there. I *wanted* her to feel things for me, even if I didn't have a single clue what that meant for the future. Having a relationship was so risky, and even thinking about having one with her was more extreme. We had our twenty-year old friendship between us, Elle, the fact we were her escape from her mom. To ruin *any* of that was too steep a price. The same burning feeling started in my chest, and I scratched over it, the gesture not doing a damn thing to ease the pain. The oven went off, and I put the fries in there.

The shower was on, and I pictured Dani in there, using my soap and towels and wearing my shirt, and my heart sped up. She fit in here, which was weird, but in a good way. Plus, she thought I was a good leader.

Scrubbing my hands over my face, I groaned because I was so confused as to what all this meant. Me needing to see her, me worrying about her, me obsessing over the fact that I'd missed her final dance routine. To keep myself busy, I cleaned the few dishes left in the sink, but it didn't work. Her comments kept repeating in my head over and over, filling me up with pride and confidence and warmth I hadn't had in a long time.

How could I return this wonderful feeling? If I could help her experience even half of what I did now, I'd feel better, but I had no idea how to do it? Feed her? Take care of her?

That would have to do.

The door opened, and she walked out wearing a large crew neck sweatshirt with a hockey logo on it. Her hair was twisted in a wet knot on the top of her head, and her long, bare legs led to her feet. Her toes were painted navy and orange, our school colors, and she smiled. "I feel twenty percent less of an idiot."

"Fries will get you up to fifty, I swear." I pulled out a kitchen chair and motioned for her to sit. My insides were going haywire, wanting to touch her and kiss her and tell her all the amazing things about her, but she was drunk. Or at least, still very intoxicated.

"I used your mouthwash twenty times, so if you wanted to kiss me, it'd probably smell better." She sat down and looked up at me with a flushed face. "I like how I smell like you right now."

My heart flipped over in my chest. "Yeah?"

"Uh huh." She sniffed the arm of my sweatshirt. "It's a comforting scent. Makes me feel warm and fuzzy inside too. Hey. Are the fries done? I'm starving. I don't remember if I ate dinner to be honest."

The buzz of her admitting she liked my smell clashed with the anger of her not eating. "Daniella, you can't drink on an empty stomach."

"I'm aware of the rules. I simply didn't care." She pulled her knees up to her chest and put them underneath the sweatshirt. "I'm in college. I'm supposed to make dumb decisions."

I snorted. "Fair enough."

She grinned up at me, smug as hell, and I bent down to kiss her. She leaned into it and kissed me back, slow and sweet. My skin fucking prickled with want and need and comfort at her touch, but it was over too soon. She pulled back and sighed. "I do like your mouth. In my top three kisses."

"Top *three*?" I did not like that, nope.

"Settle down there." She laughed as I went to check on the fries. "I doubt I even make your top ten list, so cut that macho shit out right now, Gabriel."

I snapped my gaze to hers. Her comment didn't sit right. "You're not just…you're… this means something to me."

Cool, I sound awesome.

She narrowed her eyes for a second, her cheeks dotting with her blush. "Top three then?"

I knew what she was doing, and I let her. She needed to ease the tension and that was fine. Having this conversation right now was a terrible idea. I wasn't even sure what I wanted to say or needed to communicate, and she wasn't sober. We both deserved to talk in daylight, both aware and ready. I relaxed with a clear plan and cupped her face. "Oh yeah."

"Good. Good. I can live with that." She smiled before letting out the longest, most dramatic yawn ever. "Oh fuck, I'm tired."

"Five more minutes. It'll be worth it. Here." I sat on the other chair and patted my lap. "Give me your feet."

Her eyes lit up. "A foot massage? Oh my god."

"You said they hurt." I took one in my hands and massaged the arch, fighting with my attraction to her. *Not tonight.* She leaned back in the chair and moaned for a full thirty seconds.

"Heaven. Death. I'm dead right now." She put an arm over her eyes. "Oh my fuck."

I snorted. "Glad it feels good. Relax, okay?"

She remained in the same position as I continued massaging her. I let my hands move up to her calves, and I had to fight a groan. Her legs were ripped, all tight muscles from years and years of dancing. She was tense though, and honestly, I loved having my hands on her.

I switched to the other leg and repeated the process, admiring the little orange C painted on her big toe. How fucking cute. It was so Dani—it was cold as hell outside, and no one would see her painted nails, but she'd painted that C anyway. She was adorable.

Goosebumps broke out over her skin as I kneaded the spot under her arch and the timer went off. She didn't move when I set her foot on the ground. "Dani?"

"Hm?"

"You alive?"

"Five percent."

"Could you up it to twenty? My cheese fries are worth it." I got them out and covered them with cheese. It started melting, and I added bacon bits and sour cream. "Top three things to put in your mouth, I swear."

That got her up. She laughed and rubbed her eyes. "I bet you think your cock is up there too."

"You said it, not me."

I got our plates ready and two large waters, and the simplicity of how normal it seemed worked me up. I could *see* us doing this in another month or more. The image should've scared me, but instead, I bottled it away to think about later. When it wasn't almost three am and I had a huge game the next day.

She shoveled the fries into her mouth. Sour cream got on her face and fingers, and she crossed her eyes at one point. Instead of putting me off, it endeared me to her. She was comfortable enough around me to go to town with food, and my chest warmed again.

"Van, dear lord, this is the BEST thing to ever go in my mouth."

I kept any lewd comments to myself and enjoyed my own plate. Last year, I would've been freaking out about staying up this late and eating carbs before a game, but what did I know then?

We finished our dishes and set them in the sink, Dani dragging her feet as we made it to my bedroom. She plopped down, face in the pillow, and before I could turn off the lights and get in, she snored.

I pulled her close to me, wrapping my arm around her. How was it possible to know someone for decades and never think it could be like this? So easy? So perfect? Daniella felt like she'd been mine forever, and while we'd been in each other's lives the whole time, being *with* her made sense. These feelings were new and strange and complicated. I'd never been captivated with anyone like this before. And of course, it would happen with the one girl I could never hurt. It was too risky—with Elle and Dani and my friendship changing after all these years. Fuck, I wanted her but knew it'd be hard, but too much was on the line. I didn't have any answers, but I smiled, knowing that I had to do something. Dani was a dream, and with that final thought, I fell asleep.

A wild animal woke me up. A deep groan, like a cry, had me opening my eyes, and why the hell was it so hot in my room?

It took me three seconds to figure it out. Daniella had her entire body draped over me, my shirt riding up high on her torso, and she moaned into my chest. Seeing her here in my clothes had me grinning ear to ear despite the protest in my body. I hurt from whatever angle we fell asleep in, and I ran my hands over her ass and up her spine. "Morning."

"My head feels like it got hit with a cannonball," she grumbled, shielding her eyes when I tried shaking her. "No, no movements."

She clung to me tighter, and I checked the time: 8 am. She had to leave soon, but I could enjoy the embrace a little longer. "That happens when you drink like you did."

"Okay, Gabriel. You had your moment a few weeks ago, but you're this solid, sexy muscle tank of a person, and life's not fair." She dug her face deeper into my neck. "You smell so good it's annoying."

I chuckled and continued massaging her back. I wanted to dip my fingers between her legs so damn badly. My cock ached to be inside her, but she was hungover, and I couldn't be an asshole. "Anything I can do to help?"

"Never let me drink again."

"Ah, that's your call there, baby." I ran my fingers through her hair and massaged her scalp, earning another satisfied groan from her that went straight to my dick. "I can make you breakfast and drive you to your spa day."

"Can you help me in the shower?"

Was I alive and breathing? "Fuck yeah, let's go."

She winced when I rolled us off the bed, and I held her against me. She leaned into my chest and glanced up at me with sleepy eyes. "Did I go on about a crush last night? I'm having the hangover blues where I replay everything stupid I've ever done, and this one seems like the top."

"You did, but I loved it." I placed her on the bathroom counter before starting the shower. "Arms up."

She let out another pathetic sound but lifted her arms. I took off my sweatshirt and placed it on the side, sucking in a breath at having a very naked and sexy Daniella in my bathroom. Needing help in the shower. She closed her eyes, and I kissed her forehead. "That was cute," she mumbled.

"You look pathetic. Sexy, but pathetic."

"That's my brand."

I laughed, then stripped out of my clothes before picking her up again. I set her inside the shower, and she sighed, long and hard. "Feel good?"

"Yes. I prefer to be burned alive when I'm hungover." She tilted her face toward the stream, and I stepped in behind her, getting the soap and running it over her back and arms. "Your hands are a gift to the Earth."

"Why, thank you. Dare I say in your top three favorite hands?" I teased, unable to stop smiling. I washed her neck, along her collarbone, and dipped my hands over her breasts. Her nipples were hard, and I grazed my palms over them, slowly. She gasped.

"Do that again."

I did, this time tweaking her nipples between my fingers once, twice, and a third time. Her breathing picked up, and I kissed her neck, fighting the urge to slide into her. "I have an idea of what could help that headache, Dani."

I nipped the skin where her neck met her shoulder, and she backed against me. Her ass was right along my cock, and I groaned. "Fuck, you're sexy."

She wiggled her delicious ass, and I dipped one hand between her thighs. She was tight and wet for me. "Van," she breathed, her voice needy as hell. "Touch me."

I thrusted two fingers inside her, using my thumb to circle her clit, and she gripped the side of the shower. "Hold on while I use just my fingers to fuck you."

She trembled.

"Rock your hips against my hand, nice and slow," I said, my own lust almost blinding me. "I want you to fall apart."

She shuddered and did as I asked, riding my fingers and moaning as she went faster. I propped one arm up on the wall to hold us up and then I curled my fingers at the end, hitting her G-spot. She bucked, and I bit her ear. Then her neck. Then her shoulder. Fuck, I wanted to suck every part of her skin. "Come for me."

She whined, and I hoped we didn't fall down. I used my other hand to fist her tits, pulling her sensitive nipples and that did it. She tightened around my fingers, her head slamming back against my shoulders as she came *hard*. God, her entire body shook as she cried out, and I fucking loved seeing her like this. Unhinged. Wild. Free.

"That's my girl, coming loud for me." I put my hand on her throat, twisting her so I could kiss her. The same out-of-control urge to have her hit me again as I sucked her tongue into my mouth. She moaned, and I slid out of her and spun her around.

"I love coming for you," she whispered against my lips, getting me even harder. She sucked my bottom lip into her mouth, teasing me before pushing me onto the edge of the tub. The hot water poured down on us, and the air was so thick it was hard to breathe, but Dani spread my thighs apart and stared at me with hunger in her eyes. "I'm clean, Gabe. And on the pill."

My stomach swooped with an irrationally hungry urge at what she was insinuating. My entire body buzzed with need, and I nodded. "Yes, please god. I'm clean too."

She gripped my shoulders and slowly got onto my lap, sliding down on my cock. She tensed for a beat before grinding her hips in a perfect rhythm and stealing all my thoughts. It was just her. Her sounds, her smell, her pussy. So tight and warm and bare. I shuddered this time, wrapping my arm around her lower back and using my other to hold her throat.

"You are fucking sexy." My voice was all gravel and need, and her lips parted. "Look at you riding my cock with your sexy dancer hips." Each move was a shock of pleasure with nothing between us, and I could barely breathe. I had *never* done this before with anyone, and fuck, it ruined me. The trust between us only made each stroke hotter, my need for her burning. She arched those sexy ass hips and took me deeper, her pussy tightening around me and making me groan.

She glanced down and whimpered as we both watched my dick sliding in and out of her. She set the pace, driving me mad. "Your thighs are so thick." She bent down and licked along my jawline. "I want to take a bite out of them."

"Next time, baby." God, I wasn't gonna last. Being inside her without a condom was *perfection*. Her walls squeezed around me as she went fast, and my chest heaved, her gyrations hypnotizing me. Our kisses were messy and hungry, and I wanted more of her. My arm slid off her skin from the water sliding between us, and she arched her back, taking me deeper. I reached between us and pinched her clit, her swollen nerve already so sensitive.

"Van, yes." She pulled back and watched me as she came. She never broke eye contact, and something inside my chest ripped apart at seeing her like that. She threw her head back, moaning my name, and I thrusted up into her harder. She gave me a piece of herself, and I was never returning it.

She dug her nails into my skin as she rode out the orgasm,

her eyes swirling with emotion. That did me in. I gripped her ass and came harder than I had in a long time, the tightness of her pussy sending me over the edge. My heart beat out of my chest, and my limbs burned from straining, but all of it faded to the background as nothing but pleasure rocked my core.

When I came to, I cupped the back of her head, her hair soaking wet, and kissed her softly. "Damn."

"Damn," she repeated, her cheeks bright red and her blue eyes even lighter, like the sky midafternoon. Her freckles seemed to multiply, and I kissed a line down her collarbone. She tilted up my face, staring at me with so much warmth, I felt it in my gut. "Top one. For sure."

I smiled, unable to communicate the mess of feelings in my head. Everything spun together, and I needed time to figure it out. So instead, I kissed her. "Let's get you cleaned up and fed."

She smiled as I finished washing us both. Something had shifted for me, and I knew it was important. I just couldn't think about it until after the game that night because deep down, I knew it would change *everything*.

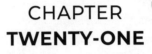

CHAPTER
TWENTY-ONE

Daniella

S unday morning, I woke up to the sound of my phone informing me of a video call. I shoved my hair out of my face, silencing my phone quickly because noise. My roomie was already at the library—on a Sunday at eight am, ugh, and I smiled at seeing Elle's face.

"Guess who's in town, bitch?" she shouted, smiling at me through the screen. "It's me."

"Hey." I ran a hand over my face, yawning. "Sorry, I swear I'm still hungover from Friday night."

"I can't wait to be there next year, living it up with you. Oh my god, I can taste it."

I laughed and felt a flicker of excitement. "It's gonna be sick."

"Can you be ready in twenty minutes? My mom is dropping me off at Gabe's because she needs to give him some papers, but I want my Dani time. Go shopping for Central State gear. Walk by our new place so I can swoon."

My brain pieced it together slowly, like how a car took a

minute to get warm in the winter. Van… Elle…" Is your brother coming with?"

"Doubt it. I'm lame, remember?" She rolled her eyes and said something to her mom. "Okay, we're almost to Van's. Be there in twenty."

She hung up before I had time to react. Seeing Elle would be amazing, and thinking about all the shit we could do together next year had me smiling ear to ear. We'd dreamt about being roommates our whole lives, and it was finally happening in June. Six months away. It was weird though to keep this entire secret from her about Gabe. I shared everything with Elle. She was my person. My best friend, more a sister. Sleeping with her brother—the biggest issue she had with girls growing up—was the biggest betrayal I could do to her. I knew she was nervous about us fake dating, and this had to be why. I was like *all the others*, thinking I could be the one who changed him.

I quickly applied my makeup, braided my hair to get it out of my face, and put on the warmest leggings I could with boots, a long-sleeved shirt, and a crewneck with a dancer on it. Knowing Elle, she'd want to go all over campus. Excitement bubbled up until I realized what it meant though—no movie Sunday with Van.

My stomach sank, and for the first time in my entire twenty years, I was mad I was hanging out with Elle. What the actual hell? My mood soured at the betrayal of my thoughts, but my time with Van was limited. Only a few weeks left until the holidays and then our ending. The thought of us breaking up made me almost throw up. The heartbreak would be brutal. I'd still have to see him from time to time, and it would be the hardest thing in the world, to smile and pretend I wasn't dying on the inside. That issue was for another day. Right now, I had to focus on my best friend because Van was always temporary, but Elle was for life.

How dare I not want to spend time with her?

I was the worst friend. She spent all her high school years

worrying about girls liking her to get closer to her brother, and here I was, sleeping with him and dreaming about him behind her back. Fuck. The guilt ate at me, and I needed air. I cracked the window, and the cool air blasted over my face. The snow melted, but the temperatures were still uncomfortable. I stared at the bleak weather, the sun not showing an ounce, and I heard them before I saw them.

Elle and *her brother* walked down the sidewalk toward the dorms, the two of them laughing at whatever he showed her on his phone. I wondered what it would be like to be with Van for real and hang out with Elle. We'd still joke around, tease, annoy him. Her and I would still be a team, but I could kiss him when I wanted. He'd hold my hand and help me get over my moments on insecurity. I could *see* it all happen, but I shook my thoughts away. This wasn't real. That daydream would remain a fantasy.

She shoved his shoulder, and he pulled her into a half-hug. My heart fully collapsed at that point and would only beat for him. The way he loved his sister and family was too much. My eyes stung—because of the wind!—and I tried not to let my emotions show on my face. Elle would know right away, but what the heck was Gabe doing here?

They'd need to be let into the dorm, so I wiped my hands on my leggings, my palms already sweating, and went to greet them. *Act chill.* My face burned as I opened the outside doors. "Hey Van Helsings."

"Daniella!" Elle threw her arms around me in a hug, and I met Van's gaze over her shoulder.

What are you doing? I mouthed, but he didn't answer. He winked.

"Come here, fake girlfriend. Where's my hug?"

Seriously, what the fuck was he doing?

"Ha ha." I forced a laugh and swatted his shoulder. "No photo ops today, boo."

"Yeah, y'all post enough. You got mom planning a wedding

and baby names at this point, so you know. Holidays are gonna be annoying. You two better be prepared."

Elle waltzed into the dorm and down the hall. She knew what room mine was and let herself in. That gave me two seconds to be alone with Van.

"What are you doing?"

"Nothing. Just hanging out." He shrugged and put his hands in his pockets. "You look good, by the way."

"Stop it. None of that." I pointed at his chest.

His lips quirked, but he didn't seem to understand we couldn't... do this with Elle around. "Behave."

His eyes danced with amusement, but I couldn't worry about him. Not with Elle in my room. Shit. His sweatshirt!

I'd worn it to bed last night and left it on the pillow. She'd notice and figure it all out. Speeding up my walk, I barged in to see her sitting at my desk, pretending to type on a laptop. "Uh, Elle?"

"Oh, just picturing what it'll be like living on my own, without having my parents there. It'll be great." She grinned wide and clapped her hands. "So, where are we off to first?"

"Is your brother tagging along the whole day?" I asked her, refusing to look at him.

"He said yes." She shrugged like it was no big deal, and I replayed all my memories of the three of us hanging out. There were a few sporadic times he would join us. So maybe this wasn't totally weird.

"You don't have *plans* this afternoon?" I asked him, making my eyes go wide.

He grinned. "I did, but they got cancelled."

"Hm."

He wiggled his eyebrows, Elle not seeing it, and I quietly went to the bed and grabbed his sweatshirt. He clearly knew what I was doing. "Oh, there's my shirt."

My face burned brighter than the sun, and I was going to kill him. Murder him with my pom-poms.

"For photos! That's why it was here."

"Right, and not because you were freezing and needed a sweatshirt. I'm not an asshole, Daniella." His tone sounded serious, but his eyes danced with humor.

Elle barely noticed or cared. She shrugged and had her own buzz of excitement going on. "Speaking of clothes, let's go to the Union and get me some gear."

"You're gonna be too much next year, aren't you?" I teased her, hating the lie that stood between us. Being with Van temporarily had been a fantasy come to life. It would take years to get over him, maybe more. He'd probably come visit Elle next year, and I'd have to see him with his flings and smile. God, what if he got serious with someone else? I gulped, knives gutting my insides. That would kill me to know he would take another girl to the movies and show them his secrets. I liked being the only one...but it wouldn't always be that way. I swallowed a ball of emotion. I'd have to deal with it. I chose this path, accepting it would hurt.

"By too much, do you mean wearing school gear every day? Going to happy hours all the time and partying and drinking too much—" Elle said.

"Okay, no. You need to be smart about it," Van said, his tone more aggressive. "Never go anywhere alone, and if you're drinking, make sure you eat dinner before."

"Ugh, fine. I know." She flipped him off. "Like you were the example of behaving."

"I've done dumb shit, but I'm not a pretty blonde girl new to campus." He narrowed his eyes at her. "The two of you will get into shit, I know it."

"I hope we do." Elle puffed her chest out, her red coat going to her knees. "Now, to the store. Mom's picking me up this afternoon, and I want to see everything."

With that, we bundled up and took off toward the Union. Sunday mornings on campus were quiet. A few students walked about, but it was really dead as we traveled toward the store. Van wore a black coat and jeans, but it was his beanie that had me looking at him. His hair escaped the sides, and it was just adorable. It didn't help that he kept touching me when Elle wasn't looking.

On the arm, hip, face—he even cupped my ass when we entered the front doors of the Union. I swatted him, but it only made him laugh.

"What's so funny?" Elle asked, her eyes moving to and from objects with our school logo. She picked up a basket and tossed in coasters, a phone case, a lanyard.

"Dani and I have been hanging out so much we have inside jokes now."

"Oh." Elle spun and narrowed her eyes us. "I don't like that at all."

"You hate being left out of everything, don't you?" Van said, something mischievous in his voice that made me nervous.

"Obviously. I can't have my best friend and brother having more fun than me." She went on shopping, her comment hanging in the air. Guilt clawed up my throat.

We had way more than *just* jokes.

Van stared at me, his dimples popping out from his smile, and I rolled my eyes. I knew exactly what he was thinking about, and damn him for being here. I wanted to kiss that smirk off his face even though my guilt about Elle physically hurt me.

We trailed Elle, me avoiding Van at all costs, and she ended up buying two hundred dollars' worth of school items. Said it was waitressing money she'd earned, and I wasn't going to bust her bubble of joy, even if she looked like a dork wearing everything orange and navy.

"Okay, now off to the apartment building."

"Could we get something eat?" Van patted his stomach. "I'm sure Dani needs to replenish nutrients after her wild Friday night."

"Shut up, I'm fine." My face heated, and Elle narrowed her

eyes at me for a beat. I prepared for a question, but none came, and I sighed in relief.

"Food works. Is there a café near our place where we can be regulars?"

"How are you going to afford all these plans, Elle?" Van asked as we walked out of the store. "This shit costs money."

"I'm getting a job the week I move in. Waitressing probably. Or bartending. That could be fun."

"I think there's a nice brunch place." I turned right. "Let's go there."

We waited in line and ordered food, Elle and I going to sit at the table while Van paid. The second our butts hit the seats, she turned to me. "Be careful."

"What?"

"You're still in love with him." She tapped her fingers on the table. "I can see it all over your face, girl. I know you as much as myself."

"Wait, what?" My throat dried up, and every cell in my body tensed, ready to flee the country. "Love?"

"Dani, you've always had a little crush on Van and it's fine." She waved her hand in the air like it was no big deal. The instant relief I felt at those words had my muscles unclench. I wasn't betraying her. Thank god.

"But you're falling for him, and I'm worried."

"I'm not. It's not…Elle, I'm your best friend, not trying to get with…It's not what you think."

"Hey, hey." She placed a hand on mine. "I know, okay? We're friends for life, the kind of friends where you're in the hospital room with me when I'm having a baby. Doesn't matter what happens, nothing changes that. I'm worried because I don't want you hurt."

"Me?"

"My brother is charming as hell. Has not unattractive features, plays hockey. I know how he operates. He'll be sweet and make you laugh, but the second you show any emotion, he's gone. He's done it a million times. Has his little timeframes for dating. Hell, maybe not even dating. Sleeping together. Do you know how many crying girls showed up at our house that he made me send away?"

The ball in my throat grew three sizes. I knew all of this already, yet hearing it again from her was like pouring gasoline in a fire.

"He's going to break your heart even if he doesn't want to. I'm not asking and never want to know if y'all hooked up. You're an adult and do what you please, but please...protect yourself. He'll always be my brother and you, my other half, but I'd hate to see him hurt you."

"Okay," I croaked out, barely able to breathe.

"Food should be here in five minutes." Van sat down next to me, his scent so familiar and comforting. I breathed him in before leaning back in my chair, putting distance between us. If he noticed, he didn't care. We ate lunch, walked more of the campus, and hung out until Elle's mom picked her up.

I somehow managed to survive the day without giving away my inner turmoil. Elle was right. Van would crush my heart unintentionally, but didn't I know that already? I couldn't tell her that it was already too late, that I was in love with him anyway and when New Year's ended, I'd be a mess.

I shoved all of it down deep when Van asked me to head to a late movie instead. It was already going to end and so what if I fell a little more in love with him before it ended?

CHAPTER
TWENTY-TWO

Gabriel

Flowers might've been too much. I wasn't sure. I stared at the red tulip display at the store, eyeing the different options. Her big night mattered, and I wanted it to be special, and flowers said *I'm proud of you.*

There was a combination of orange and red ones that I grabbed and went to check out. They reminded me of her hair, and I smiled, imagining how she'd do it tonight. Down and curly was my favorite, but her color was so pretty that it really didn't make a difference how she wore it. Wanting her to feel good about her award and seeing her smile were the goal. I paid for the bouquet and headed back to my apartment, suddenly nervous about the night.

I'd seen her every day that week, not just to hook up either. We'd grabbed lunch, and I told her about this student who wore a panda suit to class on Monday. Then we got dinner Tuesday. We worked out together Wednesday, hung around my place Thursday, and Friday, she insisted on going back to the bookstore. I honestly should've been sick of her, but instead, it was the opposite. It was an addiction. I wanted more of her. I hated dropping her off at her dorm last night because of her *rule,* but tonight was my night, the sleepover.

I couldn't fucking wait.

Dressed in a suit and black tie, I styled my hair back and even did a clean shave. Eyeing myself in the mirror, I looked good. The red swatch in my pocket was the only clue of what color Dani's dress was, and honestly, it didn't matter what kind of dress she wore. She'd look amazing regardless.

My phone buzzed.

Elle: Don't ruin this for her.

Elle: Please, Gabe.

Gabe: Do you think I'm an asshole? wtf?

Elle: The fake dating, her award night...don't hurt her.

Gabe: I would never.

Elle: Her mom literally told her getting this award wasn't as fulfilling as when she won all those beauty pageants. I just worry about her, okay? I'm not there to build her back up

Gabe: I can.

I scratched my chest, the absolute distaste for Lovely Lily making my mouth sour. What a horrible, insecure woman. I swore if I ever had kids that I'd let them be themselves. Like my parents did with me and Elle. My parents didn't even like hockey that much and weren't a fan of Elle majoring in communication and creative writing. They preferred solid careers like education, but they never stopped us or made us feel shitty for our choices.

The headspace Dani had to live with would fuck with me.

Elle's text just made me want to go over there earlier to double-check if Dani was okay, but she strictly told me four on the dot. It was three, and my nervous energy annoyed me. There hadn't been a moment in my life where I was this excited and anxious for something that wasn't hockey. I knew it had to do with celebrating Daniella and seeing her, but my feelings were still unsettled around her. She mentioned the breakup often enough for me to worry I was imagining how I felt about her.

To pass time, I went through her social feed because I was obsessed—and smiled at all her posts. They weren't all staged shots either, like I would've expected. There were messy ones and blurry faces. Her and her former dance team from a community college in our town. Her and Elle. Her and Cami Simpson. Her and some of the football guys.

I commented on ten of them, not caring if it showed her I was scrolling way down her feed. It was a supportive boyfriend role, that was all. The same burning sensation formed in my chest just thinking about how it'd feel to see her post with another guy someday. Horrible, probably. Wondering if he made her laugh as much or pleasured her as well or knew her weaknesses so he could build her up.

Okay, this was a terrible idea. I closed the app. I could take the long way there. The afternoon blended with the evening sky, the only difference being the gray air getting darker. The sun was setting earlier and earlier, casting campus in night, and I didn't mind the cold this time. My little snow slut would love the weather—there was a fifty percent chance of snow.

It was finally four, and I parked outside her dorm, my stomach bubbling with anticipation. To hold her, see her, kiss her. All of it. But mainly, I needed to look into her blue eyes to know the depth of her mom hurting her. Someone left the dorm just as I walked up and let me in. With the flowers in one hand, I knocked outside her dorm door and waited.

Soft footsteps approached the other side, and my breath caught in my throat when the handle twisted. It swung open, and Daniella stood there dressed in a fucking killer deep red dress. It hugged her curves and showed off her neckline. God, she had a great neck with her freckles and collarbone. I wanted to run my tongue in the dips along her neck, moving down her subtle cleavage. Then I noticed the slit.

Fuck. My throat forgot how to work as I trailed her long leg on full display with the dress. She even wore heels that matched, and I was gone. Done for. She stole my breath and words and ability to think.

"Well?" She twirled around and to imagine the dress couldn't get sexier was incorrect. The dress was backless, her strong muscles showing. There was a simple string connecting the fabric from one shoulder blade to the next, and I was pretty sure I grunted.

She laughed, biting her lip and gesturing to the flowers. "Oh Van, these are beautiful."

"No." She'd reverted me to straight up caveman. "You're beautiful."

"I'd like to think flowers and humans can both be beautiful in different ways. But thank you." Her cheeks pinked, and she took the flowers and smelled them. "The colors are gorgeous."

"Your hair." *Jesus, pull it together.* "I thought of your red hair."

"Be careful, Van Helsing. You're approaching cute status." She set them down on her desk and quickly poured a bottled water into a large cup. Once the flowers were secured in the cup, I held out my hand.

"Come here."

She slowly walked toward me, taking my hand before I gently tugged her closer to me. I ran my fingers over her forehead, her jawline, her collarbone before placing my hand over her heart. "You're stunning."

She blinked, her long lashes fanning over her cheeks before she glanced up at me with a watery smile. "For the first time in a long while, I feel it too. It's weird, ya know?"

"Good. You should." I couldn't stop staring at her. The way her long curly hair flowed over her shoulder, the delicate jewels in her ears, the bracelet on her left wrist. I wanted to know who gave them to her, what they meant. Did she like jewelry? I held her hand gently and lifted up the charm. A dance shoe. Of course. "I love this."

"Elle bought it for me to never forget what fed my soul." She placed her hands on my chest as her gaze moved all over me. I swear my skin prickled from her stare, and I took a shaky breath.

"You look so handsome, Gabe. A dream." She cupped my chin. "Oh, it's so soft."

"I shaved. Figured I'd look the best I could for you."

"Please." She gave a shy smile and ran her thumb over my lips. "You're perfect the way you are. I liked the scruff. Made my lips tingle."

"I'll grow it out. Give me two days."

She laughed, and I had to kiss her. I went in soft, kissing her jawline before getting to her mouth, and she leaned into me, her pillow lips meeting mine with the same gentleness. She tasted like mint and strawberries, her tongue sliding against mine with a comforting sense of heat. It wasn't new, but it was just as exciting, and I guided her closer with a hand at the base of her spine.

She groaned, and I pulled back, not wanting to spoil a single thing about the night. "Why'd you stop?"

"We need to head to the hotel." I smoothed her hair and ran a finger on the side of her mouth where her lipstick smeared. "I gotta get you there on time."

She blinked back the heat, and she straightened. "Yes, you're probably right. I do love kissing you though."

"Same, D." I waited for her to get her coat and a little purse and then we were off. I couldn't stop touching her. Tonight seemed important beyond just an awards dinner. It felt... different, like it would change things. The sixth sense I'd always had was going off, but I ignored it and focused on Dani.

"I don't really know what to expect besides food and some speeches. Coach told me it was about two hours or so." She gripped the collar of her coat. "Damn, it's cold."

"Yeah, but it's supposed to snow." I opened the passenger side door of my car, waiting for her to get in before picking up the end of her dress that hung out. She watched me with the softest, most vulnerable look, and I winked. "We would've had a kickass time at prom."

"Please." She rolled her eyes. "You had a blast at prom. There are still stories about the party you threw."

"Sure, it was fun, but I'm saying it would've been more fun with you." I actually meant the words. All my dates were temporary. Every single one of them. Maybe it was the fact I knew Daniella would always be in my life as Elle's best friend that made it different, but never had a date been this meaningful. "Watch your hands."

I shut the door, taking in a refreshing breath of winter air before getting in on the other side. Her perfume filled my car, and it hit me that I'd miss this scent—flowers and strawberries. She was just delicious, and how did we only have two weeks left?

Panic ate at my gut, like a gnawing grating feeling in my insides, and a nervous sweat broke out at the base of my neck. Two weeks. That was only two more sleepovers before we broke up. That was our plan, and we'd agreed to it, but fuck, maybe we could delay it to February?

I tapped my fingers on the wheel as we drove toward the hotel where the dinner would be held. Daniella hummed to a song on the radio, not having a clue about my inner turmoil. Why would she?

Don't be selfish. Tonight was about her and her alone. She didn't need me becoming all weird about our deal. It could wait even though the urge to beg her was right there. We could even say our ruse would go into Valentine's Day. Prevent anyone from getting ideas about me, and her mom couldn't guilt her for being single or try to set her up with another little weasel. Once we got through the evening, I'd talk to her about it.

Content with my plan, I settled down and reached over to lace our fingers together. She squeezed mine, giving me a coy look before letting out a sigh.

"What was that for?"

"This is nice." She kissed the back of my hand, and my entire body froze into a gargoyle.

No one in my entire life kissed me there. It was... everything. A simple gesture that showed so much. That she cared for me, enjoyed me. My stomach fucking swooped like I slipped on ice and was trying to catch my balance. That was what she did to me, made me feel like I was falling.

"When our two weeks is up, I want you to know this was way more fun than I would've thought, Gabe. I've enjoyed my time with you."

Her tone sounded like a goodbye, which made that panic come back. It still wasn't the time to talk about it since she should be focused on herself, so I cleared my throat and forced myself to respond. "I had fun too, Baby D."

"Two more weeks, huh?"

God. Was she intentionally goading me? I was trying to be the better person. "Yup. Two more."

"Have you thought about how we break up?"

"No, I'll let you decide." Or maybe we just don't? "We can worry about it later. Tonight is about you. No stress, just enjoy yourself, okay?"

She nodded, and I moved my hand to her thigh. Her skin was so warm and soft, and I gripped it harder than I intended to. She was trying to let me go when all I wanted to do was hold on, even if I wasn't sure what it meant. I had two weeks to figure it out though, and I made a promise to myself to do just that because there was only one Daniella, and I wanted to keep her.

And *not* as my sister's best friend. No, as *my girl*.

CHAPTER
TWENTY-THREE

Daniella

The ache from my mom's text lessened the more I was with Gabe. That happened a lot. Him shining light where dark thoughts grew. My parents should've been the first people I told about the event, but even I knew they'd dampen my mood. Against my better judgement, I'd texted them about the night that morning.

My mom's response was *cool* and my dad's was *great*.

That was it. No congrats or comments about how proud they were. Just *cool* and *great*. It was bullshit. Instead of the ire and agony of disappointing them, I let it go. It wasn't my fault that they weren't as involved in my life as I wanted them to be. They were adults and controlled their own actions.

I was proud of myself. The sophomore transfer who came here with no friends had now gotten this leadership award. Cami had my back. Van too. And this dress. I loved how I looked. It was chiffon, smooth and elegant, and I didn't give a shit if my mom thought red clashed with my hair. The color worked for me, and I smiled, running my fingers over the material as Van parked the car. His parents and Elle had reached out, gushing with pride. They were enough. *I* was enough.

The event was about me, and it felt pretty damn good, even if the looming deadline of the fake relationship was the awkward elephant in the back of my mind. It was easier to put distance between my feelings for him and our expiration date if I talked about the breakup, but he was right. We could worry about it later. Tonight? I wanted to drink and eat and enjoy my date with Van because good god, that man could wear a suit.

"Has anyone told you that men in suits and tuxes are like lingerie to women?"

"Oh yeah?" He flashed a wicked grin, one promising pleasure as soon as we left. "Want me to strike a pose?"

"Kinda, yeah." I laughed and gripped his forearm. "These meatsticks are also golden. You roll up your sleeves and flex and bam, wet panties."

"Damn, Dani, please tell me more of these little secrets."

"Doorway leaning, tight black shirts. Mm." I mimed a chef's kiss. "Also, your ass in general. Just walk real slow in front of me."

He barked out a laugh and got out of his side, pointing at me to stay put. It charmed the hell out of me that he insisted on getting my door. It made me think of his prom comment, and my face flushed. He had no idea how often I'd dreamed of going to prom with him and having him take my virginity. It hadn't happened, obviously, but this was a close second.

He wore a huge grin when he opened my door, his eyes sparkling. "It's fucking snowing."

His excitement for me was enough to have my heart stumble in my chest. He gently lifted me out of his car and spun me around. "Could tonight be any more perfect?"

I laughed as he twirled me, my life a fucking rom-com come to life. He set me down and leaned me back, kissing me real slow and creating a low tug in my gut. The pull was dangerous. Made me want to do something stupid.

A car door shut, causing me to jump and grounding me back to reality. We broke apart, but his heated smile never left his face. "My little snow slut seems happy."

"Shut up." I snorted and was grateful for the comment. It eased the sentimental feelings going through my head, trying to get through my filter and spit out love declarations.

He laughed and took my hand in his, his thumb tracing circles along my skin as we headed toward the entrance of the hotel. There were twenty tables that seated eight each, a DJ in the corner, and a small bar. It reminded me of a wedding reception without flowers. Instead, sports gear was everywhere. I recognized varying athletes from campus and nodded at one of the girls' tennis stars. These athletes were incredible and to be chosen to be here? A dream.

"Let me get your coat, Dani." Van slowly eased my jacket off and hung his and mine up on a rack. That meant there was no barrier between my lower back and his hand. His touch sizzled on my skin, and I shuddered. Our chemistry was downright wild, even after spending so much time together.

We made our way to our seats, and Jessica was there with her husband. We did introductions, and soon enough, the dinner started. Our athletic director spoke about leadership qualities and making a difference, highlighting how hard it was to be a good leader, and my chest soared with pride.

Van rubbed the back of my neck with a soft massage, sending goosebumps down to my toes. His touch was a comfort and a reassurance he was with me, and I couldn't love him more.

Food came out in various courses. First salad, then soup, then Beef Wellington and a delicious cheesecake platter for dessert. Throughout the night, coaches would go up to the podium and talk about their athlete. There didn't seem to be an order, but I scanned the program and knew I had to be soon. Twenty others had already gone, and right as I took a sip of my water, Jessica pushed out her chair.

"We met under weird circumstances, but I'm glad we did." She smiled, her perfect white teeth on display, and she winked. "Here's to you, Daniella."

Shit.

My breathing picked up as my heart beat twice as fast. She was going to talk about me. All attention on me. I could dance in front of everyone without dropping a bead of sweat, but this? It was nerve-wracking. A positive kind of attention that I struggled with. Compliments and words of affirmation made me uneasy. They were so rare and against what I was accustomed to, so my initial reaction was to brush them off. Say it was fake. Not believe it. Criticism was where my self-esteem lived, and this speech made me inexplicably uneasy. How did I react? What was a normal response? I blew out a shaky breath but then Van was holding my hand on the table, his other arm around my shoulders.

"Enjoy it, Daniella. This is such an honor. You'll remember this for the rest of your life." His breath tickled my neck, making me shiver, and he pressed a quick kiss on my cheek. "I am so fucking proud of you."

My leg bounced up and down, rattling the table, and he moved his hand to my thigh, stilling me. Jessica tapped the mic, and everyone quieted. "Good evening, everyone. I'm Jessica Jacobson, the newest dance coach. My position here came in a unique manner, and I know I haven't known the girls long. But I'm a dancer. Always have been, and there are three things that come to being a leader on the team—strength, vulnerability, and grit.

"See, our strength isn't brute force and lifting weights. It's doing the same move over and over to the point your toenails are bleeding. Then you do it again but faster. It's knowing that no matter how bad your day might be, you show up and smile. Daniella is strong every day, leading our senior veterans and motivating our freshmen. She's also real. Talks about struggles. Admits when we need help. That is also a different kind of strength. She leads by example and is the first to help out a teammate. Grit, this is my favorite thing about her in the short time I've known her. She fights for what she wants, and as a coach? What more could you want?"

A small applause went through the crowd, but my ears rang. My face burned, and my insides were all gooey with emotion. Unfamiliar emotion. I wanted to smile and cry and run and hide.

"Congrats, Daniella. You are an amazing part of the team and captain, and I can't wait to grow the program with you the next two years."

Everyone clapped, and she returned to the chair. She pulled me into a hug, and I was numb. My heart pitter-pattered, and my fingers shook. My soul seemed lighter, like it shed the heavy weight of not being enough at home. Here, I was enough. No one had ever talked about me that way, and I wanted to replay those words for the rest of my life. My voice was shaky, and a ball of emotion caught in my throat. "Thank you, Coach, oh my god."

"You deserve it." She smiled and patted my shoulder. "I have a certificate and gift for you, but it's at home. We'll get lunch soon, and I'll give it to you."

"Sure, yeah." I sat back down, dazed, and Van immediately put an arm around my shoulders, surrounding me with his scent. "Holy shit."

I turned to look at him, and his eyes blazed with heat and pride. "Best moment ever," I whispered.

He nodded, cupped my face, and kissed me softly. The gentleness of his touch had my breath catching in my throat. He pulled back and said, "Thank you for letting me be here to witness it. Top three night for me."

I smiled at our inside joke, and for the rest of the night, I floated on clouds. We stayed for the rest of the speeches and small talk. It wasn't until ten that we left and headed back to his place. We hadn't stopped touching at all. Not when we chatted with other players—the goalie from the hockey team was there who Van congratulated multiple times—and not when we walked to the car and got in. It was like we had an unwritten rule to never move from one another.

"I wish I'd recorded it," I admitted once we were on the road. "Those comments were some of the nicest I've ever heard."

"Ah, well, I did get a video of it for you."

"Gabriel." I could just marry him. "Thank you so much, oh my god." I squeezed his hand hard, and he laughed.

"I figured you might want a copy. I sure would. I am so fucking proud of you I don't know what to do with this feeling. Seriously. You're incredible, you know that?"

It was hard to describe the exact reaction my insides had to hearing him say that. Incredible. Me? From the intonation of his voice to the serious look in his eyes, Van meant it, and that had me feeling emotional. Grateful. My eyes prickled, and my pulse pounded in a good way, like it did in the middle of a dance routine where I felt happiest. Making him proud had suddenly become my first priority.

I nodded, my face flushing from his words, but it didn't last long. He stared at me at a stoplight, his expression so tender and serious I had to believe him. "Tonight is the best night ever," I said.

"It is."

We drove in silence the rest of the way back to his apartment, his hand never leaving mine as we made the journey up to his floor. Without saying a word, he led us to his bedroom where he shut the door and leaned against it.

His gaze darkened, and my pulse fluttered at the base of my neck, each beat sending a tremor through me. His intent was clear, and I knew my night was going to get even better.

"You're a dream." He pushed off the door and stood in front of me, our toes touching. He ran his hands up and down my sides, his fingers teasing my thigh exposed on the slit.

I, too, explored his broad chest and jaw. "Thank you," I whispered, my voice shaking a bit.

His brows pinched together for a beat before he spun me around. He lifted my hair off one shoulder, kissing down my spine until he got to the zipper. "Why are you thanking me? It's me who should be grateful. Look at this dress."

I laughed, but it came out more like a cry. His words were magic and his soft kisses a spell. He undid the zipper, slowly, his touch all over me. My back, shoulders, ass. The silky material tickled my skin when he undid it, and he carefully removed each strap. "Your back is so sexy, Dani."

He kissed each shoulder blade. "You're so strong."

I trembled. Then he slid the dress off me, leaving me in panties and a stick-on bra. My body throbbed with need, but he wasn't in a hurry. No. He ran his nose along my ass, legs before setting me back on the bed. My legs were spread, his face between my thighs, but he just kissed them softly, running his fingernails over my legs until he got to my shoes.

"V-van." I panted, my chest heaving. This was a slow torture.

"I know, baby. But let me enjoy you." He held my gaze as he undid the strap of my shoe, then kissed my ankle. He repeated the process before kissing up my legs toward my pussy. He breathed me in, gripping my panties and tugging them off. He dragged his nose along my calf, pressing the gentlest kisses along my skin. Each brush of his lips sent tingles everywhere. "Fuck, Dani."

His voice was soft and his touch even more so. I couldn't separate my lust from my love, and everything combined. I loved him, fully. The way he kissed me, the way he touched me and supported me. He took his time on my legs. His gaze was filled with heat as he stared up at me, holding eye contact with each kiss. He tickled the back of my knees, nipping my inner thigh with his teeth before kissing the sting away. My eyes fluttered shut when he slid two fingers inside me, slowly going in and out. The entire night was foreplay, and I was already so wet and ready for him, but I wouldn't rush it. Our touch already felt different than before, more precious.

It was in a way, since our relationship had a countdown. It made every lingering brush of a finger more special, more intense. I wanted to bottle up these feelings to save them forever, when he'd just be Elle's brother to me and me... her annoying best friend.

He licked my clit with the flat of his tongue, his deep groan of pleasure getting me even hotter. The orgasm built and built, but before I came, he stopped and moved his attention to my nipples. He sucked and teased them, the sensation making me jump off the bed. His deep laugh vibrated my skin, and he slowly dragged his tongue around each nipple, blowing on them as he stared up at me. "I love your body and how you react to me."

"I love your touch," I said, weakly. I loved everything about him, from the way his eyes crinkled when he smiled, to his movie reviews he wrote, to the way he built me up and supported me. Saying his touch was tame for the feelings I hid deep down.

He stared at me for a full minute, not saying anything, but his eyes swirled with something. Heat and...love? No. That wasn't it. He opened his mouth to talk, but I pushed up and kissed him. Fear, insecurity held me back. He might treat me wonderfully, but he never committed to anyone. Why would I be different?

The night had been a dream, and I didn't want anything to ruin it or throw it off balance. I undid the buttons of his shirt, sliding my fingers over his strong arms and chest, inhaling his scent as my tongue stroked his. He tasted like *me*, earthy, and it got me hotter. He was so selfless in bed and in life that I wished I could tell him what he meant to me. But that meant being brave, and I wasn't. I couldn't be with my heart.

He, too, roamed his hands over my body, and soon enough, we were both naked and panting.

"Need you inside me," I begged, kissing him again slow and sweet. He lowered me onto the bed and carefully thrusted into me. God, he felt good. I groaned, and he kissed along my neck. He held himself up on his elbows, staring down at me as he increased his pace.

"Love your body," he said between breaths. His nostrils flared, and his mouth was slack as I arched my hips up, taking him deeper. "Dani," he said, his voice filled with emotion.

My eyes prickled, and I wrapped my arms and legs around him, needing him closer. He went deeper but not harder, rocking into me with care. It was too much. He hit my G-spot, and the orgasm exploded through me. My toes tingled, and my thighs clenched around him as I rode it out, the pleasure almost too much to bear. He held onto me, continuing to hit me deep, and I cried out his name.

Sweat formed between our chests, and he changed his pace, moving faster as he arched up onto one arm. He sucked my nipple, then the other, then kissed me so passionately my heart thumped. There was no way he couldn't feel what he was doing to me, setting my soul and body on fire. I never wanted this to end. Him on top of me, inside me, being with me. It was perfection, and I gripped his ass as he groaned. "Come again for me, baby."

I needed more stimulation, and he seemed to read my mind. He changed his pace so each thrust added more pressure to my clit, and I squeezed my eyes shut, preparing myself for the roar of pleasure. It came, blinding me as I thrashed around. The orgasm gripped me, sending wave after wave of pure joy though me, and he went harder, holding onto me like I was slipping away. Then he tensed and let out the deepest, sexiest moan as he came.

"Yes, Van," I coaxed him, holding his gaze as he fell apart. His eyes widened, and it was the most intense experience—us coming together while watching each other. He eventually stilled and slid out of me, rolling to the side with heavy breaths. The L word was right there on the tip of my tongue, the urge to tell him what this meant to me. I bit it back, refusing to speak it. This was fake. I knew that even if my body didn't.

I rolled onto my side, running my fingers over his pecs when he opened his eyes again and sought my gaze. "Hi," I said, suddenly seeming shy with the fact that I loved him.

He grinned and leaned up to kiss me again. "How does it get better with you every time?"

I shrugged, pleased at his admittance. "It really does."

"Fuck, I love your mouth, your body." He kissed me again before pushing up. "Let me throw this away and then I'm coming back. I want to lay naked next to you all night. Need your skin on mine."

He went to the bathroom, and I tried not to overthink the fact that he'd used *love* twice. I loved food and snow and tea, but it didn't mean anything. It was typical of me to overanalyze everything and not enjoy the right now, so I shoved all thoughts of our ending and his word choice out of my head.

I was going to soak up every moment with Van, especially naked ones because our days were numbered. It didn't matter that I loved him. We had a deal, and he never went beyond it.

CHAPTER
TWENTY-FOUR

Gabriel

F inals week was a bitch. We had more practices since we had two games against Indiana right before Christmas. I hated it because it meant I couldn't drive Dani back home for break. She caught a ride with one of the dancers, basically cutting out two of the days we had left.

Because yeah, that deadline was coming up fast. One more week. And the days I had hockey games were days without seeing Dani. My phone buzzed with my alarm, alerting me it was time to leave for our team dinner *and* Secret Santa. The guys loved Cal's idea, and little did he realize I'd pulled his name. The asshole wouldn't know what hit him.

I silenced the alert, but a video call came through. *Dani.* My finger flew over the answer button. Her face greeted me, her hair in two buns and not an ounce of makeup on her. "Hey," I said way too loud, showing my pathetic eagerness. "How's home?"

"Look at this shit, Van." She pointed the camera to a bed where multiple outfits were laid out. Purples and greens and blacks, nothing like the style I was used to seeing. "My mom bought me these to wear on Christmas when you come to visit because wearing my onesie would be childish. A guy like you can't keep a girl like me with my pajamas." She put the angle on her face again, and her eyes were wild with irritation.

"The audacity."

"I know. What's funny is that I don't care. I'm not doing it. I'm wearing toe socks and an extra-large shirt without a bra, and maybe I won't shower. How do you like that? Psh, a guy like you." She bit her lip and shook her head. "It's been forty-eight hours Van, and I'm losing my mind with the comments."

"Could you go to my parents' place, hang with Elle?"

"That's the plan."

"Feel free to sleep in my bed."

"Right, because that wouldn't be weird." She frowned. "Elle would call bullshit. Better not do it especially since we only have a week left. Ugh, this went fast, but I need your ass here, Van. Lovely Lily is killing me."

"I wish I was there." I ran a hand through my hair, her comment about the week grating me. By the time I got up there, it'd be five days. That was it. The countdown made me feel desperate to cling to her. To hold onto whatever we had no matter what it took. I'd never had this strong of feelings for another person before, and it was terrifying. I couldn't lose this. I wouldn't be okay. "This team dinner is important, and Cal is really trying, but trust me, being with you sounds more fun. What are you and Elle doing today?" I asked the question as a distraction. Mainly because I knew my time was up to push off talking to some of the guys. Tonight, I had to pull them aside.

"She wants to go to the bookstore for a few hours. I'll drink all the coffee I can. The usual holiday movies."

"Hey, no snow movies without me. That's our thing."

"Yes, sir." She grinned, but it turned to a frown fast. "My mom's calling my name, sorry. I miss you, so get up here fast, okay?"

"You have no idea. I will."

She hung up, and an empty, hollow feeling grew. The guys were almost enough before. The team, playing. It still excited me, but it was different, like filling half my well instead of whole. Plus, after the season's over, I wouldn't even have that. So, what, my soul would be empty then? How would I fill all that time without hockey? My entire life was planned around practices and games and working out, so what the hell would I do then? No hockey, no team, no Daniella?

God, that future seemed too bleak. My stomach ached in longing for more.

I could think about it all on the drive up, plan what to say to her to convince her to keep at this until February. A few more months would be enough time for me to sort out if we could do this for real. Actually take a shot at being a couple, even if it meant upsetting Elle and jeopardizing our friendship. *What if it didn't work out?*

Things could get weird with her and Elle, and we were Dani's support system when her mom was horrible. If *I* got in the way of that, I'd never forgive myself. Maybe it was easier to keep it fake, so that way, she'd always have Elle and I. God this was hard. The last thing I wanted was for Dani to hurt in any way. I wanted her happy, all the time, no matter what, but was *I* the right person for her, or would I make it worse?

I couldn't figure this out. I had to think more. Make a decision later.

Right now? I had to get Cal's gift ready.

"Broooo." Jenkins hollered at the calendar of his faces. He was known for having a different expression for every occasion, and Ty had gotten him a custom calendar for his present. The guys laughed as Jenkins went through each month, and I couldn't help but enjoy it. It was creative. It was between passing out the Secret Santa gifts that I found my moment with Ty.

We stood off to the side, arranging the gifts to be passed out when I gathered my courage. He handed me a gift bag and I caught his attention. "Hey," I said, my throat thick. "You have a minute?"

"Sure." He smiled, rocked on his heels, and looked relaxed. The complete opposite of how I felt. "What's up?"

"I've gone back and forth on how to approach this with you." I gulped. "Up front is the best. Direct."

"Van, what is it?"

"It's your partying." I gripped the back of my neck, my insides twisting. What if he punched me? Got pissed? Hated me and made the drinking even worse? "We all party and have fun, but I'm concerned you're doing it too much in the season."

He frowned. "What?"

"You hit the drinks hard, like four times a week. It's making you slower on the ice, and you're not hitting your normal amount of shots. I looked at the stats. You're off from last year." God, this sucked. But I took a deep breath. "I know it's the holidays, but as your captain, I need you to rethink what's important to you. I'm all for a good time, you know me, but some our losses could've been wins if you'd played better."

His jaw tightened, his eyes darkening. I lifted up a hand, holding his gaze. My stomach rumbled with anxiety, but I had to keep talking. "Look, I'm not accusing you of anything. I'm saying something as your captain. If you want to talk about it, we can, and if not, that's fine too. But I expect you to play better. We have freshmen who are hungry for time on the ice."

"I fucking know that." Ty grimaced and looked around. "It's been a tough semester. I might be going hard, but it's not an issue, you know?"

"Didn't say you had a drinking problem. It's an issue on the ice." I put a hand on his shoulder, hoping he couldn't feel how it trembled. This sucked. Confronting him, being honest, speaking out. "Let's enjoy the party, but I'm gonna check in with you again after the holidays."

He nodded, the line between his brows deep and worrying. I couldn't focus on that. I patted him on the back and took a second to catch my breath. Christopher was next. Might as well piss everyone off before I left for a few days.

The timing was actually perfect, since it gave them a few days to deal with their emotions and reactions to me. "Christopher, could you help me get something from my car?" I'd left Coach's gifts there with the intention of having him or Ty come with me It isolated us from the team.

"Sure, Van." He had light blond hair and tried to grow a mustache and beard every year, but it never came in fully. The guy wore a knitted sweater with a Furby on it. It was weird as shit, but he was a quirky fucker.

We went through the front door of Coach's house, and the cold wind hit my face. The cold reminded me of Daniella, her love for it, and it gave me courage. I waited for the door to shut and faced him. "I have an ulterior motive here. I wanted to talk to you privately about something."

His face got all splotchy and red, and he ran a hand over his half-grown beard. "Fuck. Is it obvious?"

I chewed my lip. I could straight out say it, but curiosity got the best of me. "What do you mean?"

His eye twitched. "Uh, you first."

"Fine." I sighed, thinking about how much this was needed. "Are you using supplements you shouldn't? You've gained muscle and weight faster than you should've. We get tested randomly, dude, and if you're caught?"

He swallowed. "I haven't been caught yet."

"Is it worth it for you?" I fired back. Anger rushed through my veins at his carelessness, his callousness. "Cause you'll lose your spot. The guys will be pissed. You're one of our best defenders, and you don't need supplements, man."

His jaw tensed, and his eyes darkened. "There's no proof. Why are you doing this? Here of all places?"

"Because it's time I spoke up. This'll give you a few days to think about it. You could be tested next, and Coach could decide to test us anytime. Don't be that guy." I shook my head, ready to shoulder his anger. He could be pissed. If this altered his behavior, then it was worth it.

I walked to my car and grabbed the gifts for the coaches. He followed, his face paler than before, and I caught his gaze. "I should've talked to you sooner, but I was scared. Not anymore. I'm gonna be a lot more annoying as a captain. And if you're worried, this is between you and me."

He nodded, his lips pressed together in a firm line. "You're already annoying."

I barked out a laugh. That was a good sign.

We headed back into the house, and I watched him join the guys. He was stiff for a bit before he relaxed. Ty, too, was back to his normal self. Our dynamic might be awkward for a minute, but it was time I spoke up. Look at Cal. All it took was tough love and he was trying. It was weird, how I spent so much time worrying and anticipating the worst thing to happen when after said and done, things were okay. Cal and I had our words, and he got better. I'd waited too long, I knew that, and regret would live with me for a while. If I'd spoken up earlier, maybe we'd have more wins this year.

I chewed my bottom lip, proud that I finally said what I needed to say to Ty and Christopher, but wishing I did sooner. If Christopher had gotten caught with steroids, and I did nothing, I'd never forgive myself. Or if Ty drove drunk or did something to injure themselves drunk, I'd be pissed. This way, they knew they had support with me.

How wild that I spent more time agonizing over speaking up than just doing it. I could've avoided all the stomach cramps if I just did the damn thing. Made me think about what else I could stop avoiding out of fear.

I got Cal and handed him the bags.

Coach and Reiner chuckled as it was passed to them. We had two gifts left to give before the party started. Coaches would leave, and we'd drink, fuck around, and talk about life. It was a tradition, but the addition of the gifts was a nice touch. Cal didn't say much, kept to himself most of the night, but I swore I saw him smile twice.

Plus, he got Preston a Squatty Potty which was funny as fuck.

"Who's next?"

"Our Golden Boy, Cal." I stood up and clapped my hands. I tossed him a gift, and he caught it. "Merry Christmas, bro."

He eyed the poorly-wrapped box with skepticism, which he should, but then he tore it open slowly. The dude looked like he hadn't had a gift in years from how straight he sat. It made me sad to see his expression, like he didn't have all the family gifts and parties like we did back home. He tossed the paper to the floor and held the book and T-shirt I got him. The shirt said *I like hockey and three people*. The book was *The Subtle Art of Not Giving a F*ck*. Pretty on-brand with his personality if I didn't say so myself.

"Whatya think?" I walked up to him and put a hand on his shoulder. His silence wasn't really helpful in determining if he liked it or not. "From me to you."

"Thanks." He stood and held out a hand, like a bro-shake, but I took my shot and hugged him. It was awkward as hell, but he patted my back before pushing me off. "Enough."

"It's from my heart to yours, truly."

"The shirt should say two."

"Meaning?"

"I like hockey and two people."

I laughed, and the chatter picked up around the room. He'd never say it, but I was pretty sure Cal enjoyed the humor of my gifts. It made me super happy to see him trying. He held onto them instead of setting them on the ground, which kinda warmed me to him. He never talked about his family, friends, or girlfriend. He'd been seen with women, sure. He was drafted, and puck bunnies would sleep with the biggest asshole to get clout, but actually having someone close to him? I wasn't quite sure.

I really did hope he liked the silly gifts.

"Okay, our coach gifts." I clapped my hands, and Cal looked to me. We were in charge of collecting money and getting them. He should hand the presents off. Not me. I respected both Coach Simpson and Coach Reiner, but Cal needed to build his leadership for next season. "Cal came up with the whole thing."

"Really?" Coach Simpson said, narrowing his eyes at Cal. "Interesting."

"Yeah, hard agree. What did you do, Holt?" Reiner eyed the small packages for each coach, and Cal awkwardly tossed them to each of them.

"Merry Christmas." Cal shoved his hand in his pocket, my gifts still in his other hand, and he rocked back on his heels. He looked nervous, and when he met my gaze, I nodded.

They opened the envelopes at the same time, and Reiner let out a whoop. "Hells yeah. Two VIP tickets to a Blackhawks game? And a donation to the hockey rink? Guys, this is sick."

"Wow." Coach Simpson nodded a few times and smiled. "Thank you all so much. You did not have to do this, but damn, appreciated."

"You're always going on about the team, so might as well send you to a game on us." Cal's tone could use some work, but the meaning was clear. All the guys looked back and forth between Cal and me, and I could tell the moment they let their guard down a little around him.

"Great idea, man." Jenkins came up and put an arm on Cal's shoulder. "I would've gotten a stupid mug or something."

"I don't need any more crap," Coach barked.

"You do talk about having too much shit in your office, sir. Another mug would've been a terrible idea." Reiner laughed and hugged Cal. "Thank you."

The two of them had a unique bond, one I hadn't tried to understand before, but I was glad Cal had him. I was curious if his comment about liking two people meant Reiner was one of them. It didn't matter though. I was grateful Cal had Reiner.

Seeing all the gifts and the team tossing wrapping paper around, it reminded me I still had to get Dani a gift for the holidays. It was sad that I had never bought a gift for a girl before—one I wasn't related to. All my flings ended before a holiday because those were big no-nos. People presumed you were attached if you were together in December or February. I'd avoided holidays at all costs, but now? What did I get Dani to tell her how much I cared for her?

She liked the flowers, but those had been for her big night. *God.* That night had been incredible. I replayed it over and over because everything about it was top-notch. Her dress, her hair, the speech, the way we made love after. I knew her body head to toe now and loved every inch of it.

A spa day? No, her mom sent her to those all the time to get *ready.*

Oh. I knew it.

The perfect gift idea for her.

I quickly looked at the times the drive-in theater had films on Sunday, and sure, it'd be an hour drive there, but it was supposed to snow. I needed the universe to work with me here, but a huge grin broke out on my face. She'd love it.

"You look beautiful, Mrs. Laughlin." I leaned into the half-hug, tensing when she lingered on my biceps. It was Sunday, and after two tough wins, I was home for five days before I had to go back. "Thank you for letting me steal Daniella on Christmas Eve."

"No matter, Gabriel. You are so handsome." She fixed the collar of my black coat and smiled at me. "You are such a wonderful young man. Daniella is lucky to have you, especially since you've known her since she was in that horrible kid age. The acne, the braces, the no figure. She's past that now."

"Jesus, Mom." Dani came down the stairs wearing tall fuzzy boots, leggings, a green coat that went to her knees, and earmuffs. Her hair was in two long braids and her makeup minimal, but it was her smile that had me weak in the knees.

Relief. She was relieved and happy to see me. My gut told me it was because I was saving her from her mom, but I ignored it. Her eyes lit up. My ribcage got all tight, like I'd bruised it or something, and I rubbed it for a second.

"Hey, baby." I grinned hard. I hadn't seen her in person in three days, and I missed her energy. "Get over here."

She scrunched her nose in a smile and almost ran to my arms. She hugged me, and I kissed the top of her head.

"You smell so good." She inhaled loudly, making me laugh.

"Daniella," her mother scolded. "Manners."

"I can sniff my boyfriend, Mom." She pulled back and rolled her eyes. "Let's get away from here."

"Are you wearing what I laid out?"

"No, because I'm a twenty-year-old adult who can dress herself, thank you very fucking much." Daniella looped her arm through mine and met my gaze. "Where are we going?"

"Daniella, you cannot talk to me like that."

"She's an adult, let her enjoy herself." Her dad came into the hallway, his cheeks reddened and a glass of whiskey in one hand. "She's fine, Lily."

"But did you—"

"Have fun and be safe." Her dad jutted his chin toward the door. "Go on."

I didn't wait another minute before guiding us out of the door and to my car. Of course, I opened the passenger side door and let her in before going to my side. I loved watching how she blushed and acted like it was the most romantic thing ever to hold doors. It wasn't, but it was good manners, and my mom made sure I had those.

Once I got to my side, I slid over and cupped her face. "Give me that mouth."

She kissed me hungrily, her soft lips meeting mine in a frenzy. Three days. I hadn't seen her in three days, and starving wasn't an accurate description of how I felt for her.

"Someone's horny," she said between kissing me. She slid her tongue in my mouth and ran her fingers over my hair.

The sensation of her touch and minty taste gave me chills. The burning behind my ribcage grew, and I had to correct her. Horny wasn't right. That demeaned it. I stopped kissing her to lean back and meet her eyes. "Horny has nothing to do with it. I'm glad to see you."

"I bet you're happy, eh?" She wiggled her brows and pointed to my crotch. "Got a bone in there?"

"Daniella," I snapped, annoyed she was teasing me when my words felt so profound and meaningful…to me at least. She frowned at my tone, and I shook my head, pulling myself together. "Sorry I'm being uptight. Just anxious to get back to you and make sure you're okay."

"Yeah, I'm alright." She placed her hands on mine, her expression softening. "I'm glad to see you too."

I relaxed from her touch and let out a long breath. Being a dick was not the move, but I couldn't let her think my happiness of seeing her was just about sex for me. It wasn't at all." I have your Christmas gift night all planned out."

"Eeek! I can't wait. I've never had a gift night before."

"I've never planned one before." Our eyes met, a mutual understanding that this was new for both of us. My stomach did the little dip thing where I forgot where I was and could only see her, so I coughed just to refocus.

The theatre.

"You need to put this on." I handed her a tie.

"It clashes with my coat, but I'll wear it."

"No, as a blindfold. It's part of the allure, I swear." I handed her the tie and watched as she covered her eyes without questioning me. A part of me wanted her to remain like that so I could tease her endlessly.

Fuck, maybe I was a little horny because the thought of blindfolding her in the bedroom was a great idea. The best.

"Is this kinky? I'm down either way, but I need to know."

"No, nothing like that *yet*. I have something else planned and want you to be surprised. Now, don't cheat, please."

"I won't, Gabe. Not when you've put so much thought into this. I can't wait. Now, tell me about the games and Cal. And the talk with the guys!"

I caught her up on basically everything I hadn't already shared with her about the holiday dinner. Plus, we'd won both games so everyone had left for a quick break home in high spirits. She went through everything she and Elle did while I wasn't there and then listed all the reasons she was pissed at her mom. So, our usual chatter. And by the time I pulled up into the drive-in theatre, a light dusting had started.

A fucking miracle.

"Okay, Dani, we're here." I was fucking excited. They were showing White Christmas, and I'd already bought the tickets. There were blankets and snacks and drinks in the backseat hidden with a sheet and a small box with the gift I got her. Nerves took root, and my hands shook as I reached up to undo the tie. "Merry Christmas."

She kept her eyes closed even after the tie was off. Her lips were turned up in a smile, and I had to ask. "What are you doing?"

"Savoring this moment with you. I can almost hear your nerves. You planned an entire night for me, blindfolded me for a surprise, and no one has ever done this before. I'm so happy, and I want to remember this."

My heart about burst in my chest, and I had to kiss her. She kissed me back but then gasped. "Oh, Van. A drive-in?" Her voice got all high, and she looked at me like I'd hung the moon. "White Christmas?"

I nodded, overcome with pride at how happy she was. "I figured you'd like it, and look outside."

"IT'S SNOWING!" She squealed and threw herself over the console and onto my lap. "This is the best date of all time. Oh my god, Van." She kissed my cheeks, mouth, chin, forehead, all while squealing. "Thank you, thank you!"

Date. She said *date*. The word normally would've freaked me out, but it felt different with her. Right. Like, maybe, us dating wasn't the wildest idea in the world.

Her joy was the best thing. My body hummed from pride and joy at seeing her so damn happy. I did that for her. I put that manic smile on her face and fuck, I loved this feeling. I wanted to make her smile again and again.

"You're welcome, baby." I cupped her face, stilling her, and studied every freckle on her face. I knew them by heart, and when I kissed her this time, she trembled. I couldn't quite describe the need I had for her, the way I wanted to keep doing this and be with her. That she was the first thing I thought about the second I woke up.

It was about timing though. After the movie and present, then I'd ask.

It was the perfect plan.

CHAPTER
TWENTY-FIVE

Daniella

My leg ached from the angle, but you'd have to kill me to make me move from my spot on Van's lap. His arms were around me, resting on my waist. His chin on my shoulder. My back pressed to his chest. The radio playing the audio of the movie and our snacks in the passenger seat, already eaten. Snow fell softly all around us, and my heart pulled a Grinch and grew a million sizes.

How could I say goodbye to this? To our cuddles and jokes and our movie dates and kisses? Fuck. It was like the time Timmy punched me in the stomach in sixth grade, only somehow worse. That had healed fast, and I'd gotten a lot of attention from everyone. Even my mom was nice back then, but that was before puberty hit, so she didn't know how I'd really turn out. But this? This wouldn't heal.

I exhaled, and Van kissed my temple. I savored the feel of his lips on me and snuggled deeper. At this point, my leg had fallen asleep, but I didn't care. The movie got to the last scene with everyone watching the performance, and I just swooned. For a guy who'd never had a girlfriend and only had flings, this was perfection. Despite Elle's consistent warnings to protect my heart, it was too late, and I knew it would be the hardest thing to get over. Even though… secretly, a part of me wondered if Van wanted it to be real too.

You didn't plan this romantic of a night unless you had feelings for someone. It had to be truth. There was no one around, so it wasn't for show, and if we were fooling my mom, we could've just gone to his house, and I could've hung out with Elle. This was intentional, which had to mean *something*.

Despite seeing the movie so many times, my eyes misted when it finished, and Van hugged me tighter. He was so warm and cuddly and supportive. I leaned back into him, taking a chance. My palms sweated, and my heart beat erratically, to the point my body ached with each pulse. I could be bold and do this. Speak my truth and my goal. Like how I'd replied to my mom. Standing up for what I wanted was scary, but there was no way I'd get through life without doing it more. I squeezed his hands and said, "I don't want us to end."

He sighed and kissed my neck, a long thirty seconds of silence greeting me before he said, "I know, this is the best date night I've ever been on. It's not over yet though. Plus, you don't have a curfew, right? We could stay out as late as you'd like."

Right. My face flamed red at his misunderstanding. I never mentioned the date. If he was being obtuse, that'd be one thing, but if he intentionally made it about the movie, that was a rejection.

My eyes stung even more and thank god for the film. I scooted back to the passenger seat, picking up the wrappers and shoving them into an old to-go cup. "I'm throwing these out, be right back."

I didn't wait for an answer before opening the door and welcoming the cold night air on my skin. It cooled me down, letting me pull myself together because Van knew me too well. He'd know something was off, and I didn't want to explain it. I sniffed, closed my eyes, and inhaled the brisk, wintery scent of cement, exhaust, and dirt. It was hard to explain, but the smell of winter was one of my favorites.

The garbage can was a foot away, and I couldn't delay any longer. I'd said what I wanted, and Van hadn't responded in a similar way. That was a fact. It was unknown if he'd intentionally avoided it or not, but that left me with two choices: enjoy the night and let it go, sticking to the plan of breaking up in a week or two, or say it again and let him shatter me a second time.

Both options weren't ideal.

"Staring at all the sexy snow?" he asked, standing outside his door with worry lines on his face. "Taking you a minute."

"Sorry. Yeah, it was the snow." I turned my back to him and wiped under my eyes. No mascara came off, so I was good. I tossed the trash and rolled my shoulders back before facing him. Neither of us said anything as the wind blew snow around us. He looked so beautiful with the streetlights enhancing his features. My stomach tightened with how much I loved him, and unless I said something, he might never know.

My phone buzzed in my pocket, but I didn't bother looking. We were in a stare down, having a moment. I opened my mouth up to say something, but he beat me to it.

"Let's keep this up."

"Me and you?"

Ohmygodyesplease

"Yeah." He smiled, his dimples popping out, and my insides went wild. This was what I wanted. Oh my god. He felt something too. I knew it. My lips curved into a smile, and my heart screamed *yes, omg*. He was into me! It wasn't all fake, and I didn't have to let him go. I could live out my fantasy, in real life. Kiss him when I wanted. This was amazing. I took a step closer, ignoring another buzz.

"We keep *fake* dating?" I asked, needing him to clarify that it wasn't fake and this was real and we could legit be together.

"Yes." His smile grew wider. "Until Valentine's Day passes,

you know? We're having so much fun, and that way I won't be single leading up to the biggest couple holiday of the year. Every year I get all these damn invitations, and having a girlfriend would save my ass. What do you say, Dani? We could figure out a breakup whenever. More sleepovers and movie dates and—hey, what's wrong?"

"Oh." I sniffed, disappointment numbing me to the point I cried. I went from feeling elated to heartbroken in two seconds. This wasn't him confessing feelings. This was him prolonging the ruse, only to continue with the plan to end it later. He didn't want it to be real due to feelings for me, like I had for him.

We both could admit it was fun and we enjoyed each other, but more fake dating? No. I couldn't do it. It'd hurt even more, and I already felt like sinking into the pothole-filled asphalt and sobbing for a week.

"Why are you crying?" His voice was laced with concern, and he jumped around the car to come to me. "What did I say?"

"Oh, it's uh, the movie." I sniffed and pointed my thumb over my shoulder as my phone buzzed again. "Hang on, someone keeps calling me."

Dad: four missed calls.

My stomach dropped in an entirely different way. "Fuck. My dad called four times."

"Call him back."

I did, and he answered on the first ring. "What's wrong?"

"It's your mom. She's headed to the ER. She fell and hit her head, and I need you with me, Daniella." His voice cracked, and my entire body went on high alert.

"Yes, okay, I'll head there now. Do you need anything at home?"

"I don't know yet, just come to the ER, please. She wasn't moving, and her head was bleeding, and she was nonresponsive." His urgent, terrified tone gutted me. Felt like knives slowly sinking in between my ribs.

"Dad, are you driving there?"

"I have to."

"Call Elle or the Van Helsings. Do *not* go alone." I pleaded with Van, but he heard everything. He ushered me to the car, fast, and started it within ten seconds. We were on the road when my dad started crying. "Dad, please. You're in no state."

"Okay, you're right."

"I'm texting Elle, hold on."

I typed furiously, and she responded with in ten seconds. *On my way.* "She'll be there in two minutes. Grab a phone charger and a snack. Van and I will be there in an hour."

"I can't lose her. I know she's... you're... I love her."

"I know." I squeezed my eyes shut, my own conflicting battle raging inside my head. I could love my mom and want her healthy while also hating how she spoke to me and made me feel. It made me sick to my stomach. "Stay strong. Cry if you need to. Call me if you hear anything."

"I love you, Daniella. Tell Van to drive safely."

I hung up, and my body buzzed with adrenaline. Emergency rooms could last hours, but if she arrived by ambulance, they'd give her a room faster. Action. I needed action. "We should stop by the house, get stuff for them."

"Let's head there first and see what they need, alright?"

"But how will I get back?" My voice broke, and he reached over and laced our fingers together.

"I'm staying with you."

"Oh no, you don't have to do that."

"I'm staying with you." He squeezed my fingers. "We'll check in with your dad and make a plan afterward, okay?"

"Okay, yeah." I panted, the severity of the situation hitting me. "She was bleeding, nonresponsive. Fuck, what if... no, I can't do that. Don't let me go through what if scenarios. It'll kill me." I chewed the shit out of my nails, biting down to do something with this energy.

"She's getting the care she needs. It's completely out of your control. I find comfort in that because no matter what you do or say, it doesn't matter."

"That's… true but doesn't make me feel better."

"What would?"

"I don't know, Van." My knee shook, the adrenaline needing an escape path because I wanted to run. Nowhere in particular, but the nervous, frantic energy coursed through me to the point it hurt. I hated feeling helpless, and that was where I was. Away, unable to help. But then a small part of me felt *nothing*. How horrible was that? I'd stopped liking my mom as a person a while ago, but she was still my mom? My thoughts battled on what I should be feeling, wrong and wrong. I tapped my fingers against the side of the door, then that annoyed me.

I tried focusing on dance routines, but that didn't work. I thought I was gonna throw up or lose my mind. The car was too hot. Too small. Too *much*.

"Distract me."

"*White Christmas* isn't that good of movie. I kept my mouth shut because it mattered to you, but it's kinda boring."

"No it's not. It's awesome and has such a good story of friendship and love, and—" I paused, watching his lip quirk up on the side. "You're lying."

"Nope. I hate it."

The rest of the drive went like that, Van saying things that were completely false to get me riled up and ready to defend my opinions to death. It worked in distracting me from the crisis at home. He must've taken his time getting to the drive-in because soon enough, we pulled into the hospital parking lot.

"My dad texted that she's admitted but he doesn't have a status yet." I eyed my phone, and a wave of gratitude washed over me. Going through those doors alone, being a support for my dad and dealing with my internal struggle about my mom would've been brutal. I grabbed his forearm and squeezed. "I'm so glad you're here with me."

"Me too, Dani." Our eyes held for a beat before we both got

out of the car and ran toward the automatic doors. There weren't more than ten people sitting in chairs, and we walked up to the triage nurses. "Lily Laughlin? I'm here to see my mom."

"Follow me." The nurse with long white hair took us back and through a narrow hallway. Cries and groans carried through the curtains, and Van must've read my mind. He held me hand, giving me the support I needed.

"Right here." The nurse pulled back a curtain, and my dad sat on a chair, his head in his hands. My heart broke for him. He might've catered to my mom's neglect and hurtful words to me, but he was my dad. The guy who snuck me snacks and drinks behind my mom's back. The guy who taught me how to drive and let me play in the mud. No one was perfect, I knew that, and right now, I wanted to hug him and never let go.

"Dad, I'm here."

"Daniella." He stood up and pulled me into a bear hug. He smelled like whiskey and laundry. "They're scanning her right now."

"Good, they'll make sure she's okay and figure out what to do." I patted his back and made a small circle on it. "We're in the right space."

"What a terrible Christmas Eve, huh?" He sniffed and held out a hand to Van. "Thank you for getting her here safely."

"Of course, sir." He nodded and met my gaze. The room was small, and there was only one chair, and he sighed. "I'll let you two talk for a bit. Elle texted me she's still around. I'm gonna find her, then we can come up with a plan?"

"Sure, yes." My eyes watered, and I wanted to hug him, have him hold me so I could bury my face in his chest. Even if his comment about Valentine's Day had gutted me, he was still mine for a little bit longer. "Thank you."

His eyes warmed, and he gave me my favorite half-smile before leaving the room. I hated that he had to go, but it was the right move with my dad here. My dad sat back down, and I leaned against the wall, my stomach an absolute mess. Knots upon knots formed, and I almost whimpered in relief when a guy in scrubs came toward us.

"Family of Lily Laughlin?"

"Yes, I'm her husband, and this is her daughter. Is she okay?"

"She's awake and seems aware of where she is. We're just finishing the scans to make sure there's no internal damage." He gave us a reassuring smile. "Despite the blood and scare, my gut is telling me it's a nasty concussion and cut. We need the results to confirm this, but she'll be back here soon, and the results should take an hour."

"Will she get to go home tonight?" my dad asked.

"Depending on the results, but my guess is yes. She's stitched up and already asking questions."

"Thank god." My dad sank further into the chair, his relief tangible. I felt it too. That it wasn't life or death.

"Thank you, Doctor."

"Hang tight, she'll be back here soon."

He closed the curtain, and my dad smiled. "Just a cut and a concussion. Those aren't bad."

"Could definitely be worse, that's for sure." I, too, regained feeling in my limbs with the news that she'd be okay. "This is good, Dad."

"Yes. Yes." He stood up and squeezed my shoulder. "I haven't peed since we came because I was too afraid to miss an update. I'm going. Stay here in case she comes back, okay?"

I agreed because what else would I do? Sure, I wasn't certain I was the first person she'd want to see, but at least she was safe. Stable. Alive. My hands shook as I texted Van and Elle a quick update, but the rocky sounds of a wheelchair caught my attention.

"Alright, Ms. Laughlin, hang out in here until we get the official results." A nurse pushed her into the room, her eyes landing on me, and she sucked in a breath. She wore a loose cashmere sweater, her favorite red leather pants seeming too much for a wheelchair. Her face was paler, void of her lipstick. Her eyes were red, like she was crying or in pain, and she held an ice pack against her head. She looked exhausted and awful. Nothing like the picture-perfect woman I was used to.

"Daniella."

"I'm glad you're okay, Mom." My voice shook, and my heart thundered against my ribcage.

She studied me and frowned when she got to my puffy boots. "Where's Gabriel. Did he bring you here? I thought you were on a date, but if you're wearing those, I'm not sure."

And, pop. There went the momentary relief. Irritation flared, and this was it. Injured or not, my filter was gone. I could care for her and want her well, but the time for her bullshit comments was done. I snapped.

After twenty years, it took Christmas Eve at the hospital for me to stand up to her.

CHAPTER
TWENTY-SIX

Gabriel

What a fucking mess. I rubbed my eyes with my palms once I saw Elle in the corner of the emergency waiting room. She was watching some Youtuber and sat up straighter when I found her. "Hey."

"Dude." She shook her head and tucked her knees to her chest. Her face was red, and she looked worried. It made me want to fix everything for her, but I couldn't. Not this. It tore me up.

"You alright?"

"That was stressful as hell. He's not in a good place." She shivered. "Cried and went on about he wasn't sure what to do. I let him talk and focused on the road, but fuck, think she'll be okay?"

"I hope so." I sat next to her, absolutely gutted for Dani and her dad. I couldn't help but wonder what our family would be doing if it was our mom. Just thinking about her going in an ambulance had my stomach tightening with dread. Cringing, I forced those thoughts from my mind. "How long you planning to stay?"

"Don't know, honestly. It's weird. I've known Mr. and Mrs. Laughlin my entire life, and they should *feel* like family, but they don't? Like, Dani would be fine in the car with our parents and not at all awkward. She loves them like we do, but her parents?"

"It's a shitty situation." I leaned back in the chair and crossed one leg over the other, my foot bouncing on the tiled floor. Elle and I hadn't been alone since I'd realized I wanted to prolong my time with Dani. God, seeing her cry was the worst I'd ever felt. I'd take fucking up a hockey game over seeing her tears. Her blue eyes filled with moisture, and her face got all red, but it was the sadness, the lack of joy in her expression that stuck with me. I only wanted to give her smiles, never tears. It surely wasn't the time or place, but I had to get it off my chest. "Can I talk to you about Dani?"

She set her phone down and gave me her full attention. "What about her?"

Damn. I never realized my sister had that intense of a look. My nerves prickled at her tone and narrowed eyes, but I powered through. "Well, I'm thinking about prolonging the relationship."

"Fake relationship you mean?" she said, something flashing across her face. "Because it's all staged to help her stick it to her mom, right?"

"Yes. Fake relationship." I swallowed down the guilt and ache in my throat at considering what I felt for Daniella fake in any way. "Just until February."

"Why?"

Because I want to be with her all the time and am not ready to let her go.

"Figured her mom would be on her about a date for Valentine's Day, and plus, it's been nice getting girls to back off since I haven't been single."

"You don't need Dani to be your backup person. Grow some, man. Tell people no and mean it." She shook her head, her eyes scrunching on the sides. "I thought you were going to say you love her."

"Love her?" Alarm bells pinged in my head, my instinct to deny it making me say, "Oh no, no. Like, of course. She's been in our life forever. I care for her deeply, but love?"

Elle raised her eyebrows and waited.

Did I love Daniella? I preferred my life uncomplicated. It was why I waited so long to confront Cal and Ty. It was why the team dynamic was off for half a season because I hated drama. Keeping relationships at a distance was easier, less messy. It was what I'd done my whole life. But seeing Elle's face full of irritation, my gut twisted. I had feelings for Daniella, I knew that, but how deep? Continuing to fake date meant there was an out if it got messy, but I *wanted* messy with her.

I'd never been in love before. My chest ached, and I thought about the tears in her eyes before she got the call. She looked devastated and blamed the movie, but watching her cry felt like she stabbed me. The way she looked at me in the room with her dad, like I was her lifeline, I loved it. I wanted to be that for her every day, fake or not, but she was always talking about the deadline. *Two more weeks* or *five days left* or *how do we break up?*

Hell, I'd asked to prolong it, and she never answered. If anything, it seemed the idea was terrible to her. And it wasn't like I could just ask her via text. Even tomorrow, I couldn't bring it up. She needed to worry about her family right now, not me. I chewed my lip at the uncomfortable feeling growing inside me. It was unsettling and weird, and I shook my head, annoyed at myself. "I really care for her, Elle."

That was the truth. I did. I could create a million excuses, but I liked her. More than liked her. I thought about her every second we weren't together and got sick imagining *not* being with her. I smiled into my hand. "Yeah, I like her a lot."

"Hm."

That syllable was laced with disappointment, and I hated seeing Elle look at me like that, all sad and disgusted. Did she not *want* me to have feelings for her best friend? "Why do you seem irritated?"

"I'm not."

"Elle. Come on."

"I'm not mad." She stared at me again with wide eyes. "I think you're fooling yourself and being typical Gabe."

"What does *that* mean?"

"Afraid to do something. Stand up for something. Fight for what you want. Growing up behind you meant I watched and learned. You always prefer the easy way out or the path of least resistance. Even being a captain on the ice, you lead but don't take charge. People are going to disagree with you, and you need to be okay with it."

"Whoa." I swallowed her words, digesting them as my muscles tensed. "Did I piss you off or something?"

"Not at all. I wish you'd take a damn stand, that's all."

"So, you think I love Dani?"

"Yes, I do." She smiled for a second and laughed. "In some twisted way, it makes sense that you two belong together. I never thought... I'd ever be okay with the two of you, but I am."

"You want me to love and date Dani?"

"I'm not pushing you, but I'm saying if you're not admitting your feelings because you're worried about how I'll take it, don't. If she is who you want, really want, then 'll be thrilled for you and her. But that's the question you need to figure out."

It'd be different to have it out in the open for real. But then again, everyone except Elle and Cami thought it already was legit, so was that a bullshit excuse I created out of fear? Elle's words replayed in my head *afraid to take a stand*. Daniella said something similar to that about me being a captain.

I was twenty-two years old and afraid of rocking the boat. How fucking sad. I should fight for things I want instead of being a passive bystander. Look at what happened with the team? I built up how bad it would be for weeks instead of just doing it. What if I missed my shot with her? What if Christopher got busted for steroids and I kept quiet the entire time? Doing *nothing* was not how I wanted to live.

I had feelings for Daniella—now I needed to decide what to do about it.

Why was I having these existential thoughts at the ER when I should be focused on seeing what Dani and her family needed? I could talk to her later when this was done. We'd figure it out together. Maybe she had feelings for me too. She used to, so there was a solid chance they'd never went away... hopefully.

"Hey, is this their charger?" I pointed to a white cord on the floor.

"Shit. Yeah."

"I'll bring it back to them."

"Thanks. Hey, Dani texted us. They think a concussion and stitches but are waiting on the brain scan to make sure there wasn't internal bleeding." Elle sighed and let her feet fall noisily on the chair. "Thank god."

My breath came out a little easier with the news, mainly for how Dani must be feeling. She'd been so scared in the car. God, I wanted to fight her battles for her but was helpless. The slight trembling of her lip, the way she'd checked her phone every second. I'd never wanted to do more to make her smile. "Be right back."

I nodded in greeting to the triage nurse and held up the cord. "Dropping this off."

She didn't care at all. I traced the same path toward the room where Lily was and stilled at hearing Dani's voice.

"Enough."

"What?" *Shit, that was her mom.*

I froze, each limb on my body turning to ice at the situation because I knew Dani's tone. It was her 'I'm sick of your shit voice.' I'd heard her use it when bitching about her mom to me, safely back at school, but this was now. My fingers tightened around the cord, and I was about to step back when I heard my name.

"Don't comment on what I'm wearing. It doesn't matter what I choose to wear if I'm at home, out with Van, or Elle, or on the team. Stop trying to turn me into someone I'm not. I'm sick of it. I'm fucking sick of it."

"Daniella, your tone."

"I left the best date of my life to get here, to see you and make sure Dad was okay, and the first thing you say is about my outfit choice?"

"Gabriel is a fine man. He needs someone to suit him."

"We're not even dating, Mom. How fucked up is that?"

"Language." Lily stuttered, her gasp audible. "What do you mean *not* dating?"

"Because of you. I want this to be very clear—your comments for years hurt me, belittled me, made me not like you. I was sick of you trying to set me up and change my clothes and insist I wasn't enough because I didn't have on makeup. We faked dating so you'd get off my back."

"Pretended? So, he's not with you really?"

"Oh my god. That's what you're hearing? Yes. He's *not* with me. A guy like him wouldn't fall for a girl like me, right? You've said it a million times. I'm not curvy enough or pretty enough, and I don't wear the right clothes to match my skin hues. Well, I'm not a beauty queen like you, Mom. I never will be. I like wearing baggy shirts and toe socks. And the people who love me? They don't give a shit either."

A guy like him wouldn't fall for a girl like me. Oh god, Dani. Hearing her say those words were like gut punch. Did she really think that? Did I not do enough to show her how much I loved…yes, *loved* her? It took all my strength to not barge in there and yell at her mom. I'd fight any one of Dani's battles, and right then, I knew what I wanted: to be right by her side all the time.

"Daniella, what... I... it was out of love," her mom continued.

"Making me feel like shit was out of love? Oh, this sounds great." A chair leg scraped the floor, and a thud echoed in the hall. I snapped back to reality. I shouldn't be listening to this. Not at all. It was horrible to witness it even though Lily deserved everything Dani said. Maybe even more.

"I wanted for you to have what your dad and I have. That's all."

"By changing parts of me that I happen to like about myself."

"So, Gabriel really isn't into you?"

"No. It was pretend. Fake. We planned to break up after New Year's, but thanks to this riveting conversation, we don't have to keep it up anymore because I'm done with your shit. Did you know I have an apartment leased in May so I don't have to come home anymore?"

"Dani—"

"No. Look, I am so sorry this happened right now. You need to focus on getting better, and I am so glad you're okay. Truly. Because despite all the mental games you put me through, I love you. You're my mom. But I'm done." Footsteps shuffled, and fuck.

I tripped over my own feet as Daniella stormed out of the small room. Her eyes were blazing with emotions: anger, sadness, resentment. "I'm—"

"I'm going for a walk." She brushed by me, and I knew her anger wasn't directed at me, but it still stung to have her not lean on me like I wanted her to. I could be her person.

"Dani, wait." I caught up to her. "I didn't mean to listen. I was dropping off the charger and—"

"You heard the whole thing? Good. We don't have to pretend to date anymore. Lovely Lily knows it's fake. Ruse is off, so you can go home now. I need air." She shook her head back and forth hard before pushing the double doors and storming through them.

She loved winter and snow and cold air, so I let her go outside, not following her. She wanted space, and I could give her that, but she was a fool if she thought I was leaving her here. Plus, her dad needed a ride home.

I watched her through the window as she sat down on a bench and pulled her knees up to her chest. Her shoulders shook. *Fuck.* It was too cold for her to cry out there. Her tears would freeze.

"What just happened?" Elle stood by me, frowning at Dani's back.

"Dani finally stuck it to her mom."

"Shit. Not the time or place."

"No, but I'm glad she did." I sighed, wishing there was more I could do. "She told her about our fake dating. Then Dani said we were done and that I should *go home.*"

"Hey." She pulled on my sleeve. "She's right."

"What?" I snapped, refusing to leave her. "I'm not abandoning her here. What the fuck?"

"Van," Elle said, softly. A pitying look crossed her face, and she patted my arm. "This is a time for her best friend. Not... the guy unwilling to admit his feelings who asked her to *fake date* for another two months to keep girls away from him. You're the last person she needs to see."

"What are you saying?"

"You're my brother and I love you, but you're an idiot." She closed her eyes and exhaled. "Go home and figure it out."

"Spell it out for me, Eleanor." My temper flared at my sister talking in riddles, and I used her full name. "I'm tired, worried about Dani, and—"

"How do you think she feels? She's heartbroken over her mom, over you, probably feeling guilty as hell."

"Heartbroken?" Her words had me taking a step back. "What? How?"

"She's been in love with you since sixth grade, Van. I tried to warn her to protect her heart, but it was a lost cause. She's always loved you, and she deserves to be loved back. If you're not going to date her *for real*, then please, leave her alone."

She's always loved you. Elle saying it out loud made everything worse. If that were true, then even suggesting *fake dating* would've crushed her. Fuck. I didn't want to add to her heartbreak and hurt. I wanted to make it better, to tell her the truth. That I'd fallen for her too but was too afraid to speak up and admit it. I'd spoken in circles, avoiding big feelings because I was scared. A chicken. "Elle, wait."

"No, my best friend needs me. Go home, Gabe."

And with that, Elle walked outside and put her arm around Dani. Dani leaned onto Elle, her shoulders shaking even more, and I felt gutted. The fact I'd caused even a little bit of her hurt messed with my head, and I had to get out of there. I needed air and space to figure out a plan. I definitely, with absolutely certainty, loved Daniella Laughlin, and I had to get her to believe it.

Because she was wrong. A girl like her—perfectly imperfect, was exactly who I'd fallen for.

CHAPTER
TWENTY-SEVEN

Daniella

I woke up with my arm around a warm body. My first thought was Van, but the smell was different. Lighter. Long blonde hair was in my face, and everything about the night came back to me in aggressive, horrible waves.

The best date of my life.

Van wanting to fake date, not real date more.

The ER.

My mom.

Van hearing my outburst.

The shame.

Elle taking care of me.

I groaned and rolled onto my back, the guilt of what I did eating me alive. What I said to my mom… after her scare…how could I do that? "Fucking shit."

"Remembering last night?" Elle asked, her voice sleepy. She rolled onto her side and stared at me. "You okay?"

"No. I mean, physically yes, but I feel like I could throw up." I pushed off the bed and fanned my face even though it was cold in my room. "My mom…"

Elle nodded, my best friend wearing a look of sympathy. "You were a straight-up dick. Don't get me wrong, she deserved it. I'm glad you finally stood up to her, but—"

"The timing. God." I rubbed my chest over and over, my face getting hotter as I recalled my words. "I have to talk to her."

"Yes, you do." Elle wiped under her eyes. "Your dad too."

"Fuck." My eyes stung, and tears pooled over. Elle got up and hugged me, giving me the support I needed. It was the wrong set of Van Helsing arms, but they did the job. "What do I even say?"

"You apologize. Then listen." She fluffed my hair and winced. "Take a shower first. Put on your more comfortable clothes and then go see them."

"This is gonna suck." I swallowed down the lump in my throat, wishing I could just sneak out the window and never come back. This was hard. Harder than admitting I had major feelings for Gabe. Big ones.

A small voice in my head wanted me to reach out to Gabe, but I couldn't handle two emotional crises at once. I shouldn't have yelled at him to leave, but there was no reason for us to continue anymore. At least, there wasn't any motive on my end. *Shit.* I grabbed yoga pants and a crewneck sweatshirt and forced myself to worry about him later. My family came first, then I could deal with him.

"Want me to stay?"

"It's Christmas. You should head home and enjoy it." My voice shook, and Elle smiled. "What?"

"Your eyes are so pretty when you cry. It's annoying."

"Shut up. Get out."

"I love you." Elle put on her jacket and stuck her hands in her pockets. "Shit. This is for you. Almost forgot."

She put a small box on my bed. Guilt hit me again. "I didn't buy you anything. I thought we said no gifts, just sleepovers and binge sessions."

"It's not from me." She got quiet and pressed her lips together. "I told him I'd leave it for you this morning, okay? If you'd rather I take it, I can."

"No. No." My heart lurched. A present from Van? More than the movie date? My pulse raced, and I itched to open it and see what was inside. "Leave it."

"Mom first, then figure this shit out with Van." She pushed her hair away from her face and tied it in a messy bun. "He's been texting me nonstop about you."

"I said I wanted more, and he wanted to continue to fake-date."

"He's an idiot. I love him, but he's a real ding-dong." Elle patted my shoulders and smiled. "Let me know how the talk with your mom goes, okay?"

I nodded, the dreaded feeling weighing me down. She left me in my room, and I gave myself a few seconds to freak out. My phone buzzed, and I jumped, hoping it was Van, and my gut flip flopped at his name. There was no message, just a video clip.

The one from the awards ceremony.

Then the dots showed up.

Van: Apologizing is a display of strength. Holding your own and standing up for yourself is grit. Admitting mistakes and that you're hurting makes you vulnerable, but it's okay to show that side of yourself.

How in the world did he know I needed to hear those words? To remember how my coach and teammates saw me? That version of me was my best, and it was time I showed my parents who I was, truly was. I set my phone down and showered. I took my time, soaking in the hot water, and put on my comfiest clothes. Then, I steeled my shoulders. My insides twisted as I padded my way toward my parents' bedroom down the hall, pictures of my mom and dad lining the walls. God, they had to hate me.

How selfish and immature was I?

No. I could apologize but not obsess over it. It wouldn't help. I gulped and knocked on their door and waited. Silence greeted me but then I heard hushed whispers. They could disown me or kick me out of the house or say to never see them again. I'd have to deal with it, but I kept my mouth shut as I waited.

Then, my dad cracked the door open. "Merry Christmas, Daniella."

My unshed tears dripped down my cheeks, and I threw myself at him. "I'm so sorry for how I acted. Please understand I feel horrible and want to die inside."

He rubbed my back, laughing and kissing the top of my head. "I know you feel bad, hon."

"Why are you being nice to me?"

"Because we're healthy. It's Christmas, and I have my two girls with me." He kept his hands on my shoulders and smiled. "Last night was emotional and rough for all of us."

"But you didn't lash out and say fuck to your mom."

"No, but you stood up to her." He lowered his voice. "I don't love the setting, but this talk between you two is long overdue."

"You're not mad at me? Or disappointed?"

"None of the above. I love you, as you are, all the time. I'm shit at showing it, and I don't say it a lot, but last night scared the fuck out of me, Daniella. So, I'm not going to shy away from messy feelings anymore."

"Dad." I squeezed him again, half of my heart lightening. We'd always gotten along, and the thought of disappointing him hurt my soul. "I can't believe you said fuck."

"It's a holiday miracle."

I snorted into his chest before he pulled back and a more serious look crossed his face. "I don't know what she'll say. We barely talked about what happened. It'll be hard, but I hope you both get what you need."

I gulped, and he headed down the stairs, leaving me alone

outside their room. The fan was on, and it smelled like her lotion—eucalyptus and mint. With one final breath, I went in.

The lights were off, but she sat up in bed, her gaze trailing me as I walked farther into their room. My feet froze where I stood, right in the middle of the room, and I lifted my arms in a shrug. I didn't regret what I said, just the timing, and this weird, in-between moment battled in my head. Guilt and relief, sad and angry. "How are you feeling?"

"Tired. A headache, but it should clear up in a day or two." She looked so different than normal. No makeup, not put together. The bags under her eyes matched the wrinkles around her mouth, and god, I liked this version of my mom. She was messy. Approachable.

I sat on the end of their bed, picking at a loose string. "I came in to say that I'm really sorry for how I acted last night. There's no excuse for being unkind when you were in pain and in the emergency room. I feel horrible for the timing of what I said, and there aren't enough words to apologize."

She opened and closed her mouth, and I held up a hand. "This is important for me to say, even if it's hard. I meant everything I said. I regret the location and that you weren't doing well, but my feelings? They are true and valid and have been living with me for years." My voice shook, but the truth was out there now. No more hiding.

"Dani," she said, the use of my nickname startling me.

I looked up, and she had a half-smile on her face. "Yeah?"

"I'm sorry too. For so much."

My throat got all tight, and I fought tears. I expected more of a fight, more of her denying what she's done to me. My mom had never apologized, and my first instinct was to not believe her. I waited, pursed my lips, and needed her to extend the peace offering. I apologized for my timing, but it was her turn now. I arched a brow, my insides a fucking mess, when she sighed.

"I'm so sorry." She sniffed. "I never realized how my words

could affect you. I truly thought I was helping you, and to hear how you felt? It really upset me."

The apology felt long overdue. Nerves and guilt still had me in a chokehold, but a sliver of hope ignited. She patted the spot next to her, but I was rooted to the floor, not quite ready to take what she was offering.

"You've hurt me for *years*, mom. Years. I'm not sure I can forgive you to be honest. Every single critique has stayed with me and makes me question myself, if I'm loveable or worthy enough. I had to fake a *boyfriend* to get you to leave me alone."

She blinked, eyes all watery as she paled. "Daniella—"

"I was too afraid of disappointing you. I'm not a beauty queen, and I have too many freckles, but I love them. You made me feel so small and pathetic, and I'm neither of those things." My heart raced, and my face felt like a furnace, but I held her gaze, determined to see this through.

"That's on me, I-I..." Her voice shook, and she ran a hand over her face. "I've been cruel."

"Yes, you have. I should've sat down with you before and maybe not have done it at the ER, but it's the truth, and it's out there. I don't care if you approve of who I am. I like myself, and if you can't accept that, then I will move away. I have wonderful people in my life who accept me."

She trembled now, her face ashen. She swallowed, hard. "I deserve that. I do."

"It's not revenge or retaliation. It's me picking the people I want in my life. Why would I want someone, even if they were related to me, to be around me when all they do is criticize?"

She nodded, her breathing getting heavier like she was trying not to break down. "Not that it's a good excuse, but I have my own issues that stem back from my mom. She...raised me to feel horrible about myself physically. I was no good unless I was beautiful and perfect. Women weren't meant to do things—they were meant to be seen, an accessory. I used to go to therapy, did you know that? When you were in grade school.

Then, life got busy, and I stopped but I think I need to start again."

"I didn't know." I shifted my weight, stunned. "If you like it, you should go back."

"I did, but mainly, I think it's what I should do so we can work on our relationship. If you want that." Her eyes pleaded with me. "Even if you don't want to, I'll go. I need the help. I was so afraid of my mom, I hated her, and I became her. My worst nightmare."

I winced. "You don't have to always be like that."

"I know. I know," she said, putting her face in her hands, her shoulders shaking. "I can't believe I did the same thing to you when I swore I never would."

Wow. My pulse sped up at hearing her admit this. Her admitting she was messed up was huge. Something I'd dreamed of happening for years, but one fifteen-minute conversation didn't make up for the *years* of her behavior. Not in a longshot. I cleared my throat, debating on what to say when it hit me—the truth. I didn't have to placate her with false promises because I wasn't going to hide from her anymore. She was gonna get the real Daniella from now on.

"Listen, you're my mom. I care for you. But we're never going to be best buds like my friends have with their moms. And that's fine. But something has to change for us to have *any* relationship at all."

"I understand." She swallowed loudly. "I have a lot to make up for, I know. But can we work on us... Slowly? Maybe?"

Could I hold onto my anger forever? Sure. But could I *try* too, to see what a new relationship could look like? Yes. Would it be easy or happen overnight? Absolutely not, but to write her off without attempting wasn't who I was. People got second chances—look at Cami, Cal. What *if* we ended up working through everything?

It was that small sliver of hope that had me nodding. "Yeah, we can work on it." I smiled up at her, and she returned it. The air seemed different, less chilled and tense. I chewed my lip for a second before asking, "So, do you forgive me for yelling at you after you got a concussion?"

"Of course." She blinked fast. "I won't ask for your forgiveness yet. I have a lot work to do, but I'm sorry you felt you had to fake a relationship with Gabriel to get me off your back. You two seemed so...smitten. Genuinely."

"Well, I've been in love with him for most of my life. Wasn't fake for me." I shrugged, my mind moving onto the next dilemma now that this one was on the way to being fixed.

"I'm sorry."

"No comments or suggestions that my toe socks turned him off?" I said, unable to stop myself.

She laughed but then held her head. "Toe socks are an abomination regardless of who you like."

Hearing her typical sass almost made me smile. "I'm glad you're okay, Mom."

"You know, maybe a silver lining of this whole event is for us to mend what I broke. The thought of you never coming home scares the hell out of me. It's just the three of us, and I love your Dad, but our threesome isn't complete without you."

My throat got all tight. I couldn't believe she said that. I always felt like the third wheel, an annoyance. But being a part of their trio felt good. Like what I'd always wanted with my family. Relief flooded through me, making me emotional again.

Tears spilled over, and my dad came into the room. "These better be good tears."

He turned on the light, nervously looked at us, and smiled. "My girls are better."

We nodded, and he held up a DVD. "White Christmas, anyone? I know this is your favorite, Daniella."

God. Gabe. My eyes prickled for a different reason as we watched the film. The chat was exhausting, but last night. The date. All the things he'd done for me, not just last night but this entire six weeks together. I'd pushed him away when I wanted him closer. It seemed the right thing to do since the ruse was over with my mom, but I didn't want that. I wanted to be with him for real, as long as he'd have me. Instead of hiding, I'd have to tell him. Be the leader my coach thought I was.

And with that, we laid on their bed and watched my favorite movie. The rock in my gut fizzled away. I couldn't believe my parents didn't hate me.

One crisis was done, but instead of going to the other one right away, I enjoyed the movie and my newfound relationship with my mom and dad. Couldn't have asked for a better gift.

My dad made pancakes, and my mom hummed holiday songs. I hadn't heard her hum in years? A decade? Things felt… good, right even in our house, and Gabe's gift weighed on me.

I had to see what it was.

"I'm running to my room real quick, be right back." I skipped a step as I hauled ass up there and stared at the box. It seemed important. Too important.

My phone remained silent, no texts from Elle or Van, which was probably for the best. They'd helped out so much last night, and they deserved time to celebrate with their family and *not* mine. *What did you get me, Van?*

I flipped the box over, no clues giving it away. I could feel my heartbeat in my fingers as I unhooked the box and opened it. A dainty silver bracelet—almost identical to the one I wore now—was there with one lone charm.

A sun.

There was a square card, and my heart skipped a beat seeing his handwriting.

You're the best part of my day and a ray of sunshine. I can't get enough of you, Dani. Merry Christmas.

Oh. Oh my.

I fingered the metal, my heart in my throat, and I knew. Van wasn't bold or outspoken, so his Valentine's Day comment had just been a cover. He *wanted* more with me but didn't know how to express it. I mean, who else would write something like this and not have feelings?

Who else sat in the hospital and planned the most romantic date of all time if they didn't have feelings? Fuck the fake dating.

Fuck him hiding behind quiet gestures. If he wanted me, he had to say it. Loud and proud and bold.

And yeah, maybe I needed to tell him how I felt too, like I had with my mom. Emotions were messy, but once they were exposed, you could sort through them. There was no reason to bury them and hide them because all that caused was hurt.

I had to go see him in person.

I threw on my jacket and stomped down the stairs, both my parents eyeing me with concern. "I'm sorry. I have to take care of something, then I'll be right back, I swear."

"Does this have to do with Van?" my dad asked, his eyes sparkling.

"Um, yes. Why?"

"He's outside, waiting for you."

"How do you know?"

"Because Elle texted me. Your friends are my friends now too, kid."

With that, I rolled my eyes and dove out the front door. What met me would one of the most memorable moments in my life.

CHAPTER
TWENTY-EIGHT

Gabriel

The door swung open, and I froze, not quite done with my horribly cheesy idea. Dani stood there, her lips parted and her eyes wide, and I stopped. I put my hands on my hips and faced her. My chest swelled with how much I loved her. She was the reason I'd been happier than ever, bolder on and off the ice, and more willing to do things that could get messy. Like now, my grand gesture. "I need ten more minutes. Go back inside."

"Excuse me?"

"You heard me." I couldn't stop my smile at seeing her all flushed and with her hair down, the wind blowing it every direction. God, she was beautiful. Gorgeous inside and out, and I loved her.

Oh yeah, I finally figured it out. The weird sensation in my chest, the absolute urge to do anything for her, the fact I'd do whatever she wanted just to make her happy. Took a hot second, but I could answer Elle's question. I was one thousand percent in love with my fake girlfriend, and now I had to prove it to her. Hence, the big gesture. All rom-coms had them, where the lovestruck idiot had to prove their feelings.

Me being the idiot this time.

"Get your cute ass back inside." My grin legit hurt my face.

"You're in pajamas."

"Yeah, Elle is too." I pointed toward my sister who was on the other side of the lawn. I had roped her into this idea, and she waved. Gratitude for Elle overwhelmed me. It would've sucked if she'd disapproved of me wanting to be with her best friend. I would've fought for Dani either way, but Elle being a fan of it and helping me made the world of a difference. "Matching ones."

"Hey there, Dani."

Daniella glanced between the two of us and then to the half-made creation in the middle of the yard. Honestly, it looked like a set of very large balls. But we weren't done with the snowmen yet. It had to be perfect. I wanted to get this right.

"As much as I love this surprise visit, what are you doing?"

"For starters, I should've been way clearer last night." I continued rolling what would be the stomach of my snowman. Elle got back to work too, both of us ignoring Daniella. My plan would be great if Dani let us finish. "When I stupidly, foolishly said I wanted us to *fake date* until Valentine's Day, that was me hiding behind an excuse. An easy way out."

"He was being a shy little bastard, honestly." Elle chimed in, and I threw snow at her. "Fuck off, I'm helping you. Which, this feels like it should be weird, but it's not."

"Roll faster." I wanted to get to the main reason we were here—for Daniella. Impatience gnawed at my gut.

"Oh my god." Elle groaned and then *splat.*

A snowball hit me right in the face. Irritation danced down my spine. She was ruining the plan. "You dick."

"You're bossy right now, and I'm the whole reason you're even here. Show some respect, bro." Elle threw another one at me, but this time I ducked.

"I'm gonna kick your ass. Stop ruining my moment." I tossed one at her, then she dove out of the way, and it was a full-on war. The irritation shifted to amusement. Go with the flow was my thing, and it had made my life easier in a lot of ways. As Elle and I threw snowballs at each other, I grinned. "What side are you on, Dani?"

"Oh, I'm not doing this." Her voice rang with humor, and I snuck a glance, careful to keep Elle in my sight. Dani sat on the stairs, her face in a grin as she watched us. "Don't make me pick a sibling."

"Yeah, you'll never win, Gabe." Elle threw one harder, this time getting my chest. What a little shit. "I've been her number one for decades."

I knew I'd have the two of them to deal with if I ever messed up because I wasn't a complete moron. Elle would choose Dani every time. But I'd do my darndest to never give them a reason to beat up on me.

"I'll work my way there. Just wait." I got Elle right in the neck, and she fell to the ground, being as dramatic as possible. "Point to me. Now, Dani, what I was saying—"

Elle tackled me to the ground, and snow got into my coat. In my pants. I wasn't sure how as my sister shoved more and more white powder all over me. "You're ruining the moment. Gah!"

Elle rolled off me, her face wild with glee, and she patted my face rather hard. "Consider that payback."

"For what?"

"For taking so goddamn long to figure out that you love my best friend."

Daniella sucked in a breath, and I glared at my sister. "What the fuck, that was my thing to say."

It was out there. In the air for Dani to hear and either accept or decline me. It was a relief to not hide it inside, where it had grown silently this whole time. I just hadn't realized it.

"Per usual, you were taking too damn long." Elle stood up, patted her hands together, and smiled at Dani. "My work here is done. I'm going inside because your dad promised pancakes."

"You and my dad are buddies?"

"A chaotic, emotional drive to the ER does that to people." Elle walked up to my girl, hugged her, and spoke in a soft voice meant for Dani. The wind picked it up, and I could make out her blessing.

"I love this, so let it happen. I'll pick your side every time."

"Thanks for that, Elle. A real gem."

She flipped me off and went inside, leaving Dani and me alone. I sighed, staring at the snowmen balls and shrugged. "I was going to make two snow people and have one hold a sign asking you to be my real girlfriend. It was gonna be cute as hell. You would've loved it."

"Probably." She slowly stood up, a flash of metal on her wrist catching my eye. Seeing her wear my gift caused my chest to swell with pride. And love.

"I love you, Dani." I walked toward her, the snow crunching with each step of my boots. While the words usually would've terrified me, they felt right. Comforting even. Her answering smile made it even better. "I wish I knew the exact moment, but it happened so easily and so fast it's all a blur."

She blinked a lot, and I stood right in front of her, her face at my chest. I took off my wet gloves and cupped her cheeks, running the pad of my thumb over her bottom lip. "I've struggled to be bold, and you've inspired me to be more. A better leader, a better human, and a better partner. I shouldn't have suggested we fake-date again. I chickened out and used that as a poor excuse. I should've begged you to be mine for real because I can't picture my life without you now."

"Oh yeah?"

"Oh fucking yeah. God." I kissed her forehead. "Before we started this thing, I used to call it getting a hit of sunshine whenever we hung out. You have this contagious laugh and smile that makes me forget whatever bad thing was happening."

"Van," she said softly, closing her eyes. "I love that."

"I want movie Sundays and secret snow adventures and real dates with you. The last month has been the best of my life, and it's due to you. I love you as you are, without changing a single thing. Wear what makes you comfortable, dress how you feel. Just be my girl, that's all I want."

My pulse raced, and I sweated despite the cold while I waited. She had to answer me eventually, and while I was confident she loved me too, I really needed to hear her say it. Like, right now.

She chewed the side of her mouth before slowly nodding. "Be your girl, huh?"

"Is this payback? I'm sorry I didn't tell you sooner. Please, pull me out of this what-if scenario where you don't want me back."

"Of course I want to be with you, Van." She grinned and reached around my head to run her fingers through my hair. Her touch lit me up, calming me down and soothing every worry I had. Her touch had me shuddering, and she kissed me, soft and tame, but it sent a shiver down my body.

"Thank god." I tilted her head back, deepening the kiss, and she groaned against me. She tasted like mint and felt like home. "Missed this mouth."

"It's barely been twelve hours," she said, laughing. I picked her up and hugged her hard, needing to feel her heart beat against mine. "Van, put me down."

"No."

I held her there, breathing in deep and inhaling her scent. She was mine now. "You haven't said it yet."

"Said what?"

"That you love me too."

"Oh my god, of course I love you." She kissed my neck, her cold lips making me jump, but I wasn't ever going to complain with her wrapped around me like this. "I have for a while but was afraid to tell you. That's actually what I was about to do when I burst out the door."

"You did come out real hot."

"You weren't the only one missing someone." She looked up at me, her blue eyes so clear and vivid and filled with adoration it was like a punch to the gut. This brave, beautiful woman loved me.

How wild.

I smiled wide, and she wrinkled her brow. "Why are you grinning like that?"

"Because I'm lucky. Now, what was your plan when you stormed out."

"To drive to your parents', tell you I loved you, and demand you say it back."

"Huh. What were you wearing when you told me in this idea of yours?"

"Damnit, Van." She swatted at me, and I captured her mouth in another kiss, happier than I could've ever imagined.

"You're pretty confident that I felt the same then?"

"Yes. You use actions to show love, not words. You've been telling me for a while, whether you knew it yourself, but I pieced it together, and it clicked when I opened your bracelet. The movie dates, the coffee, shop, always giving me your clothes. The bracelet. The date last night. Driving me to the ER. Sending me that text this morning when I needed a reminder so badly. Those are how you say it."

Well fuck.

My throat got tight, and I kissed her again. She slid her tongue against mine just as the door opened. Fucking Elle.

"Okay, good, you're back together. Save that shit for later. The food is done, and Bill even added whipped cream."

"Bill? I don't like this new development." Dani laughed and scooted down my body to stand. She held out a hand, her eyes glistening. "Might as well introduce you to my parents for real now. Lily might shock you, but I can fill you in on that later. For now, I want to spend Christmas with my best friend, parents, and boyfriend."

Elle and I shared a glance, her smile matching mine. It was simple really. Dani had always been a part of our family, but now... it was official. And some day, years in the future, her and Elle could be *real* sisters.

EPILOGUE

SIX MONTHS LATER

Daniella

My bracelets dangled as I hoisted the beat-up couch into the main doors. "Three more steps, come on."

"Where is your asshole boyfriend?" Elle grunted.

"Your brother, you mean?"

"Sure." Elle set her end of the couch down and put her hands on her hips. "I'm sweating buckets. Why is it so humid?"

"Summer storm, I'm sure." I, too, wiped the sweat on my forehead and panted. Van was supposed to meet us ten minutes ago to help out, but his future boss held him back for something. He was so excited about the job working in town, staying near me for the next two years so I could graduate. I had no idea where we'd end up moving, but we both wanted to go together. So, he'd found a job at a small business in town to get real experience but to also stay close. It was perfect for where we were in our relationship: committed and all-in but realizing we had to wait before starting our life together.

"Even my feet are sweating." Elle gulped water before pointed at our couch. It was her great-aunt's, super comfy, and super old. I loved it. It felt like a turning point in growing up, having someone else's used furniture. Plus, it was ours now.

"Almost there." My muscles ached. "On three?"

"One… two… three."

We grunted just as a familiar voice snapped Elle's name. "Elle, what the fuck are you doing?"

"What does it look like?" she said between clenched teeth.

"Stop. I can help." Cal Holt strutted to her, pushed her out of the way with his hip, and lifted her end of the couch without showing an ounce of struggle. "You could hurt yourself."

"I'm not some helpless, pathetic weakling."

"No, but I'm way stronger than you."

"Yeah, I know. You're drafted and so cool." Elle's eyes flared with anger, and the tension in the hot foyer was thick enough to chop with the new kitchen knives I'd gotten.

Cal stared at her for a beat before meeting my eyes. "Where's Van?"

"Running late."

He flexed his jaw but then asked, "Which door?"

"Third on the right."

"Let's do this." He assisted me with the couch, and Elle held the door open to our new unit. It was on the ground floor, which we didn't love, but it worked. The air-conditioning was in top shape, and I smiled as we set the couch down. "You two are living here?"

"Sure are." I clapped my hands and put them on my waist. My lungs burned from straining, but the couch was done. No offense to Elle, but my dear friend had worked out three times in her entire life. The struggle was real for her, so Cal's help was appreciated.

"In this building?"

"Also yes. Come on, you're not that dense, Cal. Why are you asking this?"

He sighed and pinched the bridge of his nose. "Do you need more help?"

"No, we can figure it out on our own. Thanks for blessing us with your presence. Hockey Holiness." Elle's lip curled up on the side, her clear *fuck you very much* face on display. I'd seen that look a handful of times, and boy, she did not like Cal Holt.

A complete one-eighty from her massive crush she had last year.

Cal moved his gaze over our unit before landing on her. His nostrils flared, the muscles in his arms tightening before he pointed toward the large window. "Keep that locked. Get something to jam in it so no one can break in."

"I can take care of myself, thanks." She gestured to the door. "See your way out."

He ducked his head and marched right out the door, pausing for a second. He tapped the doorframe, his face unreadable but then he said nothing. Once he was out of earshot, I arched my brow at my best friend. "Is there a reason you hate him now?"

"He's a dick."

"Sure, but he's been getting better, and you used to be all up on that? You had a poster of him, girlfriend. I saw it."

Her face hardened, and she shook her head. "Things change. He wasn't the guy I thought he was."

"Hm, alright. Well, enough Cal Holt for today. Let's finish our place."

I put on music, improving the slightly dampened mood from Cal's appearance. I appreciated his help, but Elle did not. There had to be a story there... one that had me curious, but Elle wouldn't share it unless she wanted to. I hesitated to say there was sexual tension, but she'd stab me if I did.

A sure sign of denial.

I snickered to myself as we organized our kitchen supplies, but I kept quiet. It was a dream living with her. We'd have so much fun, *and* the transition to being Van's real girlfriend had been amazing. Zero weirdness with Elle. And my parents

278 JAQUELINE SNOWE

genuinely liked him? Not just because he was *out of my league* but because he treated me so well.

Speaking of my parents... I got my phone out and opened the group text with both of them. The uncomfortable knot still remained whenever I texted them, but it was getting smaller and smaller each time. I'd only visited twice this last semester, the urge to avoid them built into my own self-protection, but that talk with my mom had shifted things a little bit. She went to therapy twice a week. She texted me after each one with more apologies.

When Van and I visited, she was quiet and listened, letting us guide the conversation. She even complimented me on my outfits with a sincere voice. It was weird and different but better. Nowhere near perfect but improving.

Daniella: Elle and I made it and got the couch in. Still visiting with the Van Helsings this weekend?

Mom: Yes, we'll be down Sunday and bring some food.

Dad: I'll get beer.

Mom: And water.

Dad: Beer is more fun.

Daniella: See you soon.

It was wild how that night in the ER changed so much in my life. Not only had it cemented Van and my relationship, but it forced me to confront my mom. Elle and Van were proud of me for trying with her, but they weren't entirely as forgiving. Lovely Lily had years to make up for, and that was fine with me. She could work on herself and our relationship, and I'd focus on my own life. If she wanted to be a part of it, then she'd have to accept me as is.

I pocketed my phone as Van walked into our place carrying three large boxes. His nice dress shirt strained against his muscles, and he rolled his sleeves up, his perfectly strong and fist-bite-inducing forearms teasing me.

"Oh, hey, Muscles."

"You moved the couch without me? I'm sorry I'm late. Was

that Cal I saw?" He set the boxes down, adjusted his shirt, and took two large strides toward me. His eyes simmered, his dimples popping out, and my heart stuttered.

He was so beautiful, handsome, and I loved him. The good, bad, and messy parts. Dating him for real was better than any fantasy I could've imagined as a teenager. He was kind, considerate, and filthy.

"Hi," he said softly, cupping my face and kissing me. I wrapped my fingers around his forearms, and he flexed. Warm and strong and thick. Mm.

"Brought out these guns, huh? You know how to tease me. And yeah, I don't know why Holt was here, but he helped."

"I may have rolled them up for you." He smirked, placing his hands on each shoulder and grazing my neck with his thumbs. "Now, where's your bedroom?"

"Ah, you came for a quickie. I see, I see." I couldn't stop touching him. It wasn't like I hadn't seen him every day, but today...my feelings overwhelmed me. We stared at each other, grinning like fools, as Elle walked back in.

The immediate urge to push away from her brother had stopped about a month after Christmas, but it still felt a little weird to want to jump his bones with her right there. Our eyes met, and she groaned. "You two. I swear."

"I'm obsessed with my girl, Elle, so you'll see me a lot. How exciting for you." Van pulled me into his chest, laughing as we faced his sister.

"Ew. Not you, Dani, my brother." She clapped her hands. "I'm going to grab some coffees and give you two fifteen minutes to be alone. Fifteen minutes. Think that's enough time?"

"I have to head back to work, you little perv," Van said, his voice filled with amusement. But I'd love an iced coffee."

Elle nodded, walked out the door, and shut it with a click.

Van picked me up and wrapped my legs around him. I giggled against his greedy mouth, sliding my tongue inside to kiss him back. He dug his fingers into my ass, kneading it and making me moan. "Van," I panted, my body flushed and ready for him. "Work?"

"I know." He rested his forehead on mine, breathing hard. His eyes burned for me, the same intensity as always there and focused just on me. "I needed to touch you. I'm a selfish prick, alright? I'm jealous of my sister. I want to live with you, wake up with you every morning, kiss you whenever."

My insides melted. "I want that too, but—"

He hung his head, pressing his lips tight together. "No, you don't have to say anything. I'm such an ass. You and Elle have been dreaming about living together for years. This is exciting. Don't let me ruin it."

"You're not ruining it." I ran my fingers through his hair. It was longer than normal, a little unruly, and I loved it. "I can want *both* things."

"We'd get a large bed because we'd spend a lot of time in it."

"Obviously."

"And a patio or a backyard. And a big kitchen." He ran his hand down my spine, his voice going all soft. "Being with you has made me the happiest I've ever been. I want to start the rest of our lives together, so forgive me for being needy the next two years."

"I love you," I whispered, his words lighting me up even though the next two years would be hard. Finishing school, enjoying my time on the dance team, and living with his sister while also imagining the next stage of my life. "I'm excited to live with Elle, but I want all this too. A life with you. Waking up with you."

"I know, so how about I get you on weekends?"

"Oh, you and Elle share custody of me?"

He laughed, kissing me again. "I'll get whatever you want to give me baby because you have to enjoy these last two years of college. Have fun, go wild. I'll be waiting and ready for you as soon as you graduate, and I'll be by your side the whole time."

I leaned into his palm, kissing it before squeezing him tight in a hug. "Fake-dating you was the best decision ever."

"It's definitely one of my finer moments." He kissed my temple, hugging me back, and everything felt right.

My relationship with my parents. Me and Elle living out our childhood dream. Me leading the dance team as the sole captain. Me and Van...my heart swelled. I loved him, always had and always would, and yeah, I couldn't wait to start life with him, but if I'd learned anything, it was to enjoy every second.

Every movie Sunday. Every kiss. Every date he planned to *woo* me (his words, not mine), and every touch. We'd get our happy ever after, but until then? I'd just enjoy the ride.

ALSO BY JAQUELINE SNOWE:

CENTRAL STATE SERIES

The Puck Drop

From the Top

Take the Lead

Book 4 coming soon!

CLEAT CHASER SERIES

Challenge Accepted

The Game Changer

Best Player

No Easy Catch

OUT OF THE PARK SERIES

Evening the Score

Sliding Home

Rounding the Bases

SHUT UP AND KISS ME SERIES

Internship with the Devil

Teaching with the Enemy

Next Door Nightmare

HOCKEY ROMANCE

Holdout

STANDALONES

Take a Chance on Me

Let Life Happen

The Weekend Deal

ABOUT THE AUTHOR

Jaqueline Snowe lives in Arizona where the "dry heat" really isn't that bad. She prefers drinking coffee all hours of the day and snacking on anything that has peanut butter or chocolate. She is the mother to two fur-babies who don't realize they aren't humans and a new mom to the sweetest baby boy. She is an avid reader and writer of romances and tends to write about athletes. Her husband works for an MLB team (not a player, lol) so she knows more about baseball than any human ever should.

To sign up for her review team, or blogger list, please visit her website www.jaquelinesnowe.com for more information.